Be

Berckman

Nightmare chase

The Nightmare Chase

Books by Evelyn Berckman

THE NIGHTMARE CHASE
WAIT, JUST YOU WAIT
THE VICTORIAN ALBUM
THE STAKE IN THE GAME
THE FOURTH MAN ON THE ROPE
THE VOICE OF AIR
SHE ASKED FOR IT
A CASE OF NULLITY
THE HEIR OF STARVELINGS
STALEMATE
A SIMPLE CASE OF ILL-WILL
A THING THAT HAPPENS TO YOU
BLIND GIRL'S BLUFF
DO YOU KNOW THIS VOICE?
LAMENT FOR FOUR BRIDES
NO KNOWN GRAVE
THE HOVERING DARKNESS
THE BLIND VILLAIN
THE STRANGE BEDFELLOW
THE BECKONING DREAM
THE EVIL OF TIME
NELSON'S DEAR LORD

The Nightmare Chase

EVELYN BERCKMAN

In England, published simultaneously under the title
Indecent Exposure.

Doubleday & Company, Inc.
GARDEN CITY, NEW YORK
1975

Library of Congress Cataloging in Publication Data
Berckman, Evelyn.
    The nightmare chase.

    I. Title.
PZ4.B486Ni3 [PS3552.E68]   813'.5'4
ISBN 0-385-03751-1
Library of Congress Catalog Card Number 74-33082

For
Philip Maitland Hubbard
A master of the art
with humble admiration

The Nightmare Chase

I

The unpleasantness took place in a library where she was fortifying herself against an oncoming examination. This library, or rather the music section of a vast general library, was handsomely fitted up for the special requirements of those who consulted it—excellent lighting and chairs not crowded and tables broad and generous to allow of spreading out large orchestral scores or other music larger and more unwieldy than folio volumes, even.

It was this spacious positioning of chairs that made them less numerous than they might be and apt to be filled to capacity early in the day; lucky to find one free, she thought as she sat down. While ranging her armoury of pencils and notebooks neatly before her, she qualified her luck as even better than she had thought, since the bodies flanking her on either side seemed not to have streaming colds plus inadequate acquaintance with a handkerchief's uses. Nor did they seem to smell, though this quality was likely to steal upon the senses later rather than sooner. The automatic arrangement of her gear she accompanied with a glance, equally automatic, to right and left. A neat grey-haired lady was writing absorbedly on one side, with constant reference to the heavy book on the stand in front of her. An equally rapid survey of her right-hand neighbour was equally favourable. By that mysterious mechanism called *receiving an impression*—for which no direct glance is required, somehow—she got the message of a good black overcoat (he was keeping it on for all the warmth of the room), a dazzling white crepe scarf that showed above the coat's velvet collar, and an overall air of modest prosperity and respectability, and the coat so beautifully brushed and clean! As she rose to claim the books for which she had put in slips yesterday, she could see he was a rather pleasing little man in early middle age, his auburn hair closely barbered and his overall look well-groomed. Tranquil and perfectly still he sat, and to her list of benefits she added, *Not fidgety,* from long experience apprehensive of this menace to concentration. She noted also that he was not using the adjustable rack that stood before every chair, but held in his lap a large thin album of Schumann's easier piano pieces, open at the title, 'The Jolly Miller.' Even that soon . . . *odd,* flitted across some horizon beyond her own concerns, but so remotely that she only remembered it later. Now it was occurring to her that she might as well look up some items against tomorrow's needs, and to do so got up and started toward a sort of anteroom to the library proper, given over to ranks of card catalogues.

A good twenty minutes later she returned, having had to queue both at the files and at the claiming desk. Approaching from behind her right-hand neighbour, while taking her seat she could not help seeing that the album was still open at 'The Jolly Miller,' and again that sense of something odd, hardly perceived before, came a little more strongly to the forefront of her mind. For all her own piled-up work awaiting her, she took a moment to wonder what there could be in the first page of a ten-year-old's piano piece to engage this silent, unmoving attention for twenty minutes. Involuntarily she glanced full at him, at his mild abstracted pose—he never looked at her directly at any time—then glanced down curiously at the album. Opened out wide its spread was considerable, but for all the skilful and discreet way in which he held it, she could see that his fly was open its full length, and spread wide apart.

An interval passed, how prolonged she had no idea, while her first shock wore off and turned slowly to unbelief, then re-

2

vulsion, and finally, all at once, to the full heat of outrage. Yet all the while that this incendiarism was building up in her she had held her own pose—not inferior to his own—of peaceful studious absorption; finding her place in a volume, drawing a notebook toward her then scanning it while tapping her lips thoughtfully with a pencil . . .

And degrading, also, that by an intuition as abhorrent to her as the man himself she should realize his thought-processes with a knowledge approaching intimacy, an intimacy unclean and almost clairvoyant. He was not sure whether she had noticed; or whether she had noticed and was now, by her silent complicity, inviting some further demonstration. She *knew* this, absolutely. As her anger boiled higher, the more stringently she held herself to her look of studious application. Any sudden movement of hers, even a sudden glance would, she knew, alert him; fiercely she wanted him to be caught. In pursuit of this desire, from moment to moment fiercer, she compelled herself to remain sitting beside the loathsome creature for a convincing and natural interval before, with leisurely movements, she picked up a notebook and moved once more with calculated abstraction toward the anteroom.

Once through the door and out of his sight she streaked like a hungry ferret down the long marble vista of the main corridor and brought up short before two uniformed library guards who were chatting near the revolving entrance.

'I want to report a man for misconduct in the music library,' she shot at them without preamble.

Both men detached themselves from their conversation and looked her over carefully.

'Yes, madam,' the senior replied, after a pause. He was red-necked and brindled, the tougher looking of the two, both of them pretty tough. 'Yes, madam, we'll see. Now could I first just have your name and address? Just as a matter of . . . ?'

He took down Jacintha Cory, Miss, and an address, before resuming, 'Now, madam, you say this man was misbehaving? You mean flirting with you, like?'

'Flirting!' She was too exasperated by their caution to recognize it for what it was—old acquaintance with cranks, eccentrics and other sources of irresponsible accusation that haunt public buildings. *'Flirting!* He's exposing himself indecently.'

'Oh,' said the elder in a voice of total recognition. He was at once on his feet, yet not hurriedly. 'I see.' Joined to his first nuance was another, which she could not define; of resignation? resignation plus something else . . . ? 'Now he's sitting, could you tell me whereabouts—?'

'On my right, in any case there's a lady on my left. I'm in the music section, the middle table to the right of the door.'

'I see.' He sounded anything but enthusiastic. 'Well, if you'd go back to your place, madam? Then we'd spot him easy—?'

The same casual and unurgent step that had carried her out of the room carried her into it. Strolling back, taking her seat, she congratulated herself on her histrionic talents and on her cunning. The quarry had not taken the least alarm from her comings and goings; his seeming inattention was as complete as before, and on her part she sedulously refrained from glancing at him. From the corner of her eye she could see that the first page of 'The Jolly Miller' was still uppermost, and mixed with her revulsion was an exultant amusement over his stratagem, its sheer musical illiteracy. Masking himself with a symphonic score, now, could not have drawn her attention; one could sit for hours of study over one single page of a complex orchestration. But to do as this little slug was doing, sit before the same page of a child's piano piece for hours (he had been there when she came, and with the ensconced look of long tenure): to make such a blunder in a room full of people who were all musicians in some sort or degree. . . .

Her mounting vindictiveness faltered, all at once—by the same repellent clairvoyance as before—undergoing a sudden check, then a transformation. Just as she had known earlier his uncertainty as to whether she had seen him, so now by some impalpable nuance in him, some complacence . . . ? she understood that he knew she had seen, that he was telling her silently that the next move was up to her. He was waiting for the next indication of her connivance; her pleasurable assent to the game he was playing. She also knew, by the same unclean telegraphy, that he would not miss her signal of assent,

4

however minute it was. Except for his choice of music, how clever he was being, how careful—and indeed for this perilous sport the most deadly caution was not too much. By similar exercises in God knew how many places like this, he had perfected a technique of intangibles: to give and receive messages without the least movement of his body, to signal kindred souls without a glance, to spin atmospheres around himself and the chance-met accomplice without a syllable exchanged. . . .

A playmate, came to her unbidden, *he's taking me for a playmate,* while a remarkable scalding sensation travelled up her gullet to her throat. This was a variation on other kinds of whom she had heard: those whose pleasure consisted of the shock or terror they could give women. *Clever,* she congratulated her neighbour, *clever boy, but I'm clever too. You'll see, you'll see.* . . . And on the last vengeful *see* it came to her suddenly: where were the guards? She had spoken to them ages ago, well, five minutes ago at least, where were they . . .

Realization first calmed, then amused her. The guards were right to delay; their appearance in the room, hotfoot on her own, must have alerted him like a shout of warning; their separate entrances must seem entirely unrelated. Just as this vermin had perfected his techniques, they had perfected theirs, they were timing it beautifully. . . . *Clever,* she cheered them on silently, *this boy's not the only clever one.* . . . .

Then—not wanting to miss a moment of this cunning being outwitted by greater cunning—she leaned her head on her right hand and found she could see him sidewise through her fingers, see his unbroken tranquillity due to be shattered any moment, any moment now . . . Her glance had begun swivelling between him and the door, and by accident came to rest on him at the crucial moment.

A very faint start traversed him; his eyes narrowed and he closed the album with a sudden movement, the first break in his immobility since she had sat down beside him. Following the direction of his gaze, she looked toward the door. Sure enough there was her guard, the senior. Than his look nothing could be more innocent and amiable as he chatted with one of the

5

librarians; though facing toward her he had not given so much as a glance in her direction. In virtually the same instant that she realized this, she became aware that the place on her right was empty. With movements so soundless she had heard nothing, he had risen, freed himself, and eeled out of his chair. Placidly, unhurriedly, he was walking away between the row of tables. Secure in the protection of his good black overcoat wrapped about him, his pure white scarf and look of a decorous little gentleman, knowing he could not be stopped or questioned, with composed step he proceeded toward the doorway whose rather narrow dimensions must make him all but brush against the uniform standing within it. Tense, she waited for his casual assurance to break apart at the guard's equally-casual murmur, his detaining gesture too discreet to be seen, except by someone waiting for it. . . .

Staring with unbelief she followed the overcoat's serene progress past the other man, in fact blocking him momentarily from her line of vision. Just in that fraction of an instant—just before the doorway swallowed him—the pervert turned his face in her direction and treated her to an enormous display of clean white teeth. *Yes, you were clever,* said the teeth, *but I'm still more clever.* Then he was gone before she realized that what appeared to be a grin was in fact no grin at all, that in it was nothing recognizable as human, not mockery, triumph nor enjoyment. He had not even looked at her really, his eyes had been empty and unfocussed, but the flash of white in the mirthless face had been to her address and no other. A frightful creature who functioned by chain impulses of furtiveness and obliquity, who had in him no ordinary instinct of directness like other people. Belatedly too she realized why he had kept his overcoat on in a room too warm if anything, and realized also her naïveté in regretting that their seats *faced* the door, so that the guard could not come up noiselessly behind him. . . .

New and sudden hope alleviated her still-vivid shock at the grin full of teeth. A disturbance could not be risked in this tranquil and orderly archive, how stupid of her to expect it; the guard would simply follow the man into the corridor and deal

6

with him there. With renewed confidence she waited for the uniform to whip about in pursuit, and again could hardly believe her eyes when it remained static. A subtle change had come over its wearer's look and bearing, the deflation of lost purpose and accustomed resignation. After some moments he turned and disappeared, his aimless gait confirming his defeat, if confirmation were needed.

Only on his disappearance did a number of things pelt about her like hailstones. The creature was getting away with it, first of all. He was getting off scot-free because he was an old hand at the game; with the slimy divinations that were part of his gift for avoiding capture, he had perceived almost at once his error in taking her for a kindred soul, and at sight of the guard—easily, expertly, with reptilian suppleness—had been on his feet and away. His mere assurance as he walked toward the guard was in itself an accomplishment, informing her by a telepathy that was still another of his gifts, of how many times he had flouted propriety and tricked authority, and his farewell grin threw in her face the ease—insulting—with which he had slipped her clumsy trap.

An interval passed during which, trying to settle down and unable to settle down, she realized what fed the core of her rage hotter instead of letting it diminish. It was not the nastiness itself, it was not even the grin he had turned on her, it was none of those. It was his assumption, his *assumption* of her pleasurable connivance and sympathetic taste in his game, his adoption of her into an unclean masonry, himself the adept and she the willing novice; that he had joined himself with her even in thought; how dared he, how *dared* he. . . . She found she was digging her nails into her palms, and stopped; control to that extent was in her power, but not control of the desire for reprisal that interfered with her breathing. She picked up a pencil and flung it down; with hands shaking like this it was no good trying to write, let alone concentrate to any purpose; he had not only plowed her up with revulsion and frustration, he had robbed her of a whole afternoon's work.

With a rough movement that drew a glance of mild reproof from the neat grey lady she flung her belongings together, thrust

7

her chair back unquietly and left. Beside the entrance she found the same guard, now alone at his post, and marched straight up to him.

'Were you able to do anything about that man?' she demanded.

His eyes met hers vaguely; he was uninterested, but prepared to be patient.

'No, madam,' he replied.

'But—but—I mean, I *saw* him! Couldn't you have . . . ?'

He shook his head.

'You've got to catch 'em in the act.' Polite as he was, he looked ready to go to sleep. 'And you saw how it was, madam, you saw for yourself. It's next to impossible to catch 'em, they're too clever.'

She was silent, refusing to accept this, while *clever*—her own refrain of moments ago—sang mockingly through her mind.

'Don't worry, madam,' he soothed, misinterpreting her silence. 'He won't bother you again.'

'You mean—?' Her voice revived with her hopes. 'You mean you'll call a policeman next time, as soon as he comes?'

'Oh no, nothin' like that.' His patience was now weary, she felt, and he meant her to feel it. 'Turns out one of the librarians in the music section, she's suspected him before this, he's been comin' in say once or twice in the week. So next time he turns up we just ask to see his reader's ticket and he won't have one, that sort wouldn't, so then he knows we're on to him and he won't come again. So that's how we keep him out,' he reassured. 'Just handle it easy like that, nice an' quiet.'

She stood another moment in the silence of frustration; reluctant to give up her vision of seeing the man pounced on, wrenched up out of his seat, marched out and humiliated before the entire room. . . .

'And that's the best you can do?' she demanded aggressively.

Unless we'd take 'em with it hanging out. I've told you, you silly cow.

Unkindly debarred from such expression of his thoughts by convention, he merely repeated, 'Well, unless we'd catch 'em in the act. It happens in lib'ries,' he shrugged. 'Places like that.'

'He ought to be whipped,' she returned furiously.

'Oh, there's worse things, madam.' His voice, straying away like a suppressed yawn, no longer pretended even a token interest.

'Thank you,' she said witheringly. As she moved away he continued to survey unseeingly the constant stream of people arriving and leaving, his eyes glazed with the boredom of his job and the boredom—even greater—of her insistence.

*　*　*

For an unreasonably long time the episode clung about her like a dirty garment, from the beginning gnawing her dreams into various strange shapes. One of these for instance—the worst one—was that she was running. In this dream she carried something in her right hand, some heavy weapon or stick. Its shape repelled her, she felt indistinctly, but she liked its weight and solidity. Ahead of her was the pervert walking away from her, but by some deformity of dreams the face of this retreating body was turned squarely toward her, a face totally without features except for a grin full of teeth. With rage boiling vividly through the dream (it had actually shocked her out of sleep once) she pursued him, running to the limit of her strength without affecting the distance between them in the least. She heard her own sobbing breath and felt a pain in her chest, she panted and stumbled, unable to overtake, and once she heard him laughing . . . That also had woken her with a start, woken her to a long sigh and the turning of her pillow and lying down again, wide-eyed in the dark and unable to sleep again for a long time. She was eighteen years old, still young, but all the same knew that she had wandered into an alien and parched watercourse of the spirit that was hatred, genuine hatred, the like of which she had never felt for anyone. Foolish that the incident could take shape, within her, as so profound a distortion. Now if only she could dream of catching up with him; of raising the distasteful weapon, of bringing it down full and midway of the grin; of seeing the grin, with strange mathematical exactitude, split open and fall to pieces. . . . .

Then, only then, she would not need to run after him any more.

II

'My son can't wait for me to die,' said Mrs Tor to her solicitor. 'And that's the truth.'

'Oh, surely not,' he deprecated cautiously. 'Surely you can't say that.'

'I say it because it's true, John Dennison.' She stared at him, haggard and implacable. 'I'm in his way, I've lasted so long I'm a nuisance.'

'A little . . . unjust to him, you may be?'

His tone was a masterpiece, a blend of evasion and deference; evasion for his own good reasons, deference because of a client once of outstanding intellect and considerable reputation, and now going off her rocker. This decline of hers he had both experienced and heard of through the medium of gossip. Village gossip, grossly overdone or inexact in a small place like this—but he always preferred to delay judgment till she herself gave him the chance of face-to-face observation. So from the beginning of their colloquy—his first good sight of her for a number of weeks—he had watched her with covert alertness verging on dread, trying to assess the progress forward, or the reverse, of her breakdown. So far there had been nothing really significant that he could see; her strong craggy face, cruelly lined, had a desolate expression and a bad colour, but her piercing eyes, her harsh decisive utterance, still conveyed the stamp of her essential power. Thrown-on clothes and coarse grey-and-white hair straggling beneath her hat might look a bit eldritch, but apart from that her manner had been indisputably —one might almost say ruthlessly—normal . . .

'Yes, you do him an injustice, don't you?' he continued, deliberately and gently trying to draw her out for his own reasons. 'Hugh has never spoken nor acted but as a devoted son, so far as I know him.'

'So far as you know him,' she echoed contemptuously. 'And just why, may I ask, should Hubert be a devoted son? I wasn't a devoted mother.'

'As to that, of course—'

Her son was *Hugh* to the world at large; she was the only one who called him *Hubert*.

'I can hardly venture an opinion—'

'Of course you can't,' she cut across him. 'You know nothing whatever about it.'

'—but my impression is,' Dennison opposed her suavely, 'that you've always taken excellent care of him, he's been extraordinarily well looked after—'

'No expense spared,' she interrupted again, with a fearsome grin. 'The best schools and best clothes, the most expensive holidays and sporting gear. Anything that could be got with money, I was willing to give him.'

The other, seeing where the argument tended, was silent and satisfied.

'My work was my life.' Her look and tone were now remote. 'The *only* thing in my life. I shouldn't have married ever, I only did it out of boredom—between jobs.'

Casualness carried to extremes, thought Dennison; three marriages disposed of like that, though all were in the mists of time.

'Hubert was an accident,' she deplored, still in soliloquy. 'My bit of bad luck.'

A pause fell, brief but somehow bottomless.

'His bad luck too,' she pursued. 'The fact that the little boy was there, I didn't let it matter. I *wouldn't* let it matter, I wouldn't be tied down. So after neglecting him all during his

12

childhood—' her eyes returned from distance and skewered him inexorably '—after leaving him to paid household staff and paid teachers, why in the name of common sense should he be a devoted son?'

'Love—' he was aware of sounding lame. '—love isn't a matter of logic, it can survive neglect, unkindness, actual bad treatment. Sometimes it's—' his accent became firmer '—it's even stronger because of it.'

'One hears of such things.' Her smile derided him. 'For flabby temperaments that don't mind being kicked about, your theory might hold water. But for a man like Hubert—' her mocking smile spread wider '—it's bloody nonsense. That he's dying to get his hands on my money, now *that* makes sense to me. Think of what he could do with it, the thousand ways he could spread out and about.'

'He has a good life now,' Dennison pointed out. 'He's independent, he's got a job.'

'As a traveller.' Mrs Tor smiled unpleasantly. 'In wines and brandies.'

'But successful?' the other hazarded. 'Very—?'

'Moderately,' she contradicted. 'I know his tastes. He lives well, but he'd like to live better, make a splash on good independent means. That spoiled piece I hear he runs about with—that General Sir Somebody's daughter—she won't settle for what he is now, a man who's got to be constantly away on his rounds, touting for orders, worrying about competition—no, I can't see her type sitting down with a traveller in brandies. Not even,' she accompanied her parting shot with a nastier smile, 'a really successful one.'

They're engaged, all the same, thought Dennison, intrigued. *Or don't you know?*

'Actually, what does he owe me?' She had relapsed into meditation. 'Nothing—he owes me nothing. And I, I ask him for nothing. I could do with a little love and concern, yes, now I could do with them. But I've no right to ask,' she passed sentence on herself inexorably. 'So I don't ask.'

In his way, he does give you love and concern, the solicitor acknowledged unwillingly, and spared a thought for the rooted

13

differences between Hugh and himself, also the chances of a collision. *In his way, his wrong-headed way.*

'So I take that much credit to myself.' Miles away, she pursued the desert track of extenuation. 'I don't interfere with him, ever. He lives next door, but he's got his own independent house.'

Yes, rent-free, lucky bastard, Dennison commented silently. Years ago she had divided her big house in this manner.

'I give him an allowance with no strings to it.' She had stopped meditating and was bragging. 'His house is as much his own as if I'd rented it to a stranger. I don't even—' triumphantly she clinched her argument '—I don't even have keys to it. So there!'

'No keys—?' Badly jolted, he echoed the words. What if the arrangement were two-sided, what if the old lady's part of the house caught fire during the night? Or what if she were taken ill suddenly with no more help at hand than that other scatty old woman living there, and the servants probably dead asleep. . . .

'Don't worry, I beg.' Her malicious smile told how exactly she had followed the course of his misgivings. 'Hubert has keys to my side, of course. What if something happened to me, and I good as alone in the place? Mary'd be worse than useless in any emergency, that old fool.'

Well, thank God, passed through the other's mind with boundless relief, then with a lesser shock, *And this is the woman that they say's off her rocker? If this is a sample, I wish it'd take a few more the same way.*

'Naturally he's got keys to my house,' she was pursuing. 'But that . . . that doesn't mean . . . mean . . .'

The *suddenness* was what struck him a body-blow: the suddenness of it. Her voice, strong and assured, broke and faltered with an effect infinitely distressing, like seeing an old feeble person stumble and fall; she groped and produced one or two more struggling irrelevant words. Along with this foundering of her train of thought, he saw the other thing happen that he could scarcely describe, even to himself. The quality of power and dominance that held her face together ran out of

14

it like water from a sieve; the eyes went empty, the mouth fell half-open, the features loosened and spread out with witless amiability. She giggled suddenly, and the sound turned him cold to the marrow of his bones. Yet already the merriment was becoming something else; perplexity, suspicion, then anger. She scowled at him, yet shrank back in her chair as if from threat of a blow.

'W-where is it?' she whinnied at him. Like her face, her voice had become unrecognizable, high and urgent. 'You s-said you'd . . . *bring* it—!'

He wet his lips, groping for the right word, for any word. . . .

'Get it!' She had given him no time. '*Get* it—!'

'Yes, yes,' he said quickly. 'I shall.'

'M-more money?' she quavered. 'You want m-more . . . ?'

'No,' he demurred. 'No—'

'You'll—you'll—get it? P-promise—?'

'Yes,' he soothed, 'yes, yes,' and even on the final *yes* saw it happening again, in reverse. Sense and awareness flowed back into her face as it had flowed out, putting firmness and intelligence into her eyes, contracting her features into the sharp and haughty mask of Mrs Tor. In this very moment of her return, with no least pause for adjustment or transition she must have registered something in his aspect, for she demanded at once, 'Was I different? Was I—just now?'

'N-no,' he disclaimed, taken off balance.

'What did I do?' She ignored his denial. 'What did I say?'

'Nothing in particular,' he answered quickly. 'You seemed to lose the thread for a moment, that's all, a little blackout perhaps? People of our time of life—' gallantly he equalized their age-brackets '—frequently do, you know.'

'And that—' her voice and look were equally sceptical '—that was all?'

'All,' he affirmed stoutly. 'To tell you the truth, it passed so quickly that I almost missed it.'

'Not by the way you were goggling at me,' she returned calmly. 'In my opinion, you're lying.'

He smiled indulgently, yet through his relief—at her recovered sanity—he was somehow gripped by a conviction that

the attack would renew itself at any moment, there was something in her look . . . Yet how unerringly she had spotted and interpreted his look of consternation, on returning from her seizure, the mind still immaculate between its bouts of aberration. Cruel, cruel, yet beyond pity; the thing was too tremendous for pity, one might as well pity a volcanic eruption or other cataclysm of nature . . .

'He wants to put me away,' she blurted without preamble. Again her voice was not quite right, subtly undermined by some imminence. 'Have me out of sight.'

'Hugh?'

'Wants to shut me up somewhere.'

Now there, old girl, you're really off your rocker. His amusement was grim but invisible. *Ironic, isn't it, that you'd accuse him of the one thing he's begun fighting against, tooth and nail?*

'Get control of everything,' she was declaring. 'Watch me till I'm far enough gone, then whip me into a padded cell before you could say knife. With doctors' signatures of course, all correct and legal.'

My God, he thought despairingly. That *brilliant* wrongheadedness, a thousand times more unmanageable than stupid wrong-headedness . . .

'But tell him something from me,' she pursued fiercely. 'Tell my son he needn't wait long, maybe. There's a good reason why not, tell him. Because—because *I* shan't wait.' She grinned at him balefully, triumphantly. 'No, I shan't. So t-tell . . . t-tell . . . .'

It was happening again; punctual to his premonition, it had struck without warning. Again the fierce eyes nailing him had gone blank, the harsh compact features slipping, dissolving— this time into something different: a yearning, witless compassion.

'Poor man,' she mumbled. 'Yes, here's money, yes, you'll . . . . get it for me? Not easy to live, as y'say. No, no, not easy . . .'

'Mrs Tor.' He rose, his heart beating uncomfortably. Ring for her doctor . . . but who was her doctor at the moment? She quarrelled with all of them. 'Thank you very much for

coming in, always a great pleasure—' Oh Lord, now she was getting up. 'If ever I can be of help, in any way—'

She had started moving toward the door, obviously not listening.

'I've an outside appointment now, as it happens,' he lied quickly. 'May I have the pleasure of driving you home?'

On the instant a new spasm twisted her face; she turned on him, her eyes blazing, her mouth going square like Medusa's.

'Don't watch me!' she screamed. 'Spying on me . . . spying . . .' A thread of spittle meandered past her chin, yet once again—unbelievably—the face clarified itself into a half-sanity, a passing cloud-shadow sad beyond belief.

'Never thought . . . it would happen to me like this,' she mourned to someone, not him. 'Any other way . . . not this.' A laugh escaped her, an essence of desolation. 'Something . . . to live for . . .'

He stood silent, hardly daring to breathe.

'Thank you,' she said with dignity, still to someone not there, 'thank you,' and wavered from the room. With hardly a pause he shot to the door and watched her drift, in the same sleepwalking way, from the outer office. The instant she was out of sight—

'Miss Hornby,' he addressed the secretary, whose arrested hands and half-open mouth testified to what she had heard next door and what she was seeing now. 'Would you please follow—' he broke off short. '—no, I'll go myself, if there's trouble I might be of help, you couldn't. When Mr Bateson arrives tell him I'll be back shortly. Don't mention the circumstances, just apologize—'

Breathlessly he left, afraid she might have got too far ahead. No need to worry though, this huge old barracks, once a splendid house, had long and lofty staircases. Tiptoeing to the stairhead he had a good view of her negotiation of a curve beneath him, slow, slow; clutching the banister she descended step by step, somehow as if each downward step administered a jolt or slight shock all through her, sometimes making her stop dead. When she had passed outside, and himself on her heels as quickly as he dared, his next concern was her destination. If she were going to stray about for some unspecified period of time it would complicate things endlessly, what with his next client due in moments . . . Now she had turned right, thank God for that much, but whether her vague and wandering gait were tending homewards . . . . yes! with boundless relief he watched as she crossed the road with proper caution, looking left and right; followed and watched till she entered her own gate and moved slowly up the flagstone path.

* * *

Going back, his thoughts were in the state mostly following a disturbing experience, chaos more or less. Actually, when she had first arrived at his office (without an appointment as usual) he had assumed she wished to consult him about engaging a new companion, the last one having just departed in the usual flurry of agitation and hurt feelings for the usual cause, too much exposure to Mrs Tor's searing tongue. When instead, there, she had launched herself straightaway upon the secret desires and sinister intentions of her son, he had been taken by surprise, perfectly unready to reason with her till he had seen the lay of the land. Not that he had seen it, but— just possibly—had got enough idea of it to go on with. . . .

The beginning of a smile was wiped out as something else occurred to him. That bank business, those withdrawals of hers, mysterious and frequent and palpably unconnected with her household expenditure, for which she drew more or less the same cheque every week; not involving seriously large sums, but now mounting up to respectable totals. Nor did he blame her bank manager for drawing his attention, discreetly, to this most recent caper, indication of the general opinion that she was going around the bend; the man's behaviour was perhaps unethical in the strict sense, but also—perhaps—necessary. What was she doing with it? But how approach her on the subject, an imperious old woman used to running her own affairs without reference to anyone else? ruthlessly preferring, always, to be let alone . . . ?

So: nothing to do that he could see. Her money was hers, she enjoyed unquestioned access to it until declared incompetent.

18

And so long as her fool of a son held out stubbornly against imposing any restraint on her, even the gentlest. . . .

Hurrying faster, less because of his waiting client than the driving pressures of the situation—*What to do?* he repeated mentally. *What* was she doing with those healthy chunks of money, never less than fifty pounds at a time? His mind went far back to an aged client discovered tearing up ten pound notes with an air of earnest and dedicated purpose, and flushing them down the lavatory. . . . Unconsciously he shook his head in negation. She might be withdrawing those sums for some purpose foolish or unwise, but that she was moved by *purpose,* he never for an instant doubted. From her mind, once splendid, there survived too many strong and undamaged strands for him to credit her with some caprice merely imbecile. . . .

His thoughts began flashing on other, and related, aspects. He was already administering part of Mrs Tor's funds, having been appointed by Mrs Tor herself in that capacity. Could he possibly—by help of the dire experience just over—make that son of hers see that she was in crying need of care, get him to agree to a petition in Chancery? The moment had come when she was not fit to be on her own, he would *force* her son to see it . . . . then the appointment, the Chancery appointment. If he knew anything about it, what Chancery would look for was someone of good legal standing, conveniently in the protected person's neighbourhood, preferably having some personal and sympathetic acquaintance with the person herself. And who met these requirements, but . . . . . ? Of course (here he frowned) the son and no one else was the one who must petition, at this stage. Or let him delay unreasonably and see Chancery step in over his head, and *tell* him that. . . . How much, actually, was the old girl worth? What he himself was handling for her must be a trifle; she lived well, she had two servants in residence, how many could say as much nowadays? The total must be impressive, three wealthy husbands she had looted in turn as if to punish them for their presumption in marrying her at all. And look at her now, still leathery, still arrogant, but failing, failing. . . . .

19

As he entered his office he was thinking of the Chancery appointment and its benefits. Virtually complete authority over all her money, not a part; sufficient immunity from impertinent prying . . . The restrained pleasure that overspread his face was hardly changed, this time, by his recollection of the departed 'companion,' poor devil, and the fact that he must see about finding a replacement as soon as possible.

III

'Yes, yes.' With expansive good will the man threw his front door wide. 'Come in, Miss Cory, come in, good of you to do this, y'know. How'd you make it? by car?'

'No, by train.'

'But see here, what a bind for you, two changes. Why not drop me a line at least, I'd have met you at the station?'

'Oh thank you, Mr Kerwin, but that's all right. You're no distance at all from the station, and it's a lovely walk.' She was having time to assess him, the blunt features, strong build, friendly grey eyes larger than ordinary. All cordial, straightforward, prepossessing, yet what she felt for him was a sort of . . . yes, a disparagement, inexplicable . . . 'What a beautiful village this is.'

'Show village, h'm? petrified.' His amusement tuned with the rest of his manner, forthright in a naïve boyish way. 'Stone dead forever—rotten connections with London as you've seen, rotten connections with any place.' Busily he relieved her of her coat and bore it off; she was able to add to her impressions the powerful look of his shoulders and a pleasant rustic look. Then in the same moment she realized his perfect grooming as well as the fact that this rustic look was achieved by a bulky fawn sweater, obviously hand-knit, and suede trousers of a velvety fawn. Still (she argued with her unreasonable preju-

21

dice) why carp at his dressing well? why hold it against him that his healthy skin responded with a sort of bloom to the morning razor? He had a look, though, stubborn . . . ? was that perhaps the root of her unfavourable impression . . . ?

He had returned rapidly and blurted with consternation, 'For God's sake sit down, didn't I ask you? What a hell of a thing, when you've come all this way. I appreciate it too, Miss Cory, it's certainly good of you.'

'I was perfectly willing.' She suspended judgment for the time being. 'Especially since you wrote that an interview, here, was something to do with the job.'

'It's everything to do with the job,' he responded, though with solicitude not yet suspended. 'But you'll have something before we talk, h'm? Coffee, sherry,.you name it—?'

'Nothing at all, thanks.' *Come on, let's get down to it.* 'I had a pretty good breakfast not long ago.'

'Nothing, though? can't offer you . . . ?' At her firm head-shake he made a first motion of drawing up a chair, saying discontentedly, 'Rotten hospitality, you sitting there without a . . . . how's it go? no drop or crumb to stay you . . . ?'

She shook her head again, smilingly.

'All right.' As he sat down she noted that his movements were brusque and unco-ordinated, and again thought of an awkward boy. Still, grace might sit as awkwardly on a chunky body like his. . . .

'All right, Miss Cory, since you'd rather we got down to business. Only first of all, could I say one thing—?' His look combined uncertainty and apology. 'We've got to be—from the very beginning, I mean—straight with eachother. You agree, h'm? perfectly straight?'

'I don't know what you mean by straight,' she returned after a moment of surprise. 'If you're afraid I'll represent myself falsely, or offer you fake references—'

'Christ, nothing like that!' He was horrified. 'Open my mouth —put my foot—' he was working hard to reassemble himself. 'No, what I meant was. . . .'

He broke off again, and she began to realize that language came hard to him; that ease, let alone felicity, was not one of his gifts. Poor boy, getting his thoughts into words would always be a struggle for him. And why, incidentally, had she thought *poor boy* instead of *poor man . . .* ?

'It's like this,' he was saying. 'I've a bad situation here, can't call it anything else. There're things about it I can't keep back, nor I shan't even try to. So when I've—well, told you the worst—all I ask from you is a . . .' he shook his head as if fly-tormented '. . an *honest* answer. I mean, if it's no, just let me have it straight. I mean, don't try to let me down easy, don't say you'll think about it or decide later, that sort of stuff. That's wasting time, and unless I'm dead wrong time's running out, there's no time to waste . . .' He appeared to wrest himself from some dire inward vision. 'Or don't offer to have a go if your common sense tells you you can't handle it. Halfway feelings of that sort, halfway . . . *attitudes . . .*'

He brought it out triumphantly; she could guess at the effort it had cost him.

'. . . they're no help in this situation,' he was pursuing. 'What you'll give this job, if you give it at all, has got to be a hundred per cent, one hundred per cent, or nothing. That's all I meant when I said we'd got to be straight with eachother.' He stared at her in propitiation almost haggard. 'That's all I meant, Miss Cory, honestly.'

'Of course,' she murmured ashamed, also considerably undermined. 'Stupid of me to misunderstand.'

'No, why shouldn't you? It's just a matter of realizing that in this—this case—the most you can do may not be enough, p'rhaps.' His eyes explored the invisible trouble, and returned to her. 'But before we start going into it, could we—' he was suddenly diffident '—could we talk about you a little, Miss Cory? Please?'

* * *

'Of course,' she agreed warmly. 'I'd expect to give some account of myself, only it's dull—what there is of it.'

'I don't even know your Christian name,' he suggested in the same apologetic manner. 'You've always been J. Cory.'

'Jacintha. —Well, I've no family to speak of. My father's

dead, he was with a firm of solicitors near Cambridge. My mother's bought an annuity, she lives in one of those communities for the elderly. We don't often correspond, there's never been much in common between us. My father left me some insurance—one of those amounts that looks all right, till you begin taking bites out of it.'

He smiled with respectful, if rueful, understanding.

'Well, I went to Somerville and took a second in music—'

'Why, you're a musician?' he interrupted. 'Great! What d'you play?'

'Piano. Not bad, but not concert, nothing like that.'

'Mh'm'.

'But I'd always known I didn't want to teach or accompany, so I got a job in an artists' agency.'

'A secretary?' he asked.

'Not actually.' His faint air of disappointment or disparagement had not been lost on her. 'Though I'm a pretty fair typist. No, what I was in charge of was programs—being in touch with the artists about what they'd sing or play, arranging all that for the printers, then proof-reading. They're in three or four different languages you know, programs—they've got to be absolutely correct.'

'I say, I've never thought of that before.' He was pleased with her again. 'Dashed clever of you.'

'And meanwhile, I was picking up quite a lot about management—planning tours, working out trains and planes and hotels and being in constant touch with the publicity side. It's terrifically complicated but interesting, I was getting not too bad at it.' Warmed by his simple-hearted admiration, she expanded incautiously. 'Well then, through this agency I met someone—'

She broke off short, slightly dismayed.

'You met someone,' he repeated after a moment. His voice and manner, perfectly undemanding, nevertheless compelled her to finish what she had begun.

'Well, someone . . . who offered me a better opportunity.'

'Mm.' His expression had changed as his thoughts turned inward on something he viewed—obviously—without pleasure.

'What I seem to get out of all this—' his gaze, returning to her after a moment, had become as flat as his voice '—is, that you're sort of marking time? till this "better opportunity" comes through?' He paused again. 'You'd see this job with my mother as a . . . sort of stop-gap?'

'Well, yes,' she had to admit.

'Mm. Well, in that case—' his look had turned dark if not sulky '—I wish you'd made that clear at once, Miss Cory. Save time for both of us—if you had done.' He made to rise. 'Someone that's got in view to take this job for a couple of months, that's no good to me, less than no good. Well, thank you for—'

'Not a couple of months,' she blurted across his dismissal. Bragging, God, a little male admiration turned her on . . . 'A year. It'd be a year anyway.'

He continued half out of his chair, silent and palpably indecisive, before sinking back again, slowly, and saying with reserve, 'That's better.' His eyes, pinning her again, were still mistrustful. 'But how d'you know it'll be that long? a whole year?'

'I know,' she said dryly, resolved not to explain further; if her word weren't good enough, let him jump in the river. 'It's a business arrangement.'

'You promise me that, h'h?'

'Yes.'

'I can depend on it? absolutely?'

'Absolutely.' Beneath her ostensibly-regained composure, she still reviled herself; any shakiness, during a first interview, was the very worst you could do for yourself. 'It's something that can't possibly develop in less than a year. Even so, I'd give you long notice before I went.' She pulled up. 'That is, if you're still considering me for the job.'

'You bet,' he returned with medium warmth. How transparent he was with his reviving but still-tempered cordiality, afraid of believing her completely; it amused rather than offended her, along with her undeniable relief that the good tone of their conference was coming back. Also she was determined, utterly determined, not to put another foot wrong. . . .

'Sorry if I was a bit stuffy just now. I mean, showing it like that.' His apology, earnest and blundering, captured in her a first real sense of warmth toward him. 'Only you'll see in a moment why I can't leave anything in the air. I mean, leave anything to chance, not even little details.' His eyes again had that brooding look of exploring a lost battlefield, before they returned to her. 'Thank you a hell of a lot for telling me about you, and—and being so nice about my foul temper. And now—'

He sighed, an unconscious, heavy sound.

'—now, Miss Cory, let's talk about my mother.'

* * *

She waited. Waited, moreover, not only with sympathy but with a sort of growing involvement. Perhaps it was that *I mean,* repeated and repeated, that swayed her; a pathos of the inarticulate. . . . .

'My mother is Mrs Tor, Mrs Valeria Tor,' he was saying. 'Maybe you've heard of her?'

'No,' she admitted. 'Ought I to've . . . ?'

'Lord no.' He was grimly amused. 'She's old stuff, before your time—before the second war. I was a kid myself, all I remember is this sort of . . . hearing about her at second hand, something going on far off, always far off. In newspapers, and people talking to you about it, and . . . excitement generally. I was at school,' he explained, 'and she was all over the place—Spain, South America, God knows where, any place but where I was.' He smiled ruefully. 'But she was a big noise all right, for a bit.'

'I hate to sound so ignorant,' she petitioned into his pause, 'but what did she do?'

'Oh, she dug up something or other in South America, kind of a burial I expect. Don't go thinking about King Tut,' he adjured humourously. 'Nothing like that. But I seem to remember—' he frowned '—that there was some gold where gold oughtn't to be, sort of, and it raised hell among the eggheads—started them writing long letters to newspapers, abusing eachother—you know.'

26

'An archeologist,' she ventured.

'That's it. She's got medals from highbrow societies and cuttings, tons of cuttings, to prove she was front-page stuff in her day. Give some people a taste of that,' his smile was troubled, 'and they keep wanting it like a tiger wants blood. Can't get over it, you know.'

'I see,' she murmured vaguely, then realized the further change in him; he was gathering himself, now, for extended and difficult explanation.

'So I expect you can understand,' he began, with new care and deliberation, 'that mother was a brainy woman. Brilliant, actually, and did she know it. Impatient, high-handed, and the hell of a temper.' As he smiled with a sort of apology, it occurred to her that his mother, as a topic, seemed to spur his powers of description. 'But now she's beginning to have blackouts. Or maybe I'm using the wrong word for them?' he appealed. 'I mean, she's liable to forget where she is, can't recognize the person she's been talking to, I've seen it happen. —I promised you,' he digressed abruptly, 'that I wouldn't keep anything back—I'd give it to you straight.'

'Yes,' she returned slowly; his pause had demanded an answer. 'But all this doesn't sound worse than what happens to —to many old people, does it?'

'That's how it strikes you?' He had kindled with sudden hope. 'It doesn't scare you?'

'Not so far, but of course—'

'That's how I feel about it,' he cut off her disclaimer. 'Exactly how I feel. These bastards that want to make it sound bad as possible—' he sounded flustered and defenceless '—make it out as if it were insanity, or not far off—'

'How old is your mother?' she ventured.

'How old?' He emerged from his troubled vision and laughed. 'The dates she gives *Who's Who* and that lot, I've always thought she was lying by a few years, but who cares? She's eighty, that much you can bet on. A little on this side or that, but say eighty and you're close.'

'Not all that old.' Again he had seemed to expect some comment. 'Not nowadays.'

27

'No. She's all right *physically,* you know. Tough as she ever was, terrific constitution, but the fact is, she does have these spells. Can't play that down.' He shook his head despondently. 'Never did see the use of shutting my eyes.'

'I'm not a nurse,' she warned, suddenly alarmed. 'Least of all a psychiatric nurse.'

'Thank God,' he returned heartily. 'If you were peddling that sort of muck, I shouldn't be int'rested. All the same you've put your finger on it, Miss Cory,' he announced with new solemnity. *'Now* we're getting down to it.'

She waited.

'She's had companions,' he resumed. 'I think it's her solicitor who advertises for her mostly, or maybe not. The point is that these old girls from adverts, they come up against my mother and God help them—she eats them up alive and spits out the pieces. Poor old biddies, nattering about the weather and prices of this and that . . .' he shook his head despairingly.

'I can see how it wouldn't establish communication with your mother,' she assented dryly. 'Not as you've made me see her, at any rate.'

'They drive her up the wall—bring out the worst in her. And my mother's worst, Miss Cory,' he assured her weightily, 'must be seen to be believed.'

Her silence, after a moment, seemed to come home to him.

'Oh Lord, have I put you off?' he besought. 'She's not violent, you know, nothing like that. Outside of these spells of hers she's sane, most of the time. Saner than most, actually.'

Bent toward her like a suppliant, he pled his mother's cause.

'What she needs, Miss Cory, is a *friend.* Someone that's got . . . well, background. *Imagination.*' He brought it out triumphantly. 'That's what I've been trying to get at, imagination. Someone that can think up little . . . interests, occupations . . . take her mind off herself. And it'll help that you're young.' He grinned. 'God, how she hates old people. Funny, h'm?'

'Just now you said she had spells.' She by-passed his mirthless amusement, her attention caught on a word as on a projecting nail. 'What spells? What are they?'

28

'T'tell you the truth,' he said after a moment, 'I don't know exactly, I'm not here enough.' He was apologetic. 'It's just that I've heard her talk a . . . a little nonsense, maybe—'

'But what nonsense?' she urged against his dwindling voice. 'I must have some idea, don't you see? If she just springs something on me, how can I cope? Can't you remember anything specific, I don't care what? Try,' she besought. 'Please try.'

A pause fell; he had shaken his head then gnawed a thumb, obviously racking his memory. Just as she resigned herself to nothing his face changed a little, dubiously.

'It seems to me that she'll . . . take a dislike to this house now and again, not that I paid all that much attention . . .' he paused uncertainly. 'But she seemed afraid of someone, something, in the house—wanted to pull up and just get out.' He laughed distressfully. 'At her age, eh? in her condition?'

She bowed her head, sharing the ruinous vision.

'Miss Cory.' He was speaking suddenly, softly, in a voice of extremity. 'I'll tell you something. When I got your answer to the advertisement, I felt it was a . . . a sort of last hope. And now that I've seen you, talked with you, I know somehow that you're . . . you're her last chance. Her only chance.'

Flattered, undermined, she salvaged enough balance to ask cautiously, 'But you say she's not, actually, violent . . . ?'

'*God* no!' He was horrified. 'D'you think I'd run you up blind against anything dangerous, d'you think I'm that much of a rat—!'

'No, no. Well . . . .' Still wavering, with a new cowardice suddenly to the fore, she sat with her eyes on the problematic life that was being offered her '. . . if the situation's no worse than you say, if what you've told me is all of it. . . .'

His silence reached her belatedly; she looked at him and registered his latest atmosphere, dark and reluctant.

'I told you I wouldn't keep anything back,' he said after the pause, doggedly. 'There's an old girl lives in mother's house, this old bat named Mary Pargill. Mother's secretary a million years ago, well, more like a dogsbody. Not worth a damn any more and hangs on like a leech—goes on living off mother.' He paused. 'Well, I couldn't just let you run into Mary without warning.'

'You'd better tell me more,' she said coolly, over an unpleasant qualm.

'The thing is, you'd have nothing to do with her,' he pursued urgently. 'I can promise you that, Miss Cory. I understand she and mother've had some pretty vicious rows, and now she's holed up on the second floor—never comes out of her room.'

She sat blank of thought or comment, yet aware how anxiously—how painfully—his silence hung upon hers.

'I know, I know,' he assented, as if she had spoken. 'And pension her off and sling her out, no, mother won't. Won't get rid of her, just doesn't want to know. But I swear to you—' excess of earnestness dammed him up for a moment '—the woman makes no difference, chances are you might never set eyes on her—even the servants don't hardly, I understand. But she's *there*,' he summed up despondently. 'So I had to tell you.'

'She's old?' Jacintha hazarded after a moment.

'Mother's age more or less.' He shrugged. 'Have to be.'

'And demented.'

'No!' he contradicted with force. 'Absolutely nothing like that. She'll complain to anyone that brings up her food—sound off— I've heard that from the servants. But no more than that, *no!* If there were, I'd have had her taken away long ago—mother or no mother, I'd have managed it somehow.'

From mere blankness, again, her silence prolonged itself.

'Don't let this scare you away, Miss Cory.' In his low voice was an extremity of petition. '*Please* don't.'

'I'm not scared,' she returned truthfully. 'I was just thinking, I mean, let me think a moment . . .'

He subsided, his gaze remaining riveted.

She continued tossed on eddies of indecision; extra money, a year's living at almost no expense, but a strange household, *strange* . . . . . then a floating shape appeared in her cogitations, a shape of strong and stronger outline as it reappeared, for all it was unexpected. To leave this house without satisfying that shape of curiosity; to lose forever the chance of setting eyes

30

on the crumbling monument of long-gone attainments, who must have had the most astonishing life. . . .

'All this talk is no use, of course,' she announced to him, 'without your mother's seeing me first.'

'By God, you're right.' He shot up galvanically. 'Come on, let's go over—now.'

'W-wait,' she stammered with equal precipitation. 'Wait.'

* * *

He subsided again, his expectant eyes always fixed on her.

'You can't throw me at her just like that,' she argued. 'We must—we must plan some sort of approach.'

'Of course!' he acclaimed the revelation. 'We can't shove you at her, just like that—of course not.'

'So I'd have to know just a little more about her. . . .' From a comparative void, she extorted enquiry. 'Does she dislike women, as a general thing?'

'No.' He was on slightly firmer ground. 'Actually she's sorry I'm a son instead of a daughter. She's told me so more than once—made no bones about it.'

'I see. But what does she *like,* apart from her profession? gardening?'

He shook his head.

'Music?'

'No, I don't expect so. There's a big piano in her living-room, but I've never heard her use it that I remember.'

'Not very promising, is it?' Her eyes probed for other horizons. 'Well, does she ever write? about her discoveries?'

'God, not any more. She has done, but all that's deader than mutton. Anyway, at her age . . . .'

'Well—' her tone was of final recourse, without much hope '—you said that she, or her solicitor, has advertised for a companion?'

'Yes, that's so.'

'And where—in *The Lady?*'

'Now how—' his voice revived a little with admiration '—how'd you ever know that?'

'It sounds likely, for someone of her generation—and for a

job of that sort.' In her turn and without warning, she jumped up. 'I think maybe I've thought of something, but quick . . . .' She breathed as if badly winded. '. . . take me along to her now, quick—before I lose my nerve.'

* * *

The next-door house was opened to them by a maid, a dense-looking type. Surprising all the same to find that much staff in a country house, moreover in correct uniform; it took a great deal of money to maintain a style like that. After a murmured enquiry he was leading her through a hall; for all her stage-fright there reached her a sense of its handsomeness, solid ranks of old prints on the walls and a thick runner underfoot. Then, visibly bracing himself, he knocked gingerly on a panelled door, and in response to an indistinct sound within turned the knob as gingerly, advanced his head—and no more —through the opening, and addressed an unseen presence, 'Mother, a young lady to see you, Miss Cory.'

A pause fell, somehow unpropitious; after it—

'Who?' came a voice, harsh yet curiously dead.

'Miss Cory.'

'What's she want?'

'Some work, she says.'

'Work? got no work. What work?'

'Ask her yourself,' he returned with unexpected hardihood. 'She came to my door by mistake. Will you see her, or not?'

Quailing, she waited for a rebuke; nothing came, except another silence. Yet in this silence must have been some form of acquiescence, for he withdrew his head, gave her a quick hard look of incitement, and held the door wider. She passed in and heard it close behind her, all but soundlessly. Alone, defenceless before the unknown she took a quivering breath, then lessened the distance between herself and the wordless motionless presence, by a single hesitant step.

IV

Her sense of the room itself—except for its being small and bright, from french doors looking on a garden—was completely eclipsed by the occupant of a high-backed chair with arms; and again, her sense of this occupant was not of its merely physical attributes. That it should be old and gaunt, that its nose should be sharp and aquiline and its gaze noncommittal beneath untidy grizzled hair did not affect her, since she had visualized some such image. What struck her was the figure's atmosphere, far less definable than its aspect and far more daunting; its look of being crushed down into the chair by some giant weight; its look of intense, remote melancholy—leavened, mysteriously, with a suggestion of power not dead but sleeping; an ability to strike back, and strike *hard*. . . . Already longing to turn tail and flee, she blurted, 'Good morning, Mrs Tor.' Successfully, at least, she had controlled an imminent quaver. 'Thank you very much for seeing me.'

The figure took a long moment to stir very slightly; the immobility that engulfed it seemed almost too vast to overcome. Having by that much acknowledged the visitor's presence, she said slowly, 'What do you want?'

'I saw your advertisement.' Not knowing where the lie would take her, she plunged boldly yet speciously. 'In *The Lady*, an awfully old number. Very old, I'm afraid,' she admitted

33

ingenuously. 'But it sounded so—so unusual—that I thought, it mightn't hurt to—to try. I mean, if by some chance you still weren't suited . . . . ?'

She paused, holding her breath and peering to see if she had given offense. The graven image, far from responding, gave no sign that it had listened; when hope appeared to be lost, it answered, 'No, I'm not suited.' The words contained a lingering irony; the eyes, colourless with age and sunk in their pits, gave her a feeling of disquiet—as if their surveillance saw through her lies and faltering pretences, saw through them totally and all too easily . . . And no more than that, no word to help her, no question, not a syllable. . . .

'Of course I don't know your requirements.' All at once she was no longer terrified; overstrained fear had snapped and set her free. 'I don't know the kind of help you want or expect,' she pursued clearly. 'If you'd tell me, please?' Oh God, was this a little *too* bold? 'So I needn't waste your time?'

'What are you good for?' returned the harsh dull voice. The question was unexpectedly prompt, and its devastating form probably intentional. 'What can you do?'

'I . . .' The old woman's disdainful waiting, the implication of her uselessness, had unsettled her again; she had to gulp before essaying, 'I type pretty well.'

'Type.' The echo, sardonic and even derisive, nettled her into saying too quickly and defensively, 'And I can take orders and carry them out exactly. And I'm not a bad plain cook.'

'I've got a cook,' murmured Mrs Tor. 'I have no need of two.'

'No, but on her days off—? It was just my impression,' she explained, somehow with a new instinct of submissiveness, 'that what was required was someone not terribly specialized, but capable of—of not being a fool. So since I've had a sort of interruption to—to my own work . . . .'

'I see,' the old woman nodded slightly, after another pause. Not troubling to ask the nature of this interrupted work, all the same she had shown a first faint flicker of interest. 'You need other work.'

'Yes. —I'm not a nurse though,' she warned hastily, a second time.

34

'A nurse is the last thing I need,' Mrs Tor replied in her harsh dull voice. 'Or want.'

Seeming to retire to immeasurable distance, she brooded. During this period of her evident obliviousness to any outside voice or presence, Jacintha took the opportunity (with caution, so as not to be caught staring) to assess the image in detail. From this scrutiny she found herself impressed—not only deeply, but imaginatively. Former reputation of any sort could in some mysterious way (she decided) leave about its possessor an indefinable aura, capable of making its old age different from most other old age. Certainly she could still feel this old woman's distinction, still feel the power that must have emanated from her in younger days. A woman who had penetrated jungles, unearthed from jungle obliteration things lost and buried, whatever they were . . . and this was the same woman, unbelievably, this poor old bony thing with its nondescript clothes, untidy hair and hopeless look; an old dragon whose fiery breath had gone quenched and cold. . . .

In the old eyes, deep in their wrinkled nests, a slight movement could be seen as they changed focus from in-looking to out.

'You might do,' sighed the dragon, unbelievably.

Jacintha stopped breathing.

'For what, God only knows.' She was talking to herself again. 'Can't go on though . . .' Once more the voice was self-communing, the gaze fixed on disconsolateness '. . . go on this way . . . *can't!*'

A stillness came, that the other dared not break.

'Might try then, might as well . . .' came next in a lifeless murmur, with the straying focus that hardly troubled to look at her. 'When can you come?'

'At—at once, I mean almost at once,' she stammed, unready. 'I'd have to go back to London and pack,' and saw instantly—without a single word or gesture from her employer —that she was dismissed. With no word said, moreover, about pay, accommodation, duties, free time; either the old woman had the regal assurance that someone else attended to such details, or she was incapable of discussing them herself. Just as she ignored such things regally, she dismissed—regally.

The visitor got up, offered goodbyes (not answered) and suppressed a wry inclination to curtsey and back from the room. Hurrying down the splendid passage and out of the house, she thought grotesquely: was it safe to go straight next door? She paused, really worried. Unthinkable that the old woman could have stirred from that monstrous lassitude to follow quickly and spy on her, but right or wrong she must risk it . . . At her single tap, somehow as breathless as herself, the door whipped open instantly, as if he had been waiting on the other side of it.

* * *

He delayed only enough to ask her to a seat. 'Well?' he demanded, his face strained with anxiety and interrogation. 'How'd it go?'

'Not too badly, perhaps.' She was still short of breath. 'If she . . . . I mean, if she doesn't change her mind . . . she said I could come.'

'No!' he exploded. Incredulity and wonderment lit his face in succession. '*No!*'

'But don't—don't count too much on it.' She drew another unravelled breath. 'She seemed willing to let me try, that's all it amounts to.'

'But even to get that far with her—' his optimism was still high. 'I hadn't hoped for that much, honestly I—' he checked. 'Jacintha, tell me how you brought it off. What she said, what you said—tell me.'

'Honestly—' What she remembered, chiefly, was an assortment of silences. 'She said very little, asked me what I could do. And,' she smiled involuntarily, 'didn't seem to think much of it.'

'And God, is she good at that,' he returned fervently. 'Stamping you down and keeping you down.'

'Then she said did I need the work, and when I said yes—well, it seemed as if my *needing* it made some sort of difference

36

with her maybe—only maybe. At any rate, she said I could come.'

'And that's all? that's the lot?'

'Yes. Except—' She seized the opportunity and was glad of it. '—except that she never said one word about . . . about . . .'

'About your pay, your free time?' he supplied into her hesitation. 'Anything?'

'Hugh, don't think I'm worried about such details.' She had said *Hugh* without intending to; it had come about so naturally, Hugh and Jacintha. 'Only it's odd that she'd engage someone without a word about such things, not one syllable—'

'Well, don't worry.' His laugh was half-amused, half-wry. 'Her solicitor takes care of things like that—she always shoves such details on to him. He's a pleasant sort,' he amplified. 'I was just going to tell you about him, only first I wanted to—'

The peal that blasted off between them startled both equally; for a moment he let it ring, before picking up the phone and saying. 'Yes.' Implicit in his curt voice was his readiness to cut the other short, yet at once his manner became different. 'Oh hello, John . . . yes, sure, when? . . . OK, if you like, I can be with you in a few . . . Oh, here? you'd rather? . . . OK, see you.' He rang off. 'Talk of the devil.' His smile was peculiar, still wry but incongruously mixed with a relief of sorts. 'Old John himself, on his way.'

'I'd better—'

'No!' Decisively he forestalled her move of departure. 'You'd have to meet him in connection with taking the job, might as well do it now. You just sit tight, Jacintha.'

'But if he'll want to see you privately—'

'If he does, we'll arrange it.' He looked anxious for a moment. 'I wonder what he wants. Only an emergency, or what he calls emergency, would bring him to my doorstep. Actually,' he explained, 'he's never been here before.'

'I'll stop if you say so,' she said hesitantly. 'But if he wants you to sling me out, don't be embarrassed.'

'Don't you worry about that. Don't worry about anything.' A gleam escaped him, a comforting sort of firmness. 'He'll be here any moment, it's only a step away—' his eye was constantly on the bow window overlooking the road. 'Just wait and see. If he's got reasons for wanting you out of this, I may have my own reasons for wanting you here—' he broke off abruptly. 'That's his car, I think.' He was already on his feet before the doorbell had sounded. 'Sit tight now, Jacintha.' His smile in fact, while warming and steadying her, reflected an uncertainty of his own. ' 'Scuse a moment.'

* * *

Empty of thought, anticipation, of the need to brace herself—for against what, actually?—she heard from the hall the sounds of admittance and greeting, but brief and inaudible, before a man appeared in the doorway. A tall man, was her first impression, before Hugh's coming close behind him made her realize they were more or less of a height; it was the newcomer's slenderness, compared with Hugh's foursquare look, that gave him this deceptive tallness. She rose at Hugh's matter-of-fact, 'Miss Cory, Mr Dennison,' now perceiving his elegance —and feeling, likewise, his invisible check at the presence of a third, unforeseen and undesired presence at what he had thought would be a private conference. Yet with unruffled ease he seated himself at Hugh's invitation, turned upon her an impeccably courteous smile, and asked, 'Is this your first visit to our village, Miss Cory?'

To their further exchanges, inexorable as the planets in their courses, Hugh sat amiably attending; her furtive glance at him got her no more than a sense of his waiting with no anxiety or other tension. Meanwhile the small currency of politeness ran out, and if this man with his accomplished manner would never check it too abruptly, he could all the same make clear that he had no time to waste.

'Hugh,' he said, with a deprecating smile. 'Could you beg your charming visitor to excuse us very briefly, while we dispose of our tiresome business? I know that Miss Cory will forgive my mentioning—' the smile had turned her way '—that I'm a bit rushed at the moment, and our problem is somewhat urgent—'

He paused in the polite expectation that is virtual certainty; she was silent, looking toward Hugh.

38

'It's OK, John, quite OK.' His voice was cordial, ever eager. 'Anything we're going to discuss, Miss Cory had better hear, actually I'd like her to hear. So go ahead.' Clear-eyed, he met the other's gaze. 'Go straight ahead.'

'But—' for all his professional suavity, the man of law was taken aback. '—but a discussion of this sort—of this particular nature—'

'Go ahead, old man, you can say anything,' he stressed his reassurance. 'Miss Cory's just been engaged by mother, as a companion. So the more she's on to the situation, you know—' his voice turned half pleading, half propitiating '—the better.'

* * *

Dennison's pose, his sudden silence, expressed not only a check but a complicated check, its nature still unrevealed.

'Miss Cory answered an advertisement,' Hugh supplemented, and his manner of doing so engaged the bystander's admiration. He was not saying whose advertisement, he was putting it up to the other man to do so, and by every canon of civilized exchanges the other man could hardly do this, however much he wanted to. Checkmate, actually, unexpected in clumsy old Hugh. . . .

'I see,' Dennison had responded; she could feel the questions he wanted to ask, the answers he was dying to extort. . . .

'I see,' he repeated neutrally, over a cold anger. *She advertised, without telling me. Good God, what can one do with such* . . . 'A fait accompli.'

'Very,' the other returned. 'Exact word, accomplee.'

She tried to decide, vaguely, whether his accent were mere bad French or deliberate burlesque.

'There was something you wanted to tell me?' he had asked. 'Important, you said?'

'Yes,' the solicitor answered, and from his curt response and the subtle change in his manner she divined something: that he now abandoned the gentle approach and was going to lay it on the line fast and hard. 'Yesterday your mother, in my office, had a lapse—seizure, whatever you call it—of rather a serious nature. More serious, in fact, than I've ever seen.'

'Serious? how?' asked Hugh, after a pause. His face was suddenly haunted, his manner subdued. 'What did she say? or do, or . . . ?'

'She was speaking to me rationally, when all at once she lost . . . all sense of my identity, of where she was—everything.' Regarding Hugh stonily, 'Everything,' he repeated.

'Was that all?' Hugh asked, after a moment. 'I mean, all of it?'

'One might consider it enough.' His irony was unstressed. 'And when she went, she—'

'Just one moment,' Hugh interrupted. 'She left, you're saying. Was she still sort of funny, or had she snapped out of it by then?'

'Not *out* of it. She'd partly regained her power of recognition and recollection, but only partly. Then, when I proposed seeing her home,' he paused, 'she screamed at me—actually screamed.'

'Said she didn't want to be followed?' Hugh asked suddenly, on an accent of recognition.

'Yes.'

'I thought so.' He relaxed perceptibly. 'Old stuff that, you know—she's done it before.'

'Also in the course of her first seizure, while we were talking,' the other continued, his voice becoming colder, 'she was suddenly talking to someone who was trying to get money from her. I'm not sure of the exact words, but I'm sure of her manner—of acceding to demands. Demands, or quite possibly,' he appended, 'blackmail? . . extortion. . . ?'

'Extortion?' Hugh repeated, with an evident mental fumbling. 'Someone's trying to get money out of her—?'

'Evidently.'

'Then all I can say is—' his face, clearing rapidly, developed a grin '—God help them.'

'It's all you can say? then what do you say to this?' The solicitor's new manner, his driving rapidity, were eloquent of something he had kept back to the very last. 'Do you know she's been making frequent withdrawals from her bank, cash withdrawals, quite separate from her weekly household expenses? Did you know that?'

40

'No.'

He had admitted it after a moment, now patently bewildered. It was this bewilderment—its painful and helpless quality—that roused in the spectator a second feeling of support in his behalf. *Don't let him bully you,* she exhorted silently. *Don't, Hugh, don't.*

'Withdrawals?' he was asking now, his tone hesitant. 'Large ones?'

'Well, no—not over fifty pounds a time. But the frequency with which she does it—'

'How frequent? how often?'

'Well, at intervals.' The solicitor hesitated. 'Not too frequent, actually. But the fact that she does it, that she—'

'Look.' Hugh's look and tone were recovering. 'She may have her reasons—'

'Reasons!'

'It's her money.' His accent was stubborn. 'It's hers.'

'Well, and what do you say to this?' The other's tone was of a final blow, a blow delayed but at last administered. 'Did you know she's been seen with people hereabouts, various characters completely unknown and disreputable? What d'you say to that?'

Hugh was silent a moment, seeming to consider; his manner, all in all, much less shaken by this announcement than one would think. 'What people?' he asked after the pause. 'What characters?'

'I don't know.' Dennison's manner, submerging a trifle on this point, recovered. 'How would I? I can only tell you that the meetings were seen, and reported to me, by two of your mother's . . ah . . . former companions. They had to keep at such a distance, of course, that better observation wasn't possible. But the *fact* of such meetings—'

'Look, John.' With calm totally recovered, Hugh cut across him. 'This is an old old story with mother, talking to riffraff of all sorts if they happen to interest her. Gypsies, tramps, she's always done it—'

'These meetings were not casual encounters,' the other cut across in turn. 'They were deliberately arranged in out-of-the-way places. Or that's the impression both my informants had, they—'

'Your informants?' Hugh interrupted again. 'Those old girls that mother's always kicking out because of their wooliness?'

'All the same,' the solicitor retorted. A faint redness had appeared on his cheekbones. 'These meetings were observed three times, *three times,* which argues that others were un-observed—'

'All right,' Hugh interposed. 'Allow that the meetings were planned, who can say one way or the other? But whether or no, I've a new idea—wait, John, wait just a moment.'

The solicitor subsided unwillingly.

'I'm only saying—I'm only trying to say—'

Silently the audience of one applauded this hit.

'—that I've something new planned for mother. I mean, not a new plan maybe but with something new behind it. That's to say I—I—'

She sent all her sympathy to him as he groped, as so often, for words; the solicitor imperturbably waited.

'—I'm going on a new *theory* of her condition.' He had succeeded in re-launching himself. 'And the theory is . . . *lone-liness.*' He paused; the hollow sound of it seemed to expand in the room. 'I think she's lonely, and it makes her act worse, or seem worse, than she is actually. So I thought, if someone could be found who'd be a real companion to her, someone intelligent, not one of those droopy half-witted old birds you've been digging up for her. Not like one of those.'

A tightening of the solicitor's mouth, and no more, acknowl-edged this hit. She was glad to see it, yet at the same moment was aware of something not quite in line, some edge of in-congruity, sharp . . . ?

'So I advertised—*I* did it, this time—for someone with brains, educated, and I found Miss Cory. So play along a bit, would you, John? Just till we see how she handles the situation?' His tone had changed to petition, even pleading. 'Give us a little time, won't you?' He waited. 'Or let's say if Miss Cory can't help mother in five or six months, if mother gets worse . . . .'

42

The other remained silent; he continued arguing against this silence.

'. . . well then, in that case . . . .' His voice was running down. '. . . but first, I'd like to try . . .'

The other man sat impassive, then said suddenly, 'Incorrigibly hopeful, Hugh, aren't you? Even a bit artless with it?'

'That's how I sound to you?'

She sat breathless suddenly, expectant of some collision.

'OK.' Against the slurring intention, whatever it was, he had reassembled his good humour. 'OK, let it go at that.'

'By all means.' Dennison was rising. 'By all means.'

'And so far as mother meeting these people goes—' he had reverted '—well, she's not going far away to do it and she knows her way hereabouts perfectly well—'

'I've said it, Hugh,' the other responded. 'Let your mother run here and there and get into whatever she chooses, it's your affair entirely.'

'Ah, John.' He was suddenly amused, with a full-fledged grin. 'It's a village High Street out there, it's not Stepney or something. Is it? Now is it?'

* * *

When he returned from seeing the visitor out, she was on her feet.

'Sit down,' he besought, sounding alarmed. 'You're not lighting out because of him, for God's sake—?'

'No, no,' she returned restlessly. 'It's just that—just that—'

'Ah, he's upset you a bit,' he pacified gently. 'You mustn't take it like that, he's used to running things pretty much where mother's concerned, that's all.'

'Too much so,' she blurted, then could have bitten her tongue out.

'No, not actually.' He was always soothing. 'Lucky for her that she's got someone at hand, you know. And I'm not here a good bit, it's with him you'll have to deal, in case of emergency —' he broke off suddenly. 'That is, if you're still willing to take the job—?'

'Yes, I'd like to,' she responded at once. Future difficulties crowded in on her; she turned her back on them. 'I'd like to try.'

'Well, thank God.' He let out a long breath. 'And you'll come, when—?'

'Soon as possible, in a couple of days. I must give up my room, arrange one or two things—'

'Of course, of course. Now as to my part in this, my own part—' he hesitated. 'I'll be gone when you return, I'm afraid, but I'll be in touch—' he paused again, then went on rapidly, 'See here. There's a call-box just to the right, you must have passed it on your way here—'

'Yes,' she recalled, after a moment.

'—well, if you could be near it every evening, say from eight-thirty to eight forty-five—'

'That ought to be easy.'

'Well, I'll try to call you then. If I don't, well, you'll know I couldn't. But if you'd be there, between eight-thirty and—'

'And eight forty-five. Don't worry, I will if I can.'

'Fine. We'll keep in touch, somehow.' He was walking beside her to the hall. 'And don't worry about old John, if ever you can't get me and you need help—' he stopped abruptly. '—anyway you'll have to be seeing him about your pay and so-forth, only it's not my place to send you.' He grinned. 'But he'll do what he can, always, if there's any—wait!' He had stopped her as she reached to open the door. 'Mother might just be about, she's pretty unexpected—' he looked out, up and down the road. 'All clear, but don't linger. 'Bye now!'

* * *

With *don't linger!* in her ears she began to walk fast toward the station—then, as unthinkingly, stopped short. All this scramble, what for? to be out of whose way? She had left Mrs Tor sunk deep in her mysterious abstraction and deeper still in her chair; highly unlikely, for all of Hugh, that this immobility should have translated itself into action. Or again, if she happened to run once more into Hugh or the solicitor, what of it? Simply tell the truth—that she wanted to see more of the village that would be her home, virtually, for the next twelve months. At the thought she turned back decisively, passed Mrs Tor's house and her son's house and struck out toward the church standing splendid and lonely in the churchyard beyond the village's end.

A good forty minutes later, having visited this, having admired the few surviving Elizabethan houses and explored a few side streets, all petering out into countryside, she was on her way back to the station, slightly tired and vaguely dissatisfied. The village was small, clean, and wonderfully tranquil. Also—so far as she could tell—wonderfully dull. Lonely evenings stretched away from her in endless succession, and a hollowness struck at her heart. Still, the money . . . . even the thought of money did nothing to cheer her for the moment. Still, that was probably the result of evening coming on, grey and coldish, she had better get along to the station. . . . .

Instead, passing a handsome pub called the Wheatsheaf, she turned in, found the bar, and sat down at a corner table. The place was large and fairly full already, with new arrivals coming in every moment. More tired than she knew she was glad to lean back, order, and presently receive a glass of sherry. Sipping it gratefully she looked about her with interest and uninterest mixed. She might become acquainted with some of these people, well-dressed on the whole, and began amusing herself by picking out those she would like to know. That agreeable-looking young woman further along her row, for example, with the nice-looking man . . . her eyes moved to the next couple. At once, even with his back turned toward her, she was almost sure; a moment later his head turned so that she could see his profile; she had been right. His companion, facing toward her, was a blonde girl with handsome unsmiling features and an air of ruling all she surveyed; frequently she would nod at greeting and move her lips in what never became an actual smile. *Ice-cold bitch,* she thought, resolutely trying to look the other way yet stealing continual glances at the girl—who, upon one of those covert surveys, was just getting to her feet. Hugh himself had now turned; they would have to pass her on their way to the door, they were passing her now . . . . shrinking

45

inwardly she sat with lowered head and fingers around the stem of her glass. When the danger was over she raised her head and was in time to see the girl just about to pass through the door, now presenting her profile; lovely as her front face but cold, cold. . . .

Belatedly she recalled that during her stolen glances, the two of them had hardly been talking at all; still, one could hardly miss the atmosphere between them, the atmosphere and its implications. . . . .

Well, at least he didn't see me, she comforted herself illogically, then wondered why—why, in heaven's name—she should be in need of comfort.

V

'There're things about you,' said Mrs Tor, 'that I forget.'

'Oh?' queried her companion of three days' standing. Outwardly composed, inwardly alert, ready for the attack to develop in whatever direction it liked—reasonable, unreasonable or totally mindless—she waited.

'That's to say,' the old woman pursued, 'if I've ever known them.' She looked and sounded suspicious; the other, with outward composure meeting the stare of those sharp assessing eyes, waited again.

'When I engaged you,' Mrs Tor was saying, 'you told me things about yourself, only I—I've no recollection, almost no . . . my memory.' She made it a curse. 'My damnable memory.'

'We talked mostly about what I would do,' Jacintha offered cautiously. 'You asked me, you know, and I said I could type. And be useful on the cook's day off, and so forth.' Inwardly engrossed with a plan, waiting her chance yet uncertain whether to try it this soon, she slipped in a vague hint. 'That was all really, except . . . except the other thing I mentioned.'

'What thing?' She was taken up sharply. 'What other thing?'

'Just my music.' She accompanied the falsehood with an innocent, limpid gaze. 'About my music, that's all.'

47

'Music,' repeated the other, after a pause. 'Music . . . ? I seem to remember . . . something . . . but not music. Yes!' she cried suddenly, almost accusingly. 'You said interruption, that first time. That's what—an *interruption.'*

'Oh?' Surprising, this mixture of random remembrance and random forgetfulness; she herself could not recall having used the word. 'Did I?'

'What was interrupted?' the old woman pressed on forcibly. 'What?'

'Well, it's a bit of a long story—'

'If it's too long,' Mrs Tor cut her off freezingly, 'I'll tell you.'

'Well, you see—' Pausing a moment before essaying the mixture of truth and lies that had occurred to her dimly so soon as that first interview, she launched herself. '. . . I took a music degree at Somerville, but during the final examinations in piano playing, I overpractised. I hurt my arms rather badly, in fact.' She risked a glance at her auditor. 'Quite badly.'

'Oh?' said Mrs Tor. She was coming to life with a peculiar edge and glistering. 'And what then?'

'My doctor said, absolutely no practising or playing till it's all right.' The sight of the old woman reviving so curiously, so incomprehensibly, made her even more cautious. 'He says any kind of hard technical work now, and I'll never recover.' Complete silence met her; she waited, then struggled on, 'So that's that. I mean, parents who want to engage a music teacher for their children . . . well, being disabled isn't a recommendation, exactly, it doesn't inspire confidence . . .' Her voice died again at Mrs Tor's aspect. Remote, forbidding? or merely bored and inattentive? or worse, one of her frequent lapses . . . . ?

'Horrible,' said the old woman suddenly. 'Horrible luck.' Her voice vibrated with power and comprehension. 'To be kept from your work like that. *Stopped*—by mere accident. Rotten, filthy luck.'

'Yes, it was rather a blow.' Beneath her false resignation was a surge of triumph. To have divined, at such early contact with this sad old monolith, that its sympathy must somehow be invoked, as a preparation to invoking its interest; to have found, so early, a decided entering wedge. . . .

'But you—you told me you could type?' Mrs Tor asked suddenly. 'You did tell me?'

'Yes.' At once her self-congratulation turned to fright; she saw what was coming. 'I told you, yes.'

'But how can you, then?' the other demanded, querulous. 'With your arms injured, with—'

'For typing, different muscles are involved,' she improvised, badly shaken. 'But I couldn't do even too much of that.' Damn the lie, who could tell in how many ways it could trip you or throw you? 'It's just that I thought, in this job heavy typing wouldn't be required.'

Finishing with a fair degree of boldness, while still shrinking from the answer, she saw all at once that the old woman had not even listened, that she was struggling to say something else, and finally managed, 'One more . . . thing, one m-more . . .'

Jacintha waited.

'What was I going to say?' whimpered Mrs Tor. 'It's gone, it's . . . it's . . . yes, I know.' The voice of desperation calmed. 'The door, I wanted to tell you, the front door at night . . . never double locked, never.' She drew breath in the hard fight for words. 'So my . . . my son can g-get in. In case there's . . . trouble, any . . . any . . .' The thing she had been fighting overcame her; she sat with dulled eyes and vanished understanding. Yet she might, as before, recover part or all of her wits, as before. . . .

As wide awake as silent, alert to seize any glimpse that might be informative, any hint however remote, again Jacintha braced herself and again waited.

*   *   *

Her room on the first floor was spacious, even luxurious; a nice room to escape to for thinking. And plenty to think of, God knew, any number of routes that—second to her own escape routes—led back inexorably to Mrs Tor. Her powerful good sense alternating with lapses into forgetfulness, and those lapses occurring rapidly and without warning . . . still, there

49

had been nothing too difficult to cope with and certainly nothing alarming, not so far. If no worse than this developed, it should be all right . . A curious establishment this, so large, so crammed with every sort of memento of its owner's archeological career; she must examine it when she could. And come to think: now that sleep had overtaken its owner, now that her mind was overcast in some degree, why not? Her earlier newcomer's diffidence of investigation was fading away; why not now . . . ?

When she had completed a rapid survey and returned to her room, she was still wavering and indeterminate between what she wanted to do and what circumstances would allow her to do, in the light of what she had just seen. All that display of testimonies to the old woman's activities, whatever they had been; the velvet-lined case exhibiting two silver medals flanking a fat gold one; a display of artifacts (was that the word?) in clay but often in stones whose names she did not know . . . and over all of it not a look of neglect but a curious *feeling* of neglect; she was willing to swear that its owner took in it no more interest nor pleasure, not the slightest. Then she took an instant to remember the piano, a splendid Bechstein, and to regret she had not had a brief go at it. Too risky though, even with the door closed. . . .

Well, she must wait, that was all; having exhibited the first of her small baits, she had to see whether it would be taken, or disregarded for the duration. And if disregarded, what next, what next . . . the wheels went over her so depressingly that her mind cast about wildly for comfort, and ended by fleeing to the thought of Liz. Liz slaving away for her tyrant, yet with fidelity beginning to wear thin—so thin that she herself could predict her freedom in a year at most. Yet how did she know for sure, how did anyone know. . . .

She bypassed the disturbing thought of Liz for the equally disturbing thought of Herbert. Here, her expression immediately signalled her distaste. He would be trying to find her, without doubt; going from one to the other without haste and with his customary smiling, indulgent patience, that blasted *patience* of his. . . .

The knock at her door transferred her instantly to here and now; on her invitation to enter, while getting rapidly to her feet, not the presence she had expected, but another one, materialized. With this Mrs Dowling, the cook, she had (so far) only the slightest acquaintance.

'Good morning, madam,' the presence vouchsafed.

'Good morning, Mrs Dowling,' responded the other amiably. 'Sit down, won't you?'

'Oh no thank you, madam,' said Mrs Dowling, with an air of being faintly shocked. She was a vigourous-looking woman just below medium height and perhaps in the early fifties; not actually fat but just this side of it, tight and glossy with good feeding. Her dress and apron were sparkling clean, her cheeks rosy and her dark eyes lively, her teeth admirable if they were her own, her expression good-humoured. Given this impressive list of advantages it was unreasonable that the newcomer's feeling should be what it had been from the very beginning—a guarded, but instant, dislike. She disliked her manner, not quite assertive, she disliked her blandishing voice; even the broad smile came under suspicion as capable of vanishing—at need—in favour of something far less pleasant.

'I just thought I'd enquire what you liked for your breakfast,' pursued the apparition. 'Seeing that you haven't been making a very good meal of it, madam, an' I don't know your tastes and that.'

'Why . . .' somehow taken aback at solicitude so unexpected and elaborate, Jacintha blinked and responded lamely, 'Why, that's very nice of you. What you've been giving me is lovely, orange juice and eggs and coffee. Lovely,' she repeated lamely. 'Delicious.'

'And bacon with your eggs, madam, or sausage?' purred Mrs Dowling. 'Such marv'lous farm sausages we do get, such big boys, reg'lar blimps.'

'Oh, I can't eat sausage or bacon every day,' Jacintha protested. 'Once or twice a week but no more, really.'

'Oh come, madam, that's very poor eating, that is. You need a good breakfast to hold you up.' She paused deliberately, before adding, 'Here.'

On *here,* stressed obviously however faintly, she paused as if expecting her audience to pick up and chase the cue. Since her audience failed to oblige she was forced to continue.

'Kidneys an' mushrooms? grilled ham?' Already a slight displeasure was eroding her affability. 'Farm-cured ham we get, lovely. Or a nice chop . . . ?'

Surprised at the insistence as well as the menu, Jacintha took a moment to answer; her only acquaintance with such breakfasts derived from Edwardian novels about ducal houses.

'Thank you very much.' She now had the picture of Mrs Dowling complete. 'It's terribly kind of you but I couldn't face that sort of breakfast every day, honestly I couldn't.'

The following moment of silence contained assorted shiftings of mood—among them the undisguised eclipse of Mrs Dowling's smile, and its replacement by something a little more complex than mere hostility. Hostility was *part* of it without doubt, a carry-over from the unaccepted breakfasts and the unaccepted invitation to gossip. But the rest of it? anger, and beyond anger a curious new . . . . wary look? measuring . . . ?

'Well, all right,' the woman returned. 'It's up to you, innit? If that's how you like it, OK.'

The vanishing of the numerous *madams,* along with the switch from half-obsequious to half-familiar, was predictable; less so a further and abrupt change of subject and increasing deterioration of manner.

'Miz Tor is such a wunnerful lady,' she said with hateful smoothness. 'I could tell you o' some that don't appreciate good service, but Miz Tor she's not one of them. Awhile back, well, it was a good while, Miz Pargill she took to interfering, well I never, as if I needed to be told what's what. Straight to Miz Tor I went, an' I said to her, "Either Miss Pargill stops coming in my kitchen, or I go." Like that I let her have it, straight. An' from that day, why, who's been scarcer in my kitchen than my lady Pargill—?' Her triumphant smile faded; she seemed in two minds about continuing, then proceeded mellifluously, 'I wish Miz Tor ate better than she does, I do wish she would.'

It was not what she had been going to say, Jacintha could have sworn.

'She'll hardly do more'n peck, how she stays alive I can't see, hardly,' Mrs Dowling pursued. 'It's been gettin' so that you might say she starves herself, well, half-starves, anyway.'

* * *

The woman's smile of departure—of warning and contempt undissimulated and mingled—impelled in her a first blankness. This was followed by a rush of thought, as if some mental catch had been released. For the woman herself—a domestic bully, truly indispensable in this troubled house and maintaining her power by covert threats to leave—she did not give two pins; she would yield on all fronts, so long as they did not conflict with her efforts on Mrs Tor's behalf. It was an old conviction of Jacintha's (drawn from experience) that the lowest and poorest classes, once they tasted power of *any* kind, flung themselves into abuses of the most insolent and overbearing kind. A consequence of their life-time suppressions, probably, let it go at that. But Mrs Dowling's reference to the invisible dweller upstairs, whom she had all but forgotten, that was something else again. . . .

She was engrossed, now, with the unknown who lived her life in the silence of her room (rooms?) on the second floor. It was her withdrawal, undoubtedly, her solitude, that made the thought of her forbidding; existing up there behind closed doors, emerging when? how . . . ? Between a desire to glimpse the apparition if only once, and a more violent inclination to have nothing to do with it, she hung suspended for a moment. If they should meet on the steps, of course entirely by accident . . . leave it, leave it till it happened. Or it might not happen, the invisible woman would know too well the best times for slipping up and downstairs unseen . . .

With the tiredness that thinking uselessly always gave her, she removed her mind to the next point of encounter, Mrs Tor's solicitor. She had met him just twice, the second time when she went to his office (on Mrs Tor's command) to settle the matter of her pay, her free days and so forth. For this second encounter she had anticipated a crushing coldness, an inclusion of herself in his anger with Hugh. But not at all, he had been courtesy itself, though evidently not disposed to lengthen their interview by an extra syllable. . . . He was curiously distinct in her mind, his tallness, composure . . . she smiled a little, remembering how the composure had cracked against Hugh's good humour. Now undecided whether to like or dislike him, she hesitated momentarily. Suppose he tried to interfere in this household . . . no, never, his whole atmosphere was a guarantee of professional correctitude. On the other hand if he should put in an appearance, uninvited, she would at once make clear to him her intention of communicating this to Hugh. Weighted by this imagining her mind swung, ever so little, toward her first dislike . . .

Mrs Tor, she thought suddenly; Mrs Tor, beginning and end of all this complication; how much potential trouble swirled and eddied about the person of this one old woman . . . *who's had a life,* she thought suddenly, *so far and so beyond what most people have.* Again the mysterious montage inseparable from the aged sybil flashed across her mind: jungle dimness, tombs hugely and tropically overgrown, the discovered burial . . . whose burial, by the way? Some time or other she must look it up. . . .

Still, no wonder that these vast calm Suffolk skies and vast unpeopled surfaces, mysteriously conserving an ancient rural peace, should cruelly confine the bird of daring flights; no wonder that the changeless tranquillity of centuries should appear as bars on the—yes, on the falcon's cage . . . Her mind moved to her plans for the old lady; she experienced a moment of disastrous let-down. *How can nonsense like that work, for such a person,* she wondered, and with eyes gone vacant stared disconsolately at the prospect.

Well, all right, she exhorted herself harshly, *don't flap. Don't think about it, just do it,* then in search of relief tried to remember: what had she been thinking about when Mrs Dowling's incursion interrupted her?—Oh, Herbert. And let him wait, she had more present things to worry about than Herbert.

* * *

'Jacintha?'

'Yes, Hugh.'

'How's everything?'

'All right so far, I expect. Or at any rate—' she was a trifle short of breath, not knowing from what. '—at any rate, not too bad.'

'But no . . . news?'

'News?'

'I mean, have you been able to find some—some little interests for mother, something for her to do?'

'Oh, not yet.' Not for worlds would she tell of her cautious first steps in that direction, not till they succeeded decisively or failed decisively. 'Nothing yet, actually.'

'Things are just the same then? as a couple of days ago—?'

'Well, yes.' Her unpromising voice annoyed her; what did he expect in the first five minutes? 'I've got to go carefully.'

His silence was so heavy with criticism of her failure that she was inclined to say something sharp or at least defensive. Then with an effort she suppressed it; perhaps she had even imagined his condemnation. . . .

'You've had dinner?' he was asking.

'Yes.'

'And did she eat?'

'Yes, she seemed quite hungry.'

'Well, that's something,' he said with a cheerfulness that sounded to her forced. 'That's a change.'

'You mean she's got no appetite?' This was an opportunity to confirm Mrs Dowling's account of it. 'Frequently?'

'Well, Mrs What's-her-name told me,' he said uncertainly. 'The cook.'

'Oh. Well, she did eat this time—with appetite.'

'Good so far as it goes.' The renewal in his voice appeared to her still forced. 'All right then, I'll ring tomorrow or soon as I can. You might have some news for me then?'

55

'And I might not,' she replied at once, more sharply than she had intended. 'No use getting your hopes up too soon, is there?' Again he was silent, and again the quality of this silence pushed her into saying, 'I'll do my best, my very best, depend on it. So we'll see, shall we?' The uncertainty in her voice was partly, all at once, petition. 'We'll see, and just . . . just leave it at that?'

VI

'Your arms,' said Mrs Tor commandingly, without warning. 'Let's see them.'

Startled, also quaking slightly, Jacintha pulled up the sleeves of her jersey and held out both members for inspection. While doing this she registered the present qualities of the voice: its intimidating common-sense and the fact of the topic's being sprung on her as if moments had passed since their talk yesterday, and not another twenty-four hours. Finally there was the sharpness of the old woman's inspection; the eyes in their wrinkled nests peering at the presumably afflicted areas with . . . . with alarming intentness? with expertise, even . . . ?

'H'm, no inflammation,' Mrs Tor observed in her own good time. 'I'd expect inflammation.'

'There was some, at first,' the other improvised. Damn the lie again, why did it have to become more and more intricate to hold water? 'Never bad though, and it's mostly gone now.'

'And just how did you hurt them, again—?'

'I overpractised.' The prepared fiction now came readily. 'I started some heavy technical work and just . . . overdid it.'

The other said nothing, and her silence—like all her silences—was enigmatic. Silence of disbelief? of brief interest swallowed by boredom? or that other silence, ruinous, meaning

57

that the curtain had fallen between her and the outer-world. . . ?

'Let's see,' said Mrs Tor magisterially. She took an arm between her two hands and began kneading it gently. 'Tell me if it hurts, and I'll stop at once.'

'It feels wonderful,' said the patient truthfully, after some moments; the quality of the touch was what one would feel (she imagined) in the hands of an expert masseur.

'Had to do this every day in the jungle,' grumbled the old woman. 'Bearers, cooks, guides, more trouble than they were worth. Sprains, scratches, insect bites, had to do it all. Shots too, anti-malarial, tetanus, snake-bite. Let natives think you're helpless when there's trouble, and they're ready to die of fright.'

'Goodness,' murmured her companion, genuinely overawed. Jungle dusk filled her mind again, tropical denseness alive with venom and danger of all kinds, and this woman—this very woman—pitting herself against it. Spare and active she must have been, her skin leathery with sunburn. And beneath it what courage, what grim endurance, yes, and what knowledge too. . . .

'There, that's enough for one time.' The old woman let go of the arm. 'Not a good idea, to overdo it.'

'Thank you,' she murmured, rolling down her sleeves. *So far so good,* she allowed herself a cautious moment of congratulation. *This may be the right track,* and under this encouragement took courage to begin, 'Mrs Tor, the piano in your drawing-room—' The other's eyes were fixed on her with the abstraction that she would have taken, only yesterday, for prohibitive; today she knew better, and pursued boldly, 'Do you ever use it? I mean, would you like it if—' She stopped suddenly, frightened. The eyes had gone suddenly hostile and staring, their whites duskier and duskier.

'Who let you in?' the old woman demanded harshly. 'It's too soon. You said not before—not before—you said . . .'

Shock cut the other's breath off; this had happened while she was still rolling down a sleeve. As quickly as that, it could happen . . . *Oh God,* she thought, meeting the glare of hatred with an appearance of composure and scraping her wits for

58

any answer. Yet careful, careful, it must be nothing to enrage her further, stir her up to possible violence . . .

Wasted alarm, as it happened. Even as she groped in panic for a pacific answer of any sort, Mrs Tor seemed to collapse inwardly. Her threatening rigidity had gone, confusion almost tangible seemed to envelop her; she shook her head as if battling cobwebs. Still waiting, the other continued to watch mistrustfully, tense in every nerve and muscle . . .

'W-what . . . ?' the old woman asked feebly. 'What did . . . . what did I . . .' She raised a hand and feebly, inaccurately, brushed at a disordered grey strand that had fallen over her forehead. And in this gesture was such helplessness, such bewilderment, that it suddenly routed the beholder's terror and reduced her instead—or very nearly—to sudden, uncontrollable tears. In fact tears were stabbing her eyes, the last articles in the world of any use to Mrs Tor or herself. Now the old woman tottered to a chair; her head nodded, nodded lower, her body spent and flat and her breathing first irregular, then regular. Mrs Tor slept, undeniably, her head supported against the wing of a Queen Anne chair upholstered in velvet. The episode of massage had over-exhausted her, obviously, she would probably sleep for a good bit, now . . .

On a long unconscious sigh, Jacintha first sat blank, then began casting about vaguely in her mind. These seizures, at least that she had seen so far, were not too bad; they seemed to pass off into an addled state of mind, then to sleep. But suppose this developed into something more dangerous, something not to be controlled by an inexperienced or unskilled helper. . . . Realization came with a shock. She had been taken advantage of, that was the long and short of it; landed with something impossibly beyond her control. She would throw over the whole damned thing at once, no one could possibly blame her . . . . something checked her anger and her resolve simultaneously, the vision of an old woman trying to brush away a lock of hair . . . well, all right, she would wait. But get the solicitor at once, ask for the name of a doctor; how could she have overlooked this, how could Dennison have overlooked it . . . as for Hugh, when he rang her next he would hear something, she would open him up from stem to stern. . . . Her eyes, which had moved from the old lady while she canvassed her wrongs, returned to her and received another shock. Mrs Tor was awake once more, and staring at her fixedly moreover; in her regard was a stillness, a horrid slyness, as she said, 'Come.' Her voice was soft and gloating. 'I'll show you something. Come with me.'

'Oh?' Jacintha's tone was a masterpiece of calm, all things considered. 'Come where?'

'I'll show you.' The old woman was struggling from her chair, vigourous yet shaken; she rejected her recent collapse, but the collapse still had hold of her. 'Come!' She was going across to the french door, her speed pitiably eroded by weakness. 'Come, come—' she had the door open after some fumbling and hurried through; Jacintha followed hastily. This rear part of the house, the garden, she had not yet explored as it happened, the weather having been rainy, chilly, or boisterously windy. It was still windy, with fugitive gleams of sunshine, as she pursued Mrs Tor through a garden of whose surprising depth the house-front gave no hint at all; it went on and on, sloping gently always, and ended at another surprise—the stream that went sliding past with the gentlest possible chuckling of water. She had seen it passing beneath a stone bridge on the High Street, but had never suspected its existence so close to home. Cold air came off its surface; the sunshine, brightening then paling, lit crocus and daffodils to an unearthly flame, pale yellow. If she were alone she could let her mind go blank in this healing silence, breathe in the smell of earth, the bitter-sweet smell of daffodils . . . a big branch swam past at surprising speed; the full glassy surface of the water, innocently dimpled, gave no hint of the driving current beneath.

'High at this time of year.' A voice recalled her, a murmuring, gloating voice. 'Swollen in spring. And fast, fast.'

Shock held the younger woman again, the sense of something impending.

'Deep too, deeper than you'd think,' the remote voice went on. 'Drownings—there've been drownings in it.'

60

'What's it called?' asked the other, repressing a shiver. 'Has it a name?'

'The Crale,' came the answer slumbrously, after a moment. 'They call it the Crale.'

Silence repossessed them for an interval. *Your body'll last forever*, thought Jacintha, *and your mind'll give out. Sounds a picnic for someone, and it won't be I.* Her anger woke again, full-bodied. *That Hugh, that son of yours, who didn't begin to give me an idea of the situation*, she accused, simmering, then —without warning—the anger ran out into a weak *He might not have known, not known at all how bad it was*, and looked furtively at the cause of it all—to receive another shock. Mrs Tor was present again, recognizably herself; seeming oblivious of the water, which before had engaged all her attention, she tapped with a forefinger on her forehead and asked, 'Do you know how it started?' She tapped again. 'This thing?'

The cold of the water seemed to enter the other's veins; breathless once more, she waited.

'January, it was January,' pursued the voice, remote. 'A cold day, bitter cold for this climate. Maybe the cold had something to do with it, I don't know . . .' She made one of her stops—that might herald the break, some senseless digression. . . .

'I was in London.' She no longer looked at her companion; her attention was riveted on her narrative. 'I was in the City, to see my accountant. I was there just a short time, I'd only needed a word with him, actually. I stepped out of the building to the pavement, and then—right there—I knew it'd happened.'

She paused again, but briefly.

'First of all I had a sense of having spoken to lots of people in that office, and yet I'd only talked with two, the man's secretary and the man himself. But I could *hear* those other people, all those other voices talking, talking . . . on the pavement I kept hearing them, on and on . . .'

She stopped, seeming to reflect.

'Then I realized I didn't know my own name.' She was now curiously detached. 'And I didn't know where I lived. But I did remember,' her tone strengthened a little, 'I *did* remember a bus number, I even knew somehow it was the right bus to take. So I waited for one and got on, and all the way from King William Street to Knightsbridge the voices went with me. They never stopped talking, not once. And all the time—' she paused '—I was wondering where to get off, I simply didn't know. So I watched, I'd a feeling I'd recognize the stop when we came to it, and,' she wound up on a note of desolate triumph, 'I did. I did recognize it.'

Before this pitiless yet clouded lucidity, her companion's terror had changed; changed to an enormous compassion, also something else not yet definable . . .

'And when I'd got off the bus,' Mrs Tor resumed, 'I didn't know where I was. But then again I knew I had to cross the road and walk straight on—I kept thinking I'd recognize something, sooner or later. So I walked, then I saw this hotel, it looked familiar somehow, and walked in on the chance. And the girl at the desk said, "Thank you, Mrs Tor," and gave me a key, so I knew I was right. And the number was on the key, so I could find my room. But the thing didn't pass off straightaway, no, it . . . it didn't.'

She paused again, always looking at the water.

'That was the first time,' she went on tonelessly. 'And the next time was the same, only worse. Those *voices!* all talking and talking to me. And mixed up with them, in the strangest way, was this . . . this arithmetic.' She frowned bewilderedly. 'Numbers, adding and subtracting themselves. As if a *partition* had given way somewhere . . . ?' she queried distressfully. 'The mind's a lot of separate cubbyholes, isn't it? But supposing a wall breaks down between them, here and there? And the voices,' she complained, 'going past so quickly, one can't get hold of . . . of what they're saying . . .'

The indefinable thing took sudden shape: loyalty. Loyalty, enormous and immovable, bringing her again to the verge of tears; she wanted to abase herself at Mrs Tor's feet and beg to be forgiven for her treachery, her shabby, contemplated desertion . . .

'I'll tell you something,' said the voice beside her, and the sound of it—sly again, furtive and detestable—dealt her another shock. 'A secret . . . about this house. Shan't tell you now, though. No, I shan't.'

Jacintha, striving to recover balance, was suddenly aware of being alone. She turned her head and saw Mrs Tor making her way back. The path with its upward incline, uneven and pebbly, was not enough to account for the old woman's gait—pitiably scrambling, lurching, like something crippled trying to escape pursuit. She followed quickly, again thinking, *Tell Hugh? Tell him all of it? some of it?* then realized another thing: the strength of her new feeling, the loyalty with which the old woman had inspired her.

If it gets unmanageable, I'll tell him, she thought. *Only not yet, not yet.* Misgiving assailed her, promptly overridden—drowned—in the new attachment. *She told me in confidence,* she reminded herself stoutly, *you've got to respect confidence,* and passed into the house.

Mrs Tor was in the hall, supporting herself against a newel-post; her look disturbed and uncertain, the horrid slyness all vanished.

'I've been talking . . . nonsense?' she asked tremulously. 'Something I . . . I oughtn't?'

'Heavens no,' the companion returned easily. 'We've been out walking a bit, then we came back.'

'Oh.' The nuance was of dissatisfaction, even of unbelief. She remained silent, obviously grappling with some problem, then asked suddenly, 'Did someone ring me?'

'I don't know,' Jacintha answered. 'We've been in the garden.'

'Oh,' Mrs Tor mumbled again, still on the same unappeased note, then started climbing the stairs with a labouring gait. Part way up she stopped suddenly, turned and asked, 'Did someone ring me?'

'No,' the other soothed patiently. 'Not since we came in, anyway.'

Without answering the old woman turned, this time reaching the balcony. Here, halting again, she asked, 'Did someone ring me?' Her face, peering down haggardly, looked thin and haunted. 'Did someone ring me? Did someone ring me?'

* * *

'Liz?'

'You? already? What's the trouble?'

'No trouble.' *Tired of hanging about waiting for him to call, and he didn't call.* 'Just thought I'd ring.'

'Well, what's doing at this intensely secret place of yours? What's up?'

'Oh, nothing much, it's simply that I—'

'Look,' said Liz, into her hesitation. 'Give me your number. You won't have enough money for the lies or half-lies you're preparing to tell me, I can tell by your voice. Ring off—I'll ring you back.'

* * *

'Now,' she commanded vigourously. 'What's all this any-how? What've you gone and got yourself into?'

'How do you know I've got myself into any—'

'You fool,' Liz cut her off. 'Try it on with someone who doesn't know you as well as I do. Now come on—give.'

'Well.' Jacintha took a long breath. 'Perhaps I wasn't quite frank with you—about the job itself, what it consisted of—'

'You told me,' Liz interposed implacably, 'that you were going to be companion to an old girl in poor health.'

'Well, yes. At least, that's part of it—'

'Cintha, my God!' The other's mind had leaped ahead of her, as usual. 'What have you gone and got yourself into? Chaperoning a lunatic, is that it?'

'No! not a lunatic, you mustn't get the wrong impression—'

'I'm right, aren't I?' Liz was a trifle shrill. 'What do you *know* about handling such creatures, what experience have you had? My God, of all the crazy—'

'Shut up for one moment, will you, and listen? She's not a lunatic or anything like, she may be a bit unstable now and again, that's all. Did you—' she was fighting off another in-

64

terruption '—did you ever hear of her, by any chance? a Mrs Tor, Mrs Valeria Tor?'

'Mrs Tor? Seems to me I may have . . .' The name had checked another outburst, but not for long. 'Look, whoever the woman is, I can tell you've taken on something you can't handle. Hasn't this old girl anyone else, any family?'

'A son, just the one son so far as I know. He's away a lot, but he rings me. He's concerned about her,' she said defensively. 'Terribly concerned.'

The silence that followed was different, and different likewise the quality of the answer.

'I don't like it,' said Liz. 'I never did like the sound of it. The pay you told me they're giving you—it's too much, it *must* mean there's something about the job they're holding back—'

'Rot.' Her new-born fervour for Mrs Tor made her forget, genuinely, her own moments of misgiving. 'The poor old girl, whenever she goes off a little she snaps back straightaway—just wanders a bit and either goes to sleep, or she's all there again, sensible as ever. And remember, Liz, remember—' she had the sense of stemming further objections '—with what I'm getting out of this, I'll have a thousand pounds at the end of a year.' *If the job lasts that long,* occurred to her; she drove it away. 'Which means we can . . . go ahead . . . ?'

What this produced was not so much a silence as a stillness; at the end of it Liz said heavily, 'Maybe.'

'Or if we can't, quite then—' all her affection and fidelity rushed into the breach '—it makes no difference. I'll wait, that's all—I can risk a year or two, at this time of my life.' Quickly she sailed into less dangerous waters. 'Drive down here one evening, why not, and take me to dinner.'

'Where is it you've landed yourself, again—?'

'Devehurst.'

'Oh yes, I remember—show village of East Sussex. Why in hell don't you come up to London?'

'Oh, I can't.' Visions past and present mingled inextricably. 'I don't want to run into Herbert, it'd be just my luck. But the main thing's the job, I can't be away this soon. So I'll look up places hereabout where you can spend lots of money on taking me out?' she wheedled. 'Ten pounds at least?'

'All right.' Liz's voice was grim and dogged. 'I still feel there's something about the job that you haven't told me.'

'Nonsense.' The sense of escape—though from what?—hurried on her desire to ring off. 'You're crackers as usual. I'll look into the restaurant question here, then, and let you know?'

* * *

She was still wondering vaguely, much later, about her compulsion to cut off their exchanges, as if she had something to hide. Ridiculous, there was nothing, of course there was nothing . . .

The sound outside the closed door of her room brought her from her motionless trance of speculation and changed it to a trance of listening, equally motionless. That succession of small noises that indicated unmistakably a living presence, an *unseen* living presence in the house; and what time was it, after eleven. . . .

Without giving herself time to think she sprang up, hurried to the door, and with infinite precaution opened it a crack. Nothing met her eye through so infinitesimal a space; with her heart in her mouth she held it wider, which brought into view the staircase and the head and shoulders of the presence, descending and evidently carrying something. Even by that glimpse it was evident that it limped badly and breathed hard with effort; as she stared, it laboured along the staircase balcony and passed from sight.

She closed the door without a sound, and remained standing beside it, blankly. Hugh's upstairs dweller, the desiccated secretary . . . This had been her first sight and sound of the mystery; she must choose her hours of emergence cleverly to remain so well hidden, poor old thing; when they were in the dining-room, probably, or late at night, as now . . .

Her body stiffened unconsciously, ahead of the alerting of her senses. The apparition's return was worse, far worse; a panting ascent punctuated with muffled grunts and groans, a fighting for breath like a spent animal's. Listening with terror,

66

gripping the knob without daring to turn it, she stood while the presence, with more expiring sounds, took an eternity to negotiate the second flight.

On the subdued sound of the closing door overhead Jacintha, with no pause to think—no pause to let reflection get the better of her courage—was out of the room and running upstairs. On the way she remembered, belatedly, what it was that she had failed to tell Liz.

* * *

A knock too faint or hesitant would betray her cowardice; all the same, in the sleeping house, she had not intended knocking as loudly as she did. At the sound, a voice challenged, 'Who's that?' so fiercely that a pause transfixed her; while it held, the voice demanded again, 'Who's there?' this time on a cawing, faltering note, full of dread. 'Who is it, who . . . who . . .'

'Miss Pargill,' Jacintha essayed. Her own voice, held low, attempted the tone of ordinary conversation. 'This is Jacintha Cory, Jacintha, I work here and I—' quick, no more hesitation '—I was just wondering, could I speak to you for a moment?'

There was a long silence, rampant with fear, suspicion, God knows what; at the end of it the unseen occupant said, 'It's a trick.' By the sound, she had retreated farther into the room. 'Go away, go away!'

'No trick,' the visitor urged. 'Miss Pargill, I promise you there's no trick. Couldn't you—' her voice had risen unintentionally; she pulled it back. '—couldn't you just talk to me? Not let me in if you don't want, just talk—?'

She paused again; another stillness fell, broken at length by dragging, shuffling sounds. At the end of them came, 'What is it?' She was perceptibly nearer the door. 'What is it you're after?'

'I'd just like a word with you,' said Jacintha patiently. 'That's all.'

'You're that—that Miss Cory, you said?'

'Yes.'

'Who else?' came fiercely. 'Who's with you?'

'No one.' *That Miss Cory:* who could have told her? 'I'm alone.'

'You promise me?' The jerky accents had come nearer. 'You promise?'

'I promise. Put on your chain if you don't believe me, and look.'

'Got no chain,' lamented the voice, half-audible; by now it was closer still. 'Must think. Must think a moment . . .'

At the end of another silence came various metallic sounds; she had no chain indeed, but she had a bolt—bolts. Jacintha waited unprotestingly while, with infinite slowness, there appeared a crack whose hairline proportions betokened an immediate readiness to slam it shut. Refraining from looking at it directly, she had all the same a fugitive impression of an eye and a sliver of face. Again she waited under the visual inquisition till the door opened wider and the voice said low and hoarsely, 'Come in!' Slipping through obediently, she stood while locks and bolts resounded behind her; this done, her unwilling hostess came around to demand, *'She's* sent you, hasn't she?'

'No, no one's sent me.' With a mixture of compassion and misgiving she sized up the apparition that stood before her in all its pitiable belligerence and defencelessness. Mary Pargill was a shortish woman, considerably overweight, flabby with it, and unpleasantly pale. Old she must be rather than elderly, yet she seemed one of those rare types whose hair, even in advanced age, shows no trace of grey. She never left the house apparently, and chemists' deliveries of hair-dye might have been mentioned by Mrs Dowling as a morsel too delicious to keep secret. No, this pompadour was natural, at its roots was no betrayal whatever, and its darkness did nothing for her but to make her face even more ruinous and throw into prominence her ghastly pallor, the true fish-belly white . . .

'All right, let's have it,' she threw at her visitor. 'It's from *her,* or you wouldn't have come.'

'Miss Pargill, no,' countered the other. 'It's simply that the work Mrs Tor gives me doesn't take up all my time, not nearly all. So is there anything I could do for you? Anything at all—?'

Miss Pargill was staring at her; staring from pale eyes paler still under the dark pompadour, another unnerving contrast. 'The book,' she snapped, her lips opening and shutting unpleasantly. 'How've you all that much time to spend, with what you're doing on the book?'

'Well—' *the book,* she tucked away in her memory, *what book?* '—even so—'

'How's it going on?' the other pursued with dreadful avidity. 'The book?'

'You must remember I haven't been here long,' Jacintha protested. 'I suppose we'll be getting on with it more than we've done. But in the meantime, if there's anything I could—'

'Robbing her, are they?' snarled Miss Pargill, and the sudden change of theme jolted the visitor awake to something new: that her last words had not been heard, had not been listened to; that the malevolent hermit had followed her mind into some deep and better runnel of its own. 'Robbing her blind? Well, what'd she expect? When I did the shopping I controlled things. But now that woman's got it all in her hands, that Dowling—' her voice was heavy with doom and relish. '—all right, if it's frittering and squandering she wants, if it's outright stealing —all right, it's *her* money.' Again, with one of those whiplike changes, her eye was pinning Jacintha's. 'When she talks about me,' she demanded, 'what does she say?'

'Nothing,' said the intruder, then hastily—as a glare advertised to her the unwisdom of so much truth, 'Mrs Tor wouldn't be likely to discuss an old friend like you with a stranger like me.'

Miss Pargill, checkmated in one direction, found another.

'You won't last,' she declared gleefully. 'No more'n any of the others. Who knows how it is with her, but me? Who'd put up with her, but me?' She eyed Jacintha with glinting malice. 'From daylight to dark it's go, go, go, that's how she likes it. And in between times, drive you *crazy.* —How's she now?' she demanded suddenly. 'Bad?'

'Bad—?' echoed the other.

'Forgets things? screaming tempers, anything like that—?' Her hope of the worst, her half-smiling eagerness, impelled Jacintha's abrupt 'No.' She must postpone her revulsion. 'Miss Pargill, I wonder if you'd let me take your trays up and down? I mean, would you—?'

Miss Pargill, evidently jolted, as evidently postponed her own present wrath and produced a substitute variety.

'Who asked you?' she shouted. 'Who in hell asked you?'

'No one.' She was cool, pleased to feel—at last—an equality between them. 'It's no pleasure to hear you doing it, that's all. Go on if you like, till you drop the tray or fall downstairs with it—it's your affair entirely.'

For a brief explosive moment the benefits of the suggestion warred in Miss Pargill with the violent desire to refuse it. At the the end of this exercise she snarled again, 'I didn't ask you!'

'I asked you,' her visitor agreed. 'It's my suggestion, entirely.'

'Four trays a day!' Gleefully the old woman was taking her revenge. 'Breakfast, lunch, tea, dinner—!'

'All right.' Jacintha was impassive. 'I'll arrange it.'

'That *cook,* you know! devil's own—!'

'Your trays'll be up. Thank you, Miss Pargill.'

She turned to go, suddenly unable to bear it a moment longer—the old woman and the old woman's room, the room crammed to bursting with cases, knapsacks, mysterious parcels in corners or piled on top of wardrobes; a place formerly used as a port of call and used to being deserted at a moment's notice. Now that the fury and the flurry were over, it retained the shape of this confusion; still undomesticated, restless, full of movement . . .

'You won't last.' Miss Pargill, unfastening the door, was absorbed in a pleasurable, murmuring incantation. 'She'll use you, work you like a slave, then chuck you out. You'll see!' On her giggle, the door swung open. 'You'll see! You'll see!'

VII

'How are you today?' Mrs Tor demanded.

'Very well, thank you.'

'I was talking,' came astringently, 'about your arms.'

'Oh! not bad at all. Mrs Tor, will you believe—' the opening had been given her; she had to seize it, however abruptly. '—will you believe that that massage of yours, just that one time, helped me? I'm sure it helped me.'

'Why not?' Mrs Tor was dry and didactic. 'Didn't your doctor tell you to have massage?'

'No.'

'Imbeciles.' With one word she scrapped the medical profession. 'All right for piecing broken bones together, but for anything inward—anything indefinite—useless. Worse than useless, often enough.'

Jacintha smiled in cautious assent, trying to evaluate how near one of those disastrous changes was, or how far. Mrs Tor in this moment looked and sounded as in the days of her achievement, an image unblurred and inspiring little but awe. It was the other image, the helpless confused one, that inspired commiseration and a desire to help her. But help *this* woman, the one who now stood before her? As well help a flame-throwing device, as well protect an armoured tank or similar . . .

'Massage for a bad arm, of course,' she was saying authoritatively, 'should be from the shoulder. You'd better take off your jersey.'

'It's too kind of you. Only I wonder, first—' quickly suppressing her tendency to falter, she went on as quickly '—if you'd —if you'd—'

'If I'd what?'

'Well, my doctor did tell me to play a *little*. Nothing difficult, nothing technical.' This fiction had been prepared, actually, from the time that she was packing in London to come here. 'Just very simple stuff, only it's such a bore to do it alone. But I've things for four hands, that we could play together,' she continued uncertainly. 'If you could bear it? For these wretched arms of mine, I mean . . . ?'

Mrs Tor, her face expressionless, remained silent; the suppliant sat hardly daring to breathe. Did it mean that she herself was still there, that silence? or did it mean she had gone away, supplanted by that Other? As the chilling quality of *Other,* so used, came home to her—

'Let's look at the piano,' said Mrs Tor. She got up and led the way to the big handsome room; as they entered, again its smell of disuse came strong to Jacintha's nostrils.

* * *

A little later she was established in the small morning-room across the hall, keeping an ear out; she would give her a half-hour alone, unless the piano stopped. For the moment were continuing the crippled sounds of 'Invitation to the Waltz,' from the second-hand book of duets she had picked up in London against just this possibility and hardly glanced at, except to assure herself that the contents were not too difficult. There, was the piano stopping . . . ? She listened a moment, had just begun rising to her feet . . .

'Good morning, madam,' said a voice.

'Good morning, Mrs Dowling,' said Jacintha, surprised. The piano had begun again as she started to rise, and she sank back.

'I heard the pianna as I come along,' the other pursued, 'an' I made sure it was you.'

'No, it's Mrs Tor.'

'Well I never, she ain't touched that pianna ever before, not in all the time I've been here.' Mrs Dowling's comment, absent-minded, was brushed aside for the real purpose of the interview. 'Miss Cory, it's just that I wanted to tell you how it was, that Miss Pargill don't eat downstairs.' Her manner was a blend—an uneasy blend—of defensiveness and propitiation. 'You see, it's like this—'

'Mrs Dowling,' Jacintha tried to interrupt. She was astounded at this evidence of a witness, an overhearer anyway, to her late-night colloquy with the recluse. An ear pressed to the door? or a bedroom door set ajar and an avid listener in it? Whichever of the two, what a *strange* house this was; decorous on the surface, tangles of complication beneath; distrust, late-night surveillances, spying . . . 'It's all right, it's perfectly all—'

'No, madam, if I could just tell you?' She swept on, determined to have her say. 'I *offered* to send up her trays, I did, madam. I do' know what she's been telling you, but—'

'Mrs Dowling—'

'—but I did offer,' the woman pursued. 'An' talk about having my nose snapped off—! So I thought, better she stops where she is, her an' Mrs Tor was always quarrelling anyway, my, talk about cat an' dog. Only I wanted to send her trays up, madam, I wanted you to know that—'

'Of course, Mrs Dowling, of *course*. Actually I was offering to carry her trays up then, that's all there was to it.' She was deliberately conciliating. 'I was going to speak to you about it first, naturally.'

'Well, all right.' She spoke after a pause, her face gone dark and vengeful. 'But you'd ought to know how she guzzles now, two or three times what she did. For spite I reckon, stuffin' away up there. Thinkin' she'll eat Mrs Tor out of house an' home, that's what—'

* * *

For a perceptible pause, after having got rid of her, Jacintha sat perfectly still. A confused tide seemed to wash over her; new intricacies not realized, murky depths not probed. Without intending it, the woman had put into her head the thought of

Mary Pargill as a danger to the old woman downstairs, if she got the chance. She was not immobilized after all, she was capable of moving about for the commission of dirty work, she had plenty against her former employer. . . . Giving it up for the moment, escaping only partway from the ominous web, she listened again. The piano had not ceased during her colloquy with Mrs Dowling or her present reflections. With a long sigh she broke completely free of her detention, and went to see how Mrs Tor was making out.

* * *

'How's it gone?'

'Idiot's delight,' sniffed Mrs Tor. 'Bore me frantic.'

'I know, one part alone—sounds like nothing. Let's try it together now, shall we? If you'd move over, just a little?'

After a few tries they came in together; on the air rose the gentle and pellucid rhythm of 'Invitation to the Waltz.' The sound of it, for all of a slight uncertainty in the treble, refreshed the dead air of the room amazingly.

'Silly music,' said Mrs Tor, her words disparaging and her face and voice pleased. 'Silly.'

'Because we're taking it too slowly,' retorted Jacintha, glad of a chance to brandish the steel. 'Quicker, now.'

She drove Mrs Tor through two more repetitions, commanding, 'Faster! faster!'

'I can't,' protested the old woman, yet for all her flagging never taking her hands from the keys. 'I can't.'

'Yes you can,' Jacintha gainsaid ruthlessly, and as they ended, 'You see? That wasn't bad, and you'll do a lot better.' Rather late she remembered her role of beneficiary. 'Thank you, Mrs Tor, this is just what I needed. Thank you very much.'

'I haven't touched a piano since I was ten or so,' said Mrs Tor. 'Go away now, I'll do this a bit more. And close the door, will you—while I'm making a spectacle of myself.'

* * *

'Maybe I've news,' said Jacintha, with modest triumph. 'Quite good news, in fact.'

74

'Yes—?'

'Your mother's been playing the piano. I got her to do it,' she explained, 'by telling her I'd hurt my arms overpractising, and that I needed just a little bit of playing. So she's been at it.' A deep breath escaped her. 'If only she just won't drop it, for some reason or other—!'

'Well, that's good news,' he said after a moment.

'Yes.' At his lack-lustre reception of the news, her enthusiasm faltered responsively. 'So far as it goes. I only meant, to've taken her mind off herself to that extent—' she was more and more subdued '—it's not too bad.'

'Not bad! It's fine, Jacintha.'

Pretending, she thought, so as not to discourage her.

'You're a clever girl, you really are,' he was saying with false enthusiasm, 'to make her do that, you know.'

'Well.' What in hell did he expect after five minutes or so, she thought, flattened for good. 'We'll see.'

'And anything else?' he demanded. 'Anything else of interest?'

'Not . . . not specially.' He was trying to make amends for his reception of her news, she could tell; this artificial interest depressed her the more. 'She's been massaging my arms, I told her a tale about overpractising.'

'Mh'm. And she had dinner all right?'

'Yes.'

'I mean, did she eat?'

'Well, better than some other times I've seen—which isn't saying much.' She laughed uncertainly. 'But for what improvement there was, I've a feeling the practising did it. I'll keep an eye out in that direction,' she promised, always with the feeling that this was not what he had hoped to hear, 'and let you know.'

'And what's she doing now?'

'She's gone to bed—or at least, she's gone up to her room.'

'Fine. Oh, by the way.' His voice had not revived. 'Sorry I couldn't ring you yesterday, but Tuesdays and Wednesdays seem to be getting bad—all sorts of things coming up unexpectedly.'

'Of course.' She was thoroughly dispirited. 'You said you'd ring when you could. It's all right, don't worry about it.'

* * *

A beautiful morning, rapturously beautiful, with a triumphant sun faintly veiled by occasional cloud, then bursting out again in renewed glory. She tumbled out of bed and went to close the window; a shrewish breath of air chilled and warned her it was not so clement as it looked. She began dressing in a hurry, eager to see Mrs Tor, evaluate her mood, remind her how well they had played together yesterday . . . she began inventing phrases of appreciation, almost with enthusiasm, simply because the lovely day had revived her. . . .

It was while she was brushing her teeth that, very faintly, she heard the phone ringing. This was something new; she could not remember its ringing before. She listened, but it had been immediately silenced. With the brush in her hand and her teeth a welter of foam, she stood listening. No sound of a voice came to her; she finished in a hurry, cursing the luck. It might of course be someone for staff, though not very likely . . . a sense of premonition, heavier and heavier, told her that if unable to hear, she ought at least to see who had answered. In a tearing hurry she emerged from the bathroom, and again stood listening. No least sound broke the silence; she tiptoed to the stairhead and was rewarded with a view of the phone, undisturbed on its table. Had the call been taken there? or on an extension somewhere? This, she realized belatedly, must be in Mrs Tor's own room; sure to be . . . suddenly aware that to be caught prowling about in a bathrobe might dispose to suspicion or worse, hastily she made tracks to her room and finished dressing, all the while upset and angry over a misfortune, failure, something—which she felt, stubbornly, to be important.

The sight of Mrs Tor, when she descended, thickened her sense of impending trouble without defining it. The old lady was seldom on time for meals, she needed two or three proddings to get her there, yet here she was already at table, ahead of the regular hour; she must have demanded her breakfast early, and was sitting before its remains wrapped in a heavy

76

cloud. To her myrmidon's greeting she had hardly replied, and continued perfectly silent with a teapot and most of a rack of toast before her. Absently and intermittently she addressed herself to her cup while Jacintha, beginning to eat, tried a couple of gambits without getting any response. Thereafter she limited herself to furtive glances—an exercise in which she was becoming adept—trying to define the old woman's particular preoccupation. Reflection and surmise were cut short in short order; Mrs Tor threw down her napkin and rose, and a first awareness, reasonless but certain, engulfed Jacintha. Her employer had simply been waiting, killing time till a certain hour; now that the hour had arrived, she was at once on her feet.

Glancing at her own watch which said nine o'clock, and without time to think—

'Are we going to walk?' she enquired, surging up too. 'It's a lovely morning, isn't it?'

If she presumed that her question would deflect, or otherwise change the other's look of set purpose, she was instantly undeceived.

'Finish your breakfast.' Mrs Tor turned on her a new face, lethal with suspicion and enmity. 'I'm going alone.'

'But—'

'Alone, I said. Sit down!' Something dangerous vibrated in the command. 'Stop where you are!'

Subsiding, with every nerve in her body alive with protest, Jacintha sank down and watched Mrs Tor leave the dining-room, shutting the door behind her. Now possessed with preternatural alertness, yet nailed to her seat, she listened agonizingly hard for anything from the hall, any least indication . . . faint sounds seemed to indicate the old woman's departure, or was she waiting to admit someone—? After an eternity came the sound, unmistakable, of the front door closing. At once she was on her feet, racing for her bedroom and cursing the fact that she had no coat downstairs; from now on she would keep something in the hall closet, unless Mrs Tor should object. . . .

Seconds later she was outside, in the ruthless spring sunshine. Glancing hurriedly about, she perceived no trace what-

77

ever of the quarry. To the left the village street petered out to fields and the minster, to the right it ran to more houses, then the busy part of the High Street, and after that still more houses . . . She hung indecisive a moment, then—without conviction of any sort, but somehow daunted by the loneliness on her left—began walking fast into the village; here at least she might meet someone of whom she could enquire . . . As she hurried along, half running, she still connected this disappearance with the early phone call, but apart from that could get nowhere whatever. The need for spying on another person's conversations and arrangements, over a second phone, had never occurred to her; now, in the intervals of darting eyes and attention painfully on the stretch, she cursed her stupidity, her unutterable carelessness . . .

She was in the business section now, the shops open but still sparsely peopled; already tired, she drew breath and began walking more slowly, thinking what to do. Hugh was out of reach, the whole day stretched between her and his evening call. Yet unless she collected some hint of Mrs Tor's excursion, what should she tell him? The early phone call, the old woman's peculiar absorption that followed, her evident waiting and her abrupt departure? Then the pursuit, useless; no very impressive report . . . Having begun to walk fast a second time, unconsciously she slowed before a new image. Tell the solicitor . . . ? She shook her head unconsciously. Consult him for *very* serious and unmanageable trouble, certainly, but not for this. Or at least not yet, not till she had garnered some idea of what had drawn her employer outside this morning. And whatever it was, she had defended it from scrutiny with all her resolution, still formidable.

Meanwhile, perfectly abstracted, she had crossed the road and stood unseeing before a fruiterer's display. What next? where next? and the old lady perhaps getting into trouble somewhere, alone, alone . . .

'I beg your pardon, miss, but—' a voice began, and the look Jacintha turned on its owner—not quite a smile, too questioning—was evidently received with pleasure.

78

'—but wouldn't you be,' the other asked, 'the new young lady that's with Mrs Tor?'

'Yes, I am,' she admitted, then wondered too late whether more guardedness would have been advisable. At once, however, she was reassured as the speaker continued, 'I thought you must be. I'm Mrs Williams, Mr Dennison's mentioned me to you perhaps—?'

'No,' she was obliged to admit. 'I mean, not yet.'

"Oh?' The other was evidently puzzled. 'But when he interviewed you—Mr Dennison—he didn't mention—?'

'Actually,' Jacintha explained, 'I was interviewed by Mr Kerwin.'

'It was him engaged you?' Mrs Williams was clearly off centre. 'Mr Kerwin? I only ask because it's always been Mr Dennison that met the ladies and spoke to them and that.'

'Not this time.'

'Well.' Mrs Williams, obviously puzzled for a moment, dismissed the matter. 'It's just that I'm called in to stay with Mrs Tor when her ladies have their day off, so I—'

'Mrs Williams.' Clutching at the prospect of help, Jacintha had broken in without apology. Rapidly she retailed the morning's events and finished with, 'Would you have any idea where she's gone, perhaps? Any idea at all . . . ?' She ran down despairingly; the other was shaking her head.

'I wouldn't know, I'm sure,' said Mrs Williams. 'But I shouldn't worry about it too much, if I was you. She's done that with me—just flung out of the house when something didn't please her best.'

'Yes, but—but you see, this wasn't quite the same. First she was *waiting* to go out for some reason or other, then when the time came she just . . . went.'

'Well, all the same.' Mrs Williams remained untroubled. 'She went out, all right, and she'll be back. It's not as if she was crazy actually, you know, it's just that she has her spells of, well, a little bit funny. Nor she'll never explain what she's been doing,' she emphasized. 'You mustn't expect that.'

Silenced, dissatisfied, Jacintha shook her head.

'So I'd just wait,' the other concluded. 'You're upset because

79

you don't know her all that well, I can see. She hates being watched, just absolutely *hates* it, and as for being followed, well!' She rolled her eyes. 'Won't stand for it, not a single moment. Those other ladies she's had, they've told me about it—how it'd make her fly off the handle, or even bring on a spell, a bad one so they say.' She pursed her lips. 'With a lady like that, that had a big name of some sort, you can't just behave like she's ordinary, you know.' She made significant eyes. 'Careful, that's what you've got to be.'

'Suppose I've trouble with her, bad trouble,' Jacintha said bleakly. 'Could I ring you?'

'Any old time, 382, but it's in the book—William James Williams, not much imagination there.' Her laugh was clear and jolly, like her voice. 'I'm very glad to've met you, Miss Cory—my, look at the time! I'd better be pushing along.'

'And I to've met you.' Her sense of heaviness was decidedly lightened for having this auxiliary in prospect. 'Very glad.'

'So don't you go fretting,' Mrs Williams adjured vigourously. 'Not 'fore you have to, at any rate.'

'I shan't.'

'She's not grateful,' the other digressed unexpectedly. 'Never grateful, not a bit. But who cares? A woman like that, been someone in her day—she's got a little care owing to her now she needs it, hasn't she? A little patience? I'm real attached to her in a funny sort of way, I really—Lord, I'm nattering again. Ta-ta, must fly now!'

* * *

Still bemused, still with the pacifying influence of Mrs Williams upon her, she raked the street up and down. It was now much fuller of people, but still no glimpse of Mrs Tor; with a sigh of defeat she had just stepped off the kerb of an intersecting lane when she saw to her left, far down this lane, a figure approaching. Her excellent eyesight left no doubt of its identity, and her instant shrinking back was perfectly unconscious. Withdrawing into the angle of a shop-window, she waited an agonizing interval till Mrs Tor emerged from the side-road, passed her hiding-place with a reminiscent and reflective gait, and prepared to cross over. Jacintha waited, holding her breath; the instant it was plain that she had turned (at least) toward home, she had left her shelter and was flying down the lane. Unlikely that the old woman could have been very far along it, the person with whom she had had the interview might still be in sight . . .

The lane twisted suddenly to the left, and at once a change came over it. The sense of the High Street still nearby, the people moving along it, vanished; in place of all this was solitude, silence, empty fields, a feeling of desertion since the world began—not lessened, only somehow emphasized, by the solitary figure some hundred yards ahead of her. This, at first glance, she could not even be sure of as man or woman. It slouched along in the cold sunshine with no alteration of gait, having evidently all the time in the world and giving absolutely no sign of having heard her first, 'Hoi!'—a croak not loud, since she was out of breath. As she began moving faster, a succession of uneasy images and probabilities started up in her mind. Was the person deaf? Or if not deaf, pretending deliberately not to hear her, for her running footsteps must be, by now, audible? It had long hair at any rate, streaky light brown hair falling down behind, perhaps someone from a gypsy encampment nearby . . . ?

'Excuse me,' she panted, noting subconsciously that as she came alongside, the apparition quickened its gait by very little. It was a man, that much was now evident. The face that it turned upon her was white, wedge-shaped and dirty; on its upper lip was a scanty floss showing here and there a glint of pale gold. The eyes, badly red-rimmed and perfectly blank, repeated the blankness of the general expression. No interrogation in it, no apprehension, no fear; it looked half-asleep, that was it, yet in this sleepiness was there some quality, malignant . . . ?

'Excuse me,' she said again too loudly, over a suddenly-pounding heart and a frantic wish to turn tail and run; she had no right whatever to accost him in this manner, and still less wish to do so now that the picture was plain to her. He was filthy, from his rat's-nest tangle of hair to his bare feet in derelict sandals whose thongs were pieced out with bits of

81

fraying cord. Through the uncleanliness that seemed to envelop him like murk, his complexion—apart from its fishbelly pallor—stood out extremely fair; from between inflamed lids a pair of dead eyes, grey, turned a dead drugged look upon her.

'Excuse me,' she said a third time, with as good an imitation of composure as could be expected from her revulsion and breathlessness. 'I think you were—I mean, were you just now talking to an old lady who lives here?' She found herself, now, addressing a profile whose owner was once more in motion; after his single look and half-halt he had resumed the same shambling gait, not faster nor slower.

'Please,' she besought, forced to move with him and to ransack, simultaneously, her resources of improvisation. 'It's very important, and any information—would be paid for—' Dismayed, she heard herself flagrantly exceeding her brief; the instinct to hang on, to find out anything she could from the apparition, fought again with her instinct to run. '—very well paid, if you'd help—' She continued her unauthorized inducements while matching her step to his, which now (or did she imagine it) seemed to become slower; seizing on this as a readiness to stop and parley, she pursued breathlessly, 'I promise, I'll take you to . . .' to whom indeed, she wondered with her head swimming '. . . to someone who'll pay you, at once—'

He had quickened his pace instead of slowing; unready, she quickened hers.

'—he'll pay you more than—than you get from her,' she strove, now all but running beside him. 'Because she *did* give you something. Didn't she? didn't—' and stopped with a jerk as he halted without warning and turned his face full upon her, his deaf unhearing air fallen from him like so many rags.

'You want your teeth bashed in?' he asked. His voice, vicious, illiterate, grating, came through the tangled hair fallen over his face; from between reddened lids his pale eyes kindled to a paler blaze of concentrated malignity. ''Nother word outa you, y'get your wish. One more word—!'

The two of them stood, he stock-still, she in recoil; again realizing the utter desertion, the lane now petering out to a footway between fields. As their cataleptic stillness extended itself he added a word that, in spite of permissiveness, rarely achieves print. Then he swung on his heel and loped off, his long easy stride spectacularly at variance with his earlier plodding and somnambulistic gait.

She as well—a moment later, and unsteadily—had turned and was retracing her steps. Craven without disguise, she did not consider even the possibility of lingering to see him out of sight; the chance that he might look around, see himself watched, come back—here in this solitude with no living creature in sight but pasturing sheep and cows—completed her demoralization. With her heart pounding and through that feeling of dislocation and disbelief that follows any fall through the thin crust of civilization, she tried to force her mind to the next immediate problem. Mrs Tor would be home long since. With what grace would she take her employee's absence, after her virtual order to stay in? What account of herself would serve best, what subterfuge. . . . .

Stop thinking about it, she commanded herself. *Wait till you're home.* On the doorstep she took out her key, used it silently, had a cautionary peep into the hall . . . no one; silently she skimmed upstairs, disposed of her coat, smoothed windblown hair, and went down again silently, listening at every step. Nothing; closed doors, everything quiet . . . a faint sound supplied her with a clue and a return of apprehension, both; she tapped on the living-room door, and on a harsh 'Come!' entered.

'I'm having this done,' said Mrs Tor, still fingering keys at random and not looking at her. 'Tuned.'

'Oh, splendid,' returned Jacintha. 'When?'

'Today, of course.' She removed her gaze from the piano and bent it on the girl with curious intensity. Or suspicion, was it that . . . ? 'Rang them in Bowring and said if they couldn't send straightaway, I'd ring elsewhere. He should be here by one, at the latest.' Still her eyes rested on her companion with a glance undeniably disturbing; tenacious, very faintly satirical. . . . She knew about her absence from the house, of course; Jacintha braced herself to lie if questioned. Or what if the old lady's malice, half-smiling, were on some score other than her excursion? on some imaginary count, perhaps . . . ?

'Well, it's a wonderful idea.' She had to say something. 'Give us an idea of how it sounds.' She was still wary and tense, still waiting for enquiry as to her whereabouts during the last hour. 'I mean, how it *really* sounds.'

'Last night . . . .' Mrs Tor still picked out random notes; whether she half-smiled, or not, remained a question. 'Last night . . .'

She stopped; Jacintha waited.

'. . . did you,' she began again, driftingly, her hand always evoking those faint sounds of musical comment, 'did you come in late? very late?'

'I . . . ?' After her first surprise it occurred to her that her return from phoning, at about nine, might seem late to a disturbed imagination. 'How late?' she felt her way along, cautiously.

'Past one, I looked. There was someone.' Her voice had fallen very low. 'Someone here, in the house.'

It was said with an absolute sanity that refuted argument; on a faint cold chill Jacintha asked, 'And did you . . . anything . . . ?'

'I came down. I looked.'

'And—?' Fearless, thought Jacintha; such fearlessness would have been beyond her. 'Was—was there . . . ?'

'Nothing. No one at all.' Mrs Tor rose from the piano, suddenly enveloped by a sort of prescience that made her stand tall and pillarlike. With desolate eyes staring straight into Jacintha's, she intoned, 'My son wants to shut me up.'

* * *

'Mr . . . Mr Dennison?'

'Speaking.'

'This is—is—Jacintha Cory. I'm sorry to ring you so late, but I . . . . I . . . .'

'Quite all right, Miss Cory, it's not all that late. Is something wrong?'

'Well, there's been a sort of . . . of complication. Could I possibly see you, I mean . . . as soon as . . .'

'Now? would you care to come now?'

'Oh *yes!* if you didn't mind.'

'I live over my office, just ring the second bell—there're only two.'

'Thank you, I'll come straightaway. And please,' she added belatedly, 'please apologize to Mrs Dennison, but I shan't keep you more than a very few minutes.'

'I'll do that,' he promised urbanely.

* * *

'Do you mind climbing a couple of flights?' He had just let her in. 'I don't go in the office after hours, if I can help it.'

'No, I don't mind.' Scrambling up the stairs—he had waved her ahead of him—she was engrossed with arranging her tale as briefly as possible so as to restore him, with least delay, to his family. After two flights he had said, 'Excuse me,' stepping ahead of her and opening a handsome oak door. 'I'll just . . .' He preceded her, threw open another door, and motioned her in.

She took a couple of steps, and stopped short. Whatever had been in her mind, it was not this large room, comfortably furnished in out-of-date style and with a fire blazing opulently; he must have turned his family out of it to receive her . . .

'Sit down,' he was saying. 'What will you drink?'

'Nothing, nothing at all. I don't want to keep you,' she hurried on urgently. 'If I could just tell you about . . . tell you—'

He restored a glass to the side table bearing a tray of drinks, came to the opposite chair at the fireplace and seated himself, then said, 'Carry on.'

'First though—you must promise me—' of her blurting, of her bad beginning she was aware, and could not help it '—please, you must promise me not to say anything about this. Not to Mrs Tor, not to Hugh. I know it's not . . . but . . . but I mean—'

'I shan't say anything to anyone, if possible,' he put in over her incoherence. 'Go ahead.'

85

'Well.' She took a long breath. 'Early today, just after breakfast—or no!' She fell over herself in correction. 'First I've got
to tell you that we've arranged—Hugh and I—that he's to
ring me every evening, and if he doesn't, I'll hear from him
next evening. But this thing that's happened—this—this—'

'Just a moment,' he said indulgently, went to the side-table,
and brought back a tall glass full of something pale rose and
clinking with ice. 'Have a sip of this while you're thinking. Go
on, just a sip.' He watched while she picked up the glass reluctantly. 'Is it all right?'

'Yes, yes. Very nice.' She put the glass down. 'Well, this
evening he didn't ring. But earlier today, just after breakfast—'

She paused; he made no further reference to the drink, but
waited.

'Mrs Tor went out. She'd been very quiet before that, a . . .
a *waiting* quietness, you know? And all at once she got up and
started out of the room, and when I tried to go with her she
snapped my head off. So I didn't dare move, not till I'd heard
her go, then I went after her. And to make it short—' she took
another exhausted breath '—rather a long time after, I did see
her.'

'Where?'

'Coming down that lane—what's it called—Stringer's. Walking rather fast, for her, and looking . . . looking downward.
Preoccupied.' The picture was all at once more intensely clear
to her than before. 'Absorbed.'

'And then?'

'When she was out of sight, I went down the lane too. I
thought I might see to whom she'd been talking, or something—'

'And—?'

'Well, I did see him, or at least there was no one else. He
was—horrible,' she quavered unexpectedly. 'Horrible.'

'A tramp of some sort?'

'Yes—young. Quite young, anyway.'

He was silent, but the focus of his eyes had changed.

'Well, I spoke to him. I told him that whatever Mrs Tor had
given him—I took for granted that she'd given him something—

86

I said that someone would give him more. I mean, if he'd say what . . . what they'd talked about. I thought that you . . .' she explained confusedly '. . . that you'd talk to him, that you'd find out—'

'Quite. And what did he say?'

'He offered to bash me. And when Hugh didn't ring, this evening—' she drew another faltering breath '—I thought *someone* should know about it. But please, please don't tell anyone I told you—'

'Could you,' he interrupted, 'describe this man just a little more?'

'Well, he was medium height. And I think a fair complexion, but he was so filthy I couldn't be sure. I'd a sort of impression,' she added uncertainly, 'that he was some sort of idiot. But when he spoke, I wasn't sure of anything.'

He was silent again, and—again—with a silence of the recollecting variety.

'Do you know him?' she was emboldened to ask, after some moments. 'I mean, by so poor a description?'

'You may remember, during our first meeting,' he began in apparent digression, 'that I spoke to Hugh about similar encounters of Mrs Tor's—?'

'Yes.' It came back, jarringly, after a moment's thought. 'Yes, I do remember.'

'The only trouble is, that the accounts of whom she met aren't in the least like yours.' His eye was still distant, questioning bygones. 'But these two former companions of Mrs Tor's, who described the encounters, saw them from a distance.' He smiled very slightly. 'They hadn't the nerve to get as close as you did. Also, I must confess, they weren't overly bright. Still, they'd done what they could—followed Mrs Tor when she left the house.' He paused again. 'On one odd thing, they did agree: neither one was quite sure as to whether Mrs Tor'd met a man, or a woman.'

'But neither was I,' she exclaimed. 'Not till I'd caught up with him, anyway.'

'I see. But the rest of the description simply doesn't fit. One of them said the person was black-haired, the other that he was red-haired or reddish.'

A brief silence re-imposed itself; he broke it.

'I think you've done very well, very well indeed.' A smile passed between them, hers questioning, his bleak. 'Now if ever you can speak to one of these mysterious gentry without,' he weighted the word, 'without courting injury, try if you can't repeat your offer. That they'll be paid, *very* well paid, for any account of what passed between them and Mrs Tor. Bring them to my office or here, at any time.'

She nodded unhopefully to the unhopeful words.

'Nothing else we can do,' he summed it up. 'Not so long as your employer has the status of a person completely sane.'

'She *is* sane,' she blurted, without premeditation.

'Ah.' He was polite, non-combative. 'She appears so to you?'

'Well.' She withdrew inwardly, having to attempt qualification—she, not trained in qualification—to one who was. 'I only mean, she does have spells when she forgets everything. What she's been saying, or whom you are. But not more than old people do,' she pressed on against his attempt to say something. 'And she comes back from it almost at once, absolutely sane again. Sane enough, at any rate,' she added robustly, 'to impress me. To scare me sometimes, in fact.'

'If that's how she strikes you, I'm glad. Now, your drink.' His tone was at once acquiescent and dismissive. 'You've hardly touched it, or you don't like it perhaps—?'

'Oh no, it's very nice.' Obediently she took it up and sipped. 'Very nice, thank you.'

'You're sure? You'd rather not have something else—?'

'Quite sure, thanks.' She was keeping him from his family, she must be on her way . . .

'If you don't mind my asking,' he was saying, 'what has Mrs Tor been doing today, apart from meeting strange characters?'

'Nothing much,' she responded, and suppressed an inclination to mention the piano; much too premature, and what if the old girl refused to go on with it? 'She's been rather . . . sombre you might say, abstracted at times, but nothing worse.'

'How in the world,' he asked, smiling, 'do you get through the day?'

'Oh, we sit together—and talk when she feels like talking. And when I'm not wanted I walk, or read.'

'I see.' His air was again preoccupied.

'Mr Dennison,' she forged on hastily. 'Thank you very much for seeing me. And please apologize to your wife, tell her I shan't be making a practise of this sort of—'

'I've no wife,' he put in blandly. 'Don't apologize.'

'Oh!' She was already on her feet. 'Well, thank you at any rate, I shan't do this again—not unless I'm absolutely driven.'

'Miss Cory.' They were going downstairs before he spoke again. 'How am I to get in touch with you, if I need to?'

'Well.' Just in time she suppressed her first answer—that this would hardly be necessary. 'You couldn't ring me, not there.'

'I could send you a note, perhaps?'

'Oh no. Mrs Tor might just answer the door herself, by bad luck.'

'Well, by post?'

'That should be all right.' They had begun moving again. 'Friends of mine may write, after all, so if you—Mr Dennison!' He had closed the front door and come out with her. 'You needn't take me home, there's no—'

'Hush,' he returned indulgently. 'Will you walk, or be driven? You say.'

* * *

Strolling back, alone, he was divided between the intentions never very far absent from his mind, but—as well—thoughts quite unexpected. A pleasant girl. He had hardly noticed her— hardly looked at her in fact—during that earlier clash with Hugh, and during the pay-talk had still been affected by his earlier displeasure. But an attractive creature, now that he had come in closer contact with her; charming actually, well-bred, well-educated too and not too young . . . . a slight shock of surprise brought him up short, making him trace the origin of this train of thought; his prompt finding of it released a sound of amusement. Foolish, except that his single state—comfortable and pleasant, plenty of friends or near-friends when he felt the need of them—had been increasingly on his mind for some time now. A man who felt that he should marry, at the same time with no particular desire to marry, had better be pretty damned careful. This girl, however, was a decided improvement on most of the unmarried women he knew . . .

With another sound, this time of impatience, he dismissed it for considerations more immediate and oppressive. The old woman's meeting with still another of those vagabonds that she affected . . . meaningless, probably, but worrying. What to do about it, in the present state of things, he had no idea. If only he could do the obviously right thing, arrange for her some degree of confinement. . . . His mind moved to Mrs Tor's bank and his arrangements there; highly improper of course and productive of trouble if it got out, trouble not for himself but for the co-operating official . . .

He frowned as the current of his thoughts went back to the girl. Suppose her presence in Mrs Tor's house to prove a godsend? Actually he found from moment to moment that she had struck him very particularly, more so than he knew. If he indicated to her, with proper precautions, his arrangement at the bank, he felt it would go no further, its secrecy would be in no danger. Or at least, he thought—while unlocking his door—as little danger as one could reasonably ask.

* * *

She inserted her key very stealthily, stepped into the hall, listened . . . not a sound, no one stirring. Not yet absolutely certain, she stood another moment before moving again. As she began climbing the stairs she realized all at once that she was dead-tired. The episode of the vagabond; Hugh's failure to ring; her scrambling expedition to the other man, every moment of it dogged by her sense of imprudence, indiscretion, and now her effort to sneak to her own room without making a sound: all of it pushing her toward an exhaustion where she was increasingly cancelled, wiped out . . .

90

And yet in bed her mind woke again, uneasily, to her precipitate and scared irruption upon the solicitor. Tell Hugh about it . . . ? Perhaps yes, perhaps no, think later whether to . . . whether to . . . she fled for refuge to the thought of the solicitor himself, much nicer than she had imagined from seeing him that couple of times; his nose a thought too inquisitive for her taste, his self-possession a thought too absolute . . . all the same, she had begun to like him. Or rather, she did not dislike him so much as she had supposed at first, he had been . . . he had been very . . . .

An immense black cloud rolled over her, burying the next word, burying herself, and still—before she went down under it—she struggled to finish her thought: that he had been, actually, very . . . very . . .

* * *

'Jacintha?'

'Hugh! Oh, I'm so glad you've rung.'

'Why? No trouble, is there—?'

'I don't . . . I don't quite know.' It came out, suddenly, in a flood. 'Your mother met someone in Stringer's Lane—' breathlessly she stumbled along, telling the same old tale with repetitions and harkings back. '—and when you didn't ring last night, I—' just on the verge of blurting her interview with Dennison, she nearly bit her tongue out. '—I was so worried,' she substituted. 'I didn't know what to—I mean, I—'

'No, no, of course not,' he soothed. 'Anything else?'

'Not a great deal. —Oh yes! she thought someone'd got in the house, night before last.'

'Oh.' He was startled. 'And had anyone? I mean, was there any real reason she'd think so?'

'None at all.' Her sense of omission pushed her into a minor revelation. 'She said you . . . you wanted to shut her up.'

'Poor old girl,' he laughed grimly, after a moment. 'Got her lines crossed.'

'Yes.'

'You're having a bad time, aren't you? But hold on for God's sake, I'll be home tomorrow. You will, won't you—hang on?'

91

'Oh yes.'

'And how's she been, today?'

'Today was all right, quite good in fact.' She took a long breath. 'We practised awhile this morning. Oh! I almost forgot to tell you—she's had the piano tuned, she had it done yesterday.'

'Well, that's good.' His voice was unillumined. 'I suppose.'

'It's very good,' she protested. 'And it's a wonderful piano, I think she's beginning to enjoy it. Or almost enjoy it, anyway, and she may do more and more.'

'M'hm. And was there anything else you wanted to tell me?'

'Not much.' What with disappointment at his reception of the news, her own voice had gone lack-lustre. 'Would you know what time you'll be back?'

'About noon, I should think.' His sigh was immense, exhausted. 'Then we'll see what we . . . well, God knows.' He laughed comfortlessly. 'I'll get back, anyway, and we'll think of something. Or do something, h'm? We'll see.'

VIII

She came downstairs after the night's broken sleep; the curious complications all about her, beyond reach of sight or grasp, were acquiring an unpleasant power to wake her up too early. Her visit to Dennison, perhaps ill-judged, her suppression of this when she spoke to Hugh . . . it all, after a number of hours, was strong enough to rowel and disturb her. The hall was still empty, the dining-room door still closed; the morning post lay in orderly fashion on the hall table, still untouched by Mrs Tor's groping, disorderly hand. Toward this she moved with the usual automatic impulse—to see, examine, even with no prospect of anything for herself. Surprised, she saw the envelope addressed to her in a strong unknown hand; she picked it up hurriedly and—obeying an unfamiliar urge of caution—hurried into the morning-room, closed the door, and ripped it open; the postmark had more or less assured her from whom it came. *Dear Miss Cory, The person in whom we are interested drew £200 from the bank yesterday. I am telling you this in absolute confidence and beg that you'll communicate it to no one else. What can be done about this, apart from alerting you, I don't know. But if you have any chance to find out what she does with it, this might or might not be helpful. Please burn this note. Yours sincerely—*

She started, hearing a footstep in the hall, and hurriedly

crammed letter and envelope into a pocket of her jumper. Then cautiously—there being no help for it—she opened the door and looked out. Mrs Tor stood with her back partly turned to her, shoving the letters about randomly. She did not look around as Jacintha emerged and barely replied to her greeting, only murmuring, 'Nothing interesting, never. Never is, any more . . .' then with a sigh abandoned the post and turned toward the dining-room door, now open.

Her behaviour at breakfast gave Jacintha a few more turns, painful and acute, also half-comprehending. She was reminded of the old woman's manner on another morning; the same sparse and inattentive eating, the same obliviousness of what went on about her, the same waiting for . . . some advent of time, as previously? Invisibly riveted, more resolute from moment to moment, the companion waited. The instant the old girl went out, this time, she would be closer on her heels. Also the thought of the money she would probably be carrying, a sum like that, was not reassuring. . . .

Yet the anticipated exodus failed to arrive; Mrs Tor finished a scanty breakfast, rose from her chair, moved from the room irresolutely. The atmosphere of waiting was still about her, but it seemed that this new waiting attended on something *in* the house, or to come to the house . . . ? Her restless glance roamed here, there, unseeing but strangely sharp, *hungry*. . . .

'Would you,' Jacintha ventured, 'like to play a bit?' As the other seemed barely to hear her, her glance still ferreting for that undetermined thing she wanted, God knew what—'Just awhile?' she continued, carefully avoiding cajolery. 'Or if you'd prefer, later—?'

'Now,' returned Mrs Tor, her voice a curious combination of abstraction and snappishness. 'Now,' and quickly led the way to the drawing-room. At the piano she played with effort, always with that other appearance of listening, always listening . . . 'Ridiculous, this,' she commented loudly and suddenly. 'Perfectly ridiculous.'

'I know,' agreed Jacintha, over a sinking heart. 'It's so kind of you, because of my wretched arms.'

'Oh that—*yes*.' Mrs Tor was suddenly appeased. 'That

94

makes sense. Of course, of course.' With total submission—heartrending, for some reason—she settled down to play conscientiously, repeating bars and enduring correction amiably.

'I think we've had this,' the preceptress decided suddenly. 'I'll find something that'll appeal to you more.' She riffled pages to what she judged a more likely candidate for Mrs Tor's favour. 'I'll just play you the introduction, shall I, then we'll—'

A sound interrupted her, a loud whimper. As she turned her head in alarm the old woman continued in a strange broken lament, 'This house, this house! be the death of me, the end.' An awful agitation seemed to course through her, a shaking and trembling. 'I'll be *finished*. Someone . . . . hates me, someone . . . .'

'Who, Mrs Tor?' Jacintha interrupted, unable to bear the sight and sound of this disintegration. 'Who'll do that to you? Who wants to hurt you?'

The other was all at once silent, her agitation gone as suddenly as it had arisen. 'Who?' she repeated softly. Her eyes brimmed with slyness and malice. 'You don't know? Then you're stupid.' She grinned unnervingly. 'Stupid, stupid. If you don't know that, you're . . . you're . . .'

Another change had come over her, too swiftly for the moment of change to be seen. The raillery and spite melted into a look of anxiety, a waiting look for someone, something; she turned her head from side to side in a searching so distracted that Jacintha, herself unnerved, took a moment before attempting, haltingly, 'Mrs Tor . . .'

'Tired,' said the other in a rapid mumble hardly to be followed. 'This waiting, waiting, tired of . . . . mus' sleep now, yes, sleep, sleep . . .'

* * *

Issuing from the house, she looked first to see if Hugh's car stood at his end of the house; it was by no means noon, but she looked anyway. The emptiness there struck a responsive note on her own inner emptiness. She stood a moment, aimless and thinking of escape, any moment of escape. The empty fields and the church, to her left? shops and people circulating about them, to her right? She recoiled all at once from the thought of unpeopled spaces. Have a coffee somewhere, look at shop-windows, anything . . .

'Miss Cory! Jacintha!'

He had come from behind her as she turned out of the gate; he had got home, thank God . . .

'I heard you playing in there,' he announced. 'I mean, it was the two of you?' At her nod—'Well! he hurried on. 'It sounded fine, just fine. I mean, it's pretty good that you could get her interested, make her keep on with it.'

'I looked for your car, just now.' She smiled in lack-lustre fashion, yet was on the road to being cheered up. 'But I couldn't see it.'

'No, it's at a garage I rent. My house is where the garage used to be. I tried to make her change her mind about destroying it, but . . .' He shrugged; his cheerful smile returned. 'And apart from this piano stuff—how're you getting on with her, in general?'

A swarm of intentions, resolves, misgivings, assailed her at once. She should tell him everything, good or bad. But another swarm of predispositions—fidelity, affection, whatever it was—stopped and silenced her. Or at least, she compromised with herself, tell him the good news first, keep the bad till later . . .

'Quite well, I should say.' She had replied with no perceptible hesitation. 'Pretty well, actually.'

'I mean, beside the piano.' Gloom seemed to overtake him again. 'She'll do that, you know. Go on with it for a bit, then for no reason just . . . chuck it.'

'Not this time, I think.' As he turned on her an uncomprehending look, she was forced to reveal, if ever so little, her strategy. 'I told her a hard-luck story to make her start playing with me, and all I can say is, she's kept it up so far.'

'What d'you mean?' He had stopped in his tracks. 'What hard-luck story?'

'Well, it's nothing much.' For fear of claiming any benefit, prematurely, she suddenly longed to say nothing more. 'I mean, I'd like to try it out a little longer before I—'

'But Jacintha.' He had stopped dead again. 'I must know, don't you see? If there's improvement of any kind I've got to know. If only,' he argued, 'to deal with arguments for . . . well, restraint and soforth if they come up.' He took her arm firmly. 'Look, here's the Wheatsheaf. We'll go in and have a drink and you tell me all about it.'

'It's early for a drink,' she started to object.

'Well, tomato juice, coffee, anything—well! look who's here. Hoi! John!'

The man addressed checked in his ascent of the inn's three steps, turned about politely; it was somehow plain to her that he had seen them but preferred to avoid them.

'Come here!' Hugh was bellowing jubilantly. Having no choice the other came, bowing to her and murmuring, 'Miss . . .' in the form proper to a distant acquaintance.

'I think Jacintha has something important to tell us,' Hugh was burbling meanwhile. 'Are you meeting someone here?'

'No, I'm just after coffee.'

'Come on then.' The invitation was urgent. 'It sounds damned int'resting, we both ought to hear it. Come along!'

In the next few moments they were sitting at a table and Hugh, scooping up obligations of hospitality, had ordered; the instant they were served he commanded, 'All right, Jacintha, go on. What you were telling me, from the very beginning—go on.'

'Well,' she essayed a trifle awkwardly. 'It's just—' With all her heart she wished that the second man were not at the same table, fixing her with polite, empty eyes. 'Well,' she repeated, in tones suddenly ringing and defiant, 'it's just that I thought, from the very first time I met Mrs Tor—I thought that the main thing about a woman like that, and always would be, was her sense of—of purpose.' She came out with it on a gusty breath. 'Just trying to amuse her, keep her amused with this trifle and that trifle—it wouldn't do. She wouldn't have any use for nonsense like that, she never would have. So before I came here I got a book of piano duets. Not,' she explained hastily, 'that she'd ever be interested in playing them, I didn't think that. But I told her a yarn, that I'd strained my arms overpractising, that in fact I'd hurt them rather badly.' The reserve that impeded her had vanished. 'But I told her, also, that I needed to play just a little, to keep them from stiffening up. And straightaway—' she could not restrain a glimmer of triumph '—she was interested.'

'Yes,' said Hugh, hanging wide-eyed on her words. 'Go on.'

'Well, that's how it's been so far. She's not only continued to work at these duets—though the music bores her,' she explained in parenthesis, 'but straightaway she offered to massage my arms, she said she'd done it a lot for her native helpers. And *then*—she had the piano tuned.' She looked at them proudly. 'I didn't suggest it, I never said a word about it, she did it completely on her own. And—and that's all, up to now.'

'Well, John,' commented Hugh largely. 'And how do you like that?'

'Promising,' said the other, with a peculiar tonelessness. 'Rather promising.'

'*Rather* promising?' echoed Hugh, with unrestrained mockery. 'It's a damned sight more than that. In my humble opinion, it means we're on the right road—at last.' His look was challenging; the solicitor sustained it imperturbably. 'Those old girls that you engaged for her, those harmless old biddies, I always knew they were worse than useless. I *knew* it would take someone with brains, imagination—someone that could put herself in her place and come up with—with something to interest her, keep her interested.' He gazed at Dennison, his triumph even more unconcealed. 'How does it strike you, old man?'

'Good,' said the other, again with approving words that held no hint of approval. 'Very good indeed.'

'Ah, come off it,' said Hugh jovially. 'You wouldn't be a bit jealous, would you—'

'Oh!' she broke in on the exchange; her sudden misgiving had veiled its faint unpleasantness. 'But you won't give me away to Mrs Tor, will you?' She looked distractedly from one to the other. 'If she ever knew it was a trick about my arms— if she ever suspected—'

98

'Count on me,' Hugh interrupted. 'All right with you too, John? Don't worry about it, Cintha, don't give it a thought. And by the way, John—'

He had broken off suddenly, on another change of expression.

'—that yarn of yours, about mother's chinning with tramps now and again, remember? Well,' he pursued at his nod, '*I* remembered something that happened a million years ago when I was a kid, out walking with her. Which didn't happen very often,' he subjoined with a faint grin, 'but on this red-letter occasion I remember her stopping to talk with some mangy type, some beggar or gypsy maybe. Whether it was or wasn't,' he laughed briefly, 'I stood there ready to die, stinking little snob that I was. So about her taking up with types like that, I told you it was an old story.'

'You've remembered that conveniently,' said Dennison, with a regal inclination of his head. 'Very conveniently.'

'Well—not quite, old boy.' He turned on the other a face so unresentful—of innuendo no less than maternal stricture—that she was suddenly angry and sore on his behalf. 'I really didn't remember it before. And that first time, when Jacintha'd just accepted the job—well, to tell you the truth, I was mostly worried that hearing such things would make her back out—sling the job back at me. So I was in a sweat to get you out of there before you could come out with any more scary items, it's all I was thinking of.' His look and tone were apologetic. 'It's only later that I recalled this habit of hers, talking to all sorts of scruffy bods. The scruffier, the better.'

Her own encounter was in her mind, naturally; she glanced at Dennison, expecting him to mention it. Strangely he sat impassive, obviously with no intention of doing so; she gave him the least, sliding black look, and said to Hugh, 'Your mother met someone like that up Stringer's Lane, not long ago.'

'Did she?'

'Yes, but I've an idea—' her anxiety to clear her conscience obscured his glance at his watch '—an idea it was a pre-arranged thing, sort of, it—'

'Did you see it?' he interrupted. 'Or what?'

'Not the meeting, but I followed the man and—and tried to talk to him.'

'And then—?'

'He—he offered to bash me.'

'Good God!'

'So I went back,' she continued. 'There wasn't anything I could—'

'Look,' he said earnestly. 'Thank you for going after this type, but for God's sake don't do it again. Get yourself hurt maybe, where's the good? Don't you agree with me, John?'

'Decidedly.'

'I shan't again,' she said cravenly. 'I promise.'

'Good. Just so I shan't be worrying about you. Chatting up tramps is an old thing with mother, but not with—oh Lord!' He had glanced at his watch again. 'Have to be shoving off now, sorry—'

'The other half,' Dennison objected. 'What were you drinking, whiskey—?'

'Thanks, another time.' Plainly in a hurry to be gone, Hugh delayed long enough to add, 'You'll have the field to yourself, John, you're used to it.' Suddenly, for an instant, their eyes locked in a tight unbroken silence and as quickly separated. 'See you, Jacintha.' He was moving away; her eyes followed him involuntarily as he disappeared through the people now entering in streams and droves. When they returned to her companion, still sitting silent, she was angry again—with him, with herself?—and attacked at once. 'You didn't tell him about that money—that she drew from the bank.'

'I told him before, that first time we met,' he objected mildly. 'You yourself saw how much good it did.'

She was silenced a moment, thinking of her own silence—far more culpable—on the episode of Mrs Tor and the Crale. *That's different,* she thought stubbornly, *that's different,* and insisted, 'But this withdrawal—such a big one.' Still racked by that unreasonable fury without objective, she pressed on, 'I think you should have told him.'

'You do?'

'Yes.'

In the slight pause that followed her next, unuttered *If you don't tell him, I will* was loud in the silence.

'Goodbye,' she said, and started getting to her feet.

'Well,' he said calmly, as if not noticing the gesture. 'If you feel you must tell him, by all means do so.' He shrugged. 'But remember, if on this information he starts enquiries at the bank, on who's giving out this information about his mother . . .'

'Well,' she said a trifle nastily, as he stopped. 'Why shouldn't he?'

'Quite.' He shrugged once more. 'But if he does, please remember—again—the two unpleasant consequences. The trouble my informant will get into, of course needn't concern you. But the second is, that if this source of information is cut off—' he paused slightly '—I'll be completely in the dark about her goings-on, which are becoming odder and to my mind, more alarming. These financial capers of hers at least I'm able to get wind of—for her own protection if the need should arise, and by all the signs it may do.' Another pause. 'But if you still feel compelled to tell Hugh about it, you must please yourself.'

In the moments that followed she sat entangled and confused. By no wish of her own she was entrapped with this man, bound with him in a conspiracy of silence and concealment that she disliked as much as the man himself. Yet not so violently as she might have expected . . . . while she strove with the reason for this failure of resentment—

'I mean that, you know,' he said gravely. 'Tell him, if you feel you've got to.'

She nodded unhearingly, not looking at him; suddenly remembering Mrs Tor and the Crale and her own silence about this. Culpable? not culpable . . . ?

'Poor girl,' he said in a voice perceptibly amused. 'See here, would you have lunch with me?'

'Oh!' Surprise mixed with her distrust, her own shortcomings, reduced her to idiocy. 'Thank you, but—but I couldn't.'

'No?' he murmured. 'You're quite sure?'

'I can't leave Mrs Tor on her own.' She had made an effort

and was again self-possessed. 'She always has lunch. Goodbye now, and thank you anyway—'

'Would you,' he interrupted, rising as she did, 'have dinner with me, one evening?'

Surprised again, she looked awkward.

'I'm asking at a bad time, aren't I?' His smile deepened. 'A bad moment?'

'Well, I don't—I mean—' she began stammering.

'Any evening?' he urged gently. 'Whenever you please?'

'Not just now, but I'll—' She was blurting, anxious to get away. 'I'll ring you.'

'You've promised,' he said smiling. 'Remember you've promised.'

* * *

With whirling wits she hurried home, under the weight of her new commitment to deception. And again it was no worse, maybe not as bad, as her own concealment of the old woman's strange monologue in the garden. . . . she suddenly realized something else: her extremely present dread of encountering, at lunch, Mrs Tor still gripped by her sudden fear and dislike of the house. And on top of everything her remembrance, tardy, that even now Miss Pargill's tray was probably waiting for her in the pantry . . . From a gait already hurried she burst, more or less, into a run.

* * *

'I'm fond of this house,' Mrs Tor observed dreamily, toward the close of lunch. 'Very, very fond.'

Jacintha, dumbstruck, waited.

'If nothing's left for you but to die,' the old woman pursued, 'at least you've somewhere agreeable to do it in. Somewhere pleasant.'

Sitting watchfully and not daring to utter a syllable, she offered a smile of agreement that (she was perfectly aware) went unnoticed.

'I'm well off, considering,' Mrs Tor pursued her largely-untrodden path of euphoria. 'For an old hag, an old nothing, I really shouldn't complain.' Some darker thought crossed her face, some shadow. 'Except for the thing, the one *thing* . . .' She lapsed into reflection, staring at her unknown trouble and occasionally shaking her head.

'Could I help you, maybe?' Jacintha ventured perilously. 'If you'd tell me what's worrying you . . .' Her feeling for the poor old wreck, again, swelled her heart with that enormous pity indistinguishable from devotion. 'If you'd care to tell me—?'

Mrs Tor remained silent; the other began doubting that she had been heard. At the end of her silence, however, the old woman observed unexpectedly, 'You said you could type? you did say, one time—?'

'Oh yes.'

'Well.' She heaved a sigh. 'Maybe one day. Maybe, maybe.'

Jacintha waited a considerable moment for any development of this theme; as nothing more came, she added cautiously, 'Would you care to play? Now, for a bit?'

'Later,' said her employer, again on a sigh. 'Later.'

'My arms are much better,' Jacintha tried a bold distraction. 'Whether it's your playing with me or the massage I don't know, but they're beginning to feel fine.'

'Yes,' the old woman murmured as if not hearing at all; still imbedded deep in her trouble, whether real or illusory.

* * *

The sight of the luncheon tray, dumped outside the door, momentarily jolted her from the new perplexities in which she wandered. *Nothing like taking service for granted,* she thought with a gleam of saturnine amusement, and was just bending to take up the horridly disordered mess when the door was whipped part way open. Mary Pargill stood over her as she stooped; framed in the doorway she looked enormous, bloated, in a dark quilted dressing-gown.

'Come in,' she whispered harshly. 'Come in a moment.'

Jacintha, suddenly aware how the woman must have been listening for her, also vaguely uneasy about this listening, hesitated, still bent.

103

'Got somethin' to tell you,' persisted the other in a loud harsh whisper. 'I've got to tell you. Come in!'

Abandoning the tray Jacintha stood up, reluctantly passed through the door and heard it instantly clapped to behind her. As she turned—

'Tell me,' the other hissed. 'Do they *know* she's crazy? Do they say so?'

'Not that I've ever heard,' returned Jacintha, coolly and at once. Her course of action was at once clear to her; give no information whatever, at all costs remain unsurprised; in a setting like this, one might expect anything.

'Is she too crazy to make a Will?' was the next essay. 'Or— or will they let her make one?'

'I wouldn't know,' disclaimed the other. 'Actually I'm the last person in the world to ask about things like that.'

'No!' Only a whimper, it came out like escaping steam. 'No, you're not. She likes you, she plays the piano with you. She's never done that with anyone before, never—!'

Been spying? thought Jacintha, with a vision of the huge body hanging perilously over the banisters, and a more lethal vision of its horrible fall from leaning over too far. *Spying on us, have you?*

'Listen,' panted the great flabby creature, and came nearer. 'I've worked for her, if you knew! She'd wear you to rags, she'd *use* you till there was nothing left. And poor pay always, or a bit extra when she felt like it. Board and lodging she gave, very cushy too—I thought I was well off. One did, you know, twenty and thirty years ago, when people who employed my sort gave what they pleased. And now she wants me to go, does she?' The red-rimmed eyes flamed in accusation. 'Fed up with me, is she? wants to get rid of me? I'll see her in hell first, and tell her that—' With obvious panic, she caught her breath. '—no, no, don't tell her, I didn't mean—'

She dragged herself closer; her voice fell to a note both muttering and lamenting.

'She's amused,' she whimpered. 'Amused to think how I'm caught here, *caught*. But I'd get out and willing if she'd . . . a small annuity, nothing much, she could afford it a thousand times over . . .' She took hold of Jacintha's sleeve. 'Remind her how I . . . how I *slaved*. . . .' The great mottled face came unpleasantly close, her fingers increased their grip on the sleeve. 'She'll listen to you, she likes you. Will you?' she petitioned with starving intensity. 'Will you?'

'Miss Pargill.' Rent with pity she knew what a refusal would invite, and braced herself to meet it. 'I'm here on a temporary job, I'm nothing and nobody. How can I take it on myself to—to approach Mrs Tor on a subject like that, how can I—'

'You could, you could,' the other broke in, clamouring suddenly. 'She'd listen if you'd ask her, she'd—'

'I can't,' Jacintha broke in despairingly. 'I simply can't.'

'Then get out!' shrieked Miss Pargill. 'You're like all of them, cowardly—' she seemed to be grinding her teeth. 'Get out, get out, she—she—and had the piano tuned!' she screamed in sudden derision. 'What for, it's ridicu'lous, ridic— You tell her!' she reverted with no less fury. 'Tell'r she'll help me if she knows what's good for her. And tell me what she says, d'you *hear?* Tell me—tell me—'

Jacintha moved fast toward the door, the deluge still going full tilt, and got through it. Picking up the tray she went down at dangerous speed for anyone carrying anything so heavy, while faintly behind her the incoherent volley went on, racked now by a harsh sobbing. As she reached the first floor it faded or all but, thank God, but at once her ear was taken by another sound from the ground floor; a sound that seemed to indicate . . .

Rapidly she tiptoed to the stairhead, listening hard. From where she stood there was no chance of seeing the phone, but Mrs Tor's voice—for all its paucity of utterance—came clearly to her. *Mh'm,* she said, low and unaccented, then a second time, *Mh'm,* both of . . . of agreement certainly, but of something else, disappointment perhaps . . . ? then the sound of ringing off, then a deep silence.

Caught in this silence, somehow hypnotized, Jacintha stood bereft of motion. Nothing to do, nothing at all, her only immediate concern was whether the old woman still lingered beside the phone, or had left it; on carpeting so thick, sounds were not very informative. She might retreat to the back stairs if she had not—on her first use of them—received from Mrs Dowling a polite but unmistakable hint that she was trespassing. Meanwhile the ache in her arms reminded her unpleasantly of the tray; there being no help for it, she descended. The hall was empty, thank God; she only wished that this emptiness were suggestive of what Mrs Tor was up to, at present. . . .

Cautiously regaining the hall from the pantry she stood a moment, her previous suspension of mind now replaced by tumult. The old woman's first meeting with that tramp or gypsy . . . that meeting had also been preceded by a phone call. Supposing that this one meant, again, that her employer had gone out . . .

She had just whipped about to get her coat from the closet when she was stopped by the voice behind her; a voice—she noticed even then—curiously dead. 'We'll practise,' it said. 'We'll practise now.'

* * *

'That was good,' she ventured carefully, 'very good,' and looked furtively to see whether Mrs Tor had emerged from the deep depression following (perhaps?) the phone call. And whether or no, her mood had not lifted; she sat bowed in a blackness so unrelieved that it slowed the companion's words more and more with uncertainty. 'Are you tired?' escaped her imprudently.

'Don't talk nonsense,' said the elder in that dull dead voice. 'Again, we'd better.' She turned the pages to the beginning, and a new qualm of understanding, unexpected, smote Jacintha; as in the jungle Mrs Tor, whatever weight was pressing on her, would go on till she dropped. She had just brought her own hands into position when she became aware—a moment after it had happened—of the change in her companion; the sudden stiffening, the dangerous alertness, the clear and definite look as though she had come out from behind a veil.

'Yes, Hugh,' she said, having barely turned around. 'What d'you want?'

'Good day, Mother. Good day, Miss Cory. I, ah, in fact—'

he was essaying, smiling nervously '—it sounded so good from my side, this performance of yours, that I—I thought I'd just look in and tell you.'

'Kind of you,' said the old lady. 'Was there anything else?'

As the lethal politeness of her words produced a silence Jacintha started to slither from her chair, possessed by the single idea to melt away, evaporate somehow . . .

'Miss Cory,' said the same quiet voice in which command lay heavy as lead. 'Sit down please, we've not nearly finished.' As the signs of escape subsided, once more she turned the guns of her deadly courtesy on her son. 'Why did you come in now? You could hear we were practising.'

'Yes, well.' Apology and uncertainty were now eroding him. 'I just wondered if I could sit for a while, and listen . . . ?'

'Certainly not,' returned the old woman, with no lessening of her inimical courtesy. 'We're practising, not performing in public. Don't interrupt like this again, Hugh, not ever.'

'All right, Mother,' he said after a pause, then added, 'Only I'd never heard you play before.' In his tone were such dignity, patience and unresentfulness that sudden tears stung the unwilling witness's eyes, and her heart contracted with pain. *You wicked old hag,* she thought, *I wouldn't even be here if it weren't for him, you old devil,* and sat slightly sick with shame at being forced to stop and see his humiliation, deliberately—*deliberately*—inflicted. . . .

'I'll say goodbye then, I was here for only a few hours,' he had continued, and even with her avoidance of looking at him she knew that this message was for her.

'Goodbye,' said his mother with the accent of a door closing. The other one, not looking, heard his footsteps going away, then an actual door closing, then nothing. . . .

'Stupid,' muttered the old woman. 'Stupid, stupid.' Her hands were already on the keys, prepared to resume; mechanically Jacintha placed her own, silently asking, *Why did you have to do that? Why, why?*

'I can't,' said Mrs Tor suddenly, starting up. Her face was all at once trenched with despair, her eyes black and empty. 'Not just now, can't—I can't.'

'All right,' said the other, scared witless.

'He did that on purpose,' the old woman accused, now loudly. 'He did, he did—'

'Mrs Tor,' Jacintha attempted, senseless with distress.

'He knows I don't want to see him, he *knows* . . .' All at once she seemed submerged in a fathomless resignation. 'Yes, yes, he's my death, my death—'

'Mrs Tor,' repeated Jacintha loudly. As if drowning she snatched at a single, instinctive knowledge within her grasp— that her employer must not be allowed to depart in this ruinous frame of mind. 'Could you possibly do my arms a little, just a little? I think I've played a bit too much. Could you?' she entreated, 'just a little?' and cringed invisibly; this appeal at the wrong moment, might it snap some last barrier—against who knew what anger, what violent accusations and suspicions . . . ?

The footsteps halted; Mrs Tor, already on her way out, stood with her back to Jacintha for a moment, then said, 'Well.' In her tone was neither consent nor refusal. Yet after a moment she turned, said, 'Sit down,' and waited till the other had taken off her jersey. Then with mechanical skill she began running the muscular gamut, pressing, kneading—then all at once let the arm drop, something she had never done before. 'That's enough now,' she said, barely audible. 'Go out now if you like. A walk, why don't you, a nice long . . .'

Her dragging step as she left the room forbade—like her dragging voice—the least further essay of speech, of any kind whatever.

IX

She took her coat from the downstairs cloak-room where she kept it now—without objection so far, but there was always the first time. Her air as she put it on was unseeing and unhearing. While failing to pinpoint her frame of mind exactly, she only knew that Mrs Tor's latest mood had roused her, again, to the risks in her determination of secrecy, well, of *certain* secrecies. The knowledge lay heavy on her as she let herself out then paused, staring at Hugh's end of the house. After an instant she went to his door, rang, rang again, waited. . . .

She began walking toward the village with a blind hurried step. Someone should be warned about the old woman's plunge into sudden black depression, suicidal . . . the final word pulled her up short; after this her gait, now much slower, again echoed her growing distraction. She had better tell Hugh everything when he rang. Yet would he ring, so soon after leaving home . . . but *someone* should be warned, went on beating heavily through her like a pulse; someone should know . . .

She stopped dead again, thinking of Mrs Williams. Telling Mrs Williams would be different. She had been, and would be, in attendance on the old lady; she would never talk about her, nor use her knowledge for purposes such as she felt, dimly, in regard to that Dennison . . . She took another few steps. Visit

Mrs Williams now, confide the latest developments to her, take counsel about possibilities, dangers . . .

'Good day, Miss Cory,' said a voice gently, and she looked up with an invisible start. He was smiling at her, the smile whose character she did not name to herself till much later. 'You were thinking?' he pursued amiably, also with an indulgence that annoyed her. 'Thinking hard?'

'Well, I was.' Her abruptness wiped the smile from his face. 'Hard enough.'

'Can I help?' he asked seriously, after a moment. 'At all?'

'It—it—oh Lord!' A deep breath was forced from her. 'I don't know, I don't know.'

'But—' he began; she cut him off with, 'I don't want to talk about it yet, I mean . . . I've got to think.'

'Well,' he said after a long moment. His air of concern was displaced by a disapproval almost too faint to be seen, displaced in its turn by resignation. 'Could I at least serve as a small distraction? You promised to ring me about dinner, you know, and you've never done it. Could you, by any chance, this evening?'

Taken by surprise, she hesitated.

'You could probably get Mrs Williams to stay with Mrs Tor,' he was suggesting.

'Yes, actually I was just—just wondering if—all right, I'll try,' she blurted. 'I'll try now.'

'What time shall we say then? and where—?'

'But see here,' she interrupted, hardly hearing him. 'Not till —till pretty late, and perhaps not then. I'm sorry to—to do it like this,' she apologized incoherently, 'but you see I can't—I can't help—'

'Yes, yes. But if you can do it at all,' he said evenly, 'tell me what time's best for you.'

'Well . . . not till after eight-thirty.'

'Good. And in case you are able to do it, suppose we meet at the Wheatsheaf, and go on from there? Better than my calling for you at the house.'

'All right. And if I don't come,' she struggled on, 'you'll know I couldn't—couldn't help—'

'Go see Mrs Williams at once, why don't you,' he said with that imperturbable gentleness. 'See if she'll come this evening.'

'Yes.' His calm steadied her unconsciously. 'Yes, I'll do that.'

* * *

Before he saw her she saw him, waiting before the Wheatsheaf. Something in his attitude touched her faintly and fleetingly with a . . . a self-reproach? a new softening of her prejudice against him? *Imagination,* she scorned this, *he looks the way he's always looked.*

'Ah.' His pleasure, or otherwise, was hardly evident; a man temperate in all things, this one. 'My car's over here.' He took her arm, but very lightly. 'We'll move farther along.'

'Where are we going?' she asked without much interest, and he answered, 'You'll see. I hope you'll like it.'

Part of the time, as he drove, she was attentive to the route, belatedly remembering that this might be a useful resource against Liz's coming. Part of the time, again, she thought of Hugh's failure to ring, her stubborn dismay over this failure; what a thing she was making of it, what a fool she was being . . . she stared emptily through the window, then forced her attention again to the route.

* * *

'What did you say this place was called?'

'The Colchester Arms.' As their cocktails arrived he added, 'I gather, by your presence here, that Mrs Williams turned up all right.'

'Oh yes, she did.'

'Well, that's all right then. Ah!' A presence was hovering over them with menus. 'Thank you, Luigi. Now let's see what's for dinner.'

* * *

The evening, of which she had expected little, against expectation got better and better. The comfort, the excellent food, the cheerfulness and animation of a place extremely full, yet different in atmosphere from a crowded London restaurant—

111

she sensed again, here, a feeling of settled local familiarity. Some of these people must have come from far afield, of course, but many others appeared to be local, which created that social quality personal instead of impersonal. At any rate it was a change—a lovely change—to be here in a becoming dress; how intelligent of her to have brought at least one along. Best of all (she acknowledged grudgingly) was the companionship of a presentable man, instead of an erratic or disturbingly cryptic old lady; the mere change from female ambience to male was in itself electrically reviving. Nor was it unpleasant that this male was obviously well known in the restaurant, respectfully addressed by name and offered the most attentive and unremitting service . . .

The male, on his side, was employing a skill highly developed and frequently used, in surrounding her with constant deference to her tastes. It was his experience that a woman, relaxed by unobtrusive flattery, would presently speak of things she had had no intention of mentioning in the first place. Added to this professional gambit was his earlier feeling—by no means dismissed, at least not entirely—that he might come to have a deeper feeling for her, if he decided he wanted it; he had not yet made up his mind. But for the present, first things first; the more so in that he had realized, earlier on, how reticent she was about Mrs Tor, and how extremely unforthcoming as to herself; accordingly he counted on the present atmosphere to erode her taciturnity on both counts, having a well-tested idea of its powers in that direction.

She on the other hand, while indistinctly realizing some of this, threw caution to the winds increasingly. Drained—already —by living next to a threatened but originally voracious intelligence, drained with trying to guess or anticipate its needs, all at once she found herself with a companion who wordlessly invited her to discourse on *her* opinions, *her* preferences and— as dinner progressed—on her experiences. The more nonsense she talked, in fact, the better he seemed to like it; always keeping her going with another question when she began flagging. Never once did he mention Mrs Tor and the problems arising from Mrs Tor, in fact Mrs Tor had vanished from her own mind. This was toward the end of dinner when she had already overpassed her limit—two glasses of wine—in addition to a couple of cocktails; her eyes had become brighter, her laugh a little louder and attractively silly, the edges of various vowels and consonants a little damaged.

'But a girl like you,' he said casually, at this point, 'with the musical training that you've described—' While hoping for a possible let-down in her caution, he also appreciated the charming quality of her tipsiness; he knew any number of women not charming in like circumstances. '—I wonder that you'd take a job like this one.'

'I'll tell you why.' She put down her glass and looked at him owlishly. 'I don' want to teach an' I don' want to accompany—'s'all that's open, to my kin' of talent. But I've a frien'—a *wunnerful* frien'.' She fixed him with an overmeaningful eye. 'She 'n' I, we . . . we wanna open an agency.'

'I see.'

'She'll do the theatre end of it,' she continued, ' 'n' I'll do the music—artists an' soforth.'

'Interesting,' he murmured.

'Int'resting? I hope,' she said rather challengingly. 'Thanks awf'lly much.'

'I only mean,' he soothed, 'if you can make it go.'

'No if 'bout it.' She was now a bit loud. 'Li—' She stopped herself in time. 'I mean, this frien' of mine—even this soon she's got a following, some very well-known—' again in time, but only just, she stopped. 'I mean, if someone of her 'bility can't make it go—' she took a sip of wine, her eyes bright and bold over the glass '—then somethin's crazy. Jus' abs'lutely crazy, tha's all.'

'And what has this to do,' he asked unurgently, 'with your taking a job with Mrs Tor?'

'Money, of course.' On another sip of wine came the thought that she was drinking too much. To hell with it though, she was celebrating . . . celebrating what, her dying common-sense demanded, and she answered it, *Nothing 't all,* and considered roaring with laughter . . .

'Money?' he was suggesting.

'Oh! yes. I mean, I can save like mad.' She took a defiant swig. ' 'm not goin' into this thing without—'thout puttin' something into it.'

'You're going into this thing—you mean—on a shoestring?'

'Who said so?' She had now graduated into quarrelsomeness. 'Li—I mean, my frien'—she's pretty well-off, she shoul' be after *years* with—' her instinct of caution, though dying, hauled her up again. 'I mean, compared to me, she's rollin'.'

'Why wait then?' he enquired unurgently. 'Why not start the agency now?'

'She couldn'. Couldn' jus' walk out on . . .' Her voice fell away. 'Couldn', thassall.'

He looked at her, assessing her far-away look, her wide vague eyes and flushed cheeks, her fingers restless on the stem of her glass. The outline of her lips remained charming, again unlike most women he knew, whose mouths in any stage of drunkenness went thick or blurred, ruinously . . . he felt a stir of desire, ignored it for more pressing considerations, and asked casually, 'And how are you getting on with Mrs Tor?'

'Mrs . . . ?' She repeated it mechanically, her eyes still fixed on distance.

'How are you going along with her?' he pursued softly. 'With Mrs Tor?'

A pause fell, a long-drawn-out moment; he felt rather than saw something happen to her, since there had been no movement at all in her body. But he saw flowing into her again the mysterious fact of balance, realization, whatever it was, and in the same instant her eyes came back to him.

'I'm talking too much,' she said, almost in her normal voice. 'Much too much.'

'Of course not. Would you care for anything, a brandy?'

'No thanks, nothin' more—' She was peering at her wrist, not without trouble, and suddenly made it. 'Oh! Mrs Williams— I promised her I'd be back by ten-thirty at the lates', and now it's—'

'Just on, it's just barely on,' he calmed her flurry. 'She won't mind if you aren't on the dot, she won't mind at all.'

As he escorted her to the car he gave no sign of displeasure either with her behaviour or her hurry. The car fled through country silences with the modified speed imposed by the roads always winding and turning; in no time he was helping her out, accompanying her to the door, and saying, 'Thank you.'

'Thank *you*,' she returned. A flood, confused but dismaying, rose and overwhelmed her with memory of bad manners, outright rudeness for all she knew . . . as apologies rose to her lips she became aware that he was holding his hand out; with a feeling of shame she put hers in it. 'I think I've been behaving like a fool, and I'm so sorry,' she offered. 'Forgive me if I've had no manners, and thank you very much for a lovely evening.'

He said nothing, smiling that half-smile of his perhaps, but in the dark one could not be sure. At the same time he detained her hand—but so lightly, so questioningly somehow, that it left the next step entirely up to her.

'It's been lovely,' she repeated too gaily, and withdrew her hand. 'Thank you again.'

'Good night,' he said amiably, delayed a moment to see that the door was opening to her key, and went down the path. She let herself in liking and disliking him and hating herself, a state of mind not helped by this failure to keep a promise.

* * *

'I'm sorry, I'm *so* sorry—'

'That's all right, you're not more'n a few minutes late,' said Mrs Williams with undiminished cheerfulness. With her coat and hat already on, she rolled up and put in her bag a woolly object. 'Got caught up with my knitting, I'm always behind with it.'

'And how's everything? all right . . . ?'

'Quiet—quiet as the grave.'

'She didn't ask for anything? want anything?'

'I haven't seen her at all,' said the other. 'She's been in her room all evening.'

'But—' Jacintha blurted, with a beginning of cold all over her.

'Don't worry, miss, I've been sitting where I had a good view

115

of her bedroom door, no fear. There's no way out except past me—I've been here before, you know.' Mrs Williams was cheerful as always. 'She did open her door and peep out, just the once—and didn't she slam it to when she saw me, my goodness! I'd no chance to say a thing, she banged it proper. No, she hasn't been out of her room, not once.'

* * *

She took off her coat with slow movements, relieved by the news; again she was tightly bound by aftermath of contact, try-ing to remember what imprudences had escaped her to this man whom she liked and disliked, what betrayals if any . . . none occurred to her at the moment, but again—at the mo-ment—she knew she was not quite sober, not yet. Had he got her to this state deliberately, before making his attempt to get information about Mrs Tor? For he *had* made the attempt, un-mistakably. He had got nothing out of her, unless her memory misled her. Yet the thought of him waiting carefully, observ-ing carefully all during dinner, till she was a little sloshed . . . her earliest dislike began reviving smartly, till she remembered the moment of their parting. That faint, faint suggestion of a change in their relationship; a change that waited, of course, on her acquiescence, her consent . . . mollified like any other woman yet not mollified, still confused, half-dreaming, she started to emerge from the cloak-room, and stopped dead. It was the sense rather than the sound of movement, the source of it just out of sight above the staircase balcony; with unthinking alarm she stepped backward into the cloak-room again, and waited.

An instant later Mrs Tor slowly came in sight, with a curious halting, peering gait; she hesitated a long moment at the head of the final flight, then stole down with the same care and furtive-ness. All at once, paralyzingly, she streaked like an arrow across the hall and was through the living-room door in a rush. At once Jacintha, without mind or will, was on her heels; hurtling through the dimness of the big room, then the small one in which the garden door swung open. She tore through into a garden darkly in movement under a high wind; a cloud-tarnished moon cast a tarnished yellow light, often eclipsed. By this half-light, just before it vanished, she saw movement not of foliage nor branches, and realized it as Mrs Tor hurrying down the path to the stream.

Neither then nor later had she any notion of the process that sped her in pursuit. She was flinging herself down the slope; bare earth, bruising stones and grass were under her feet; her only conscious fear was a turned ankle or worse. The old woman barely had a start on her, yet what she had might be enough; grotesque in the play of light and shadow she jolted along, tripping now and again then pressing on in a hurry, a frantic, feeble, *determined* hurry . . .

With a couple of feet to spare the pursuer caught her up, laying violent hands on her person or on her clothing, no time to tell which, and wrenched her backward. Silently they struggled; the slippery verges underfoot, constantly splashed by the hurrying water, an additional peril. Blank and unbelieving, in the otherness of impossible nightmare, she set her teeth and hung on. Her fingers, dug deep where they had laid hold, hurt badly; if she were giving the other considerable pain as well, neither of them knew it. Her chief consciousness in their un-willed and disgusting bodily contact was—ludicrously—bones; Mrs Tor felt much thinner than she looked, she was startlingly, painfully thin . . .

'I won't go back there!' she shrilled suddenly. 'Won't go . . . in that house—!' then all at once, at the fiercest climax of their threshing, went limp. At this fluid sagging, whose energy had been desperate a moment before, Jacintha slipped and nearly carried the old woman down with her before she could steady herself. Both motionless, they stood breathing loudly; the cap-tor relaxed her aching fingers a trifle, but was far from letting go. Fury flooded her, a wild desire to shake the old skeleton till it fell apart . . .

Wordlessly manoeuvring so that they were side by side, she started leading the way to the house very slowly. What she was now helping up the path was an old, old woman, stumbling, submissive, shrunken; was it her mere fancy that Mrs Tor had grown smaller—as if collapsed upon herself, the characteristic

117

collapse after violence . . . ? Recalling her first sight of the fugitive, still preternaturally vivid in her mind, she realized now what feebleness had been in her erratic humping flight, from the first; the effort of it must have weakened her so that she could be caught, just as her present weakness made it possible to handle her . . .

Only in the hall, having steered her that far, did she let her go—but cautiously, ready to seize her again if need be; prepared for that and empty of all else. Mrs Tor also stood silent; a blankness seemed to envelop both of them, yet in the old woman's aspect was a faint return, a faint awakening . . .

'Wanted to . . . to end it,' she said feebly but sensibly.

'Why?' begged Jacintha. 'Why?'

The other looked at her, a glance of paralyzing irony—quickly disappearing as she said, 'Don't tell. Don't tell anyone. Will you promise?' she implored with sudden, terrible urgency. 'Promise me—?'

Jacintha, nailed between knowledge of what she should do and what she was being asked to do, looked at her levelly.

'I won't again,' the old woman contended with the look. Her weariness was lethal, her voice breaking and renewing itself like a thread. 'I've had a . . .' the word that followed was almost inaudible; it might have been *disappointment*. 'I won't again. I swear I won't, not like this. Will you promise me not to tell? Promise . . . ?'

Jacintha still looked at her with a regard, steady, that appeared to come from an inward steadiness. In reality she was shaken to the core, confusedly aware of having . . . *missed* something, important perhaps . . . ? Too disintegrated and beset by conflict to pursue it as she should, she was harried by an immediate question. Make this bargain she was being asked to make? enter into agreement with a (possible) madwoman . . . ?

'Wait awhile, it's all I ask,' Mrs Tor importuned strangely. 'Only a little while, will you? . . . wait . . . ?'

'If I do—' said the other, after a moment. Her voice came out extinguished. 'If I do wait, you must promise—you must *promise* me—'

'Yes, I—I—' the culprit's eagerness was dissimulated by the faintness of her speech. 'I promise. I do, I do.' Their joint weakness of utterance, suddenly striking her companion, almost reduced her to wild laughter; what a picture the two of them must make, hissing at eachother in voices wasted by shock . . .

Mrs Tor had turned about; feebly and with obvious effort, clutching the banister, she went up the stairs, crossed the landing, and disappeared. Jacintha, standing like stone till the sound of the bedroom door came, emerged a degree from her cataleptic stillness and tottered back to the morning-room. Here she closed the door still swinging viciously in the wind, locked it, then turned out the hall light and went upstairs. Still in shock, half-removed and half there, she stood for a long moment at the old woman's door. Had she better establish herself here all night, ready to intercept another attempt? But what of the next night, and the next . . . ? A deathly fatigue flooded all through her, her knees were no longer there. Lie down, lie down, she had to. Catch up on sleep a bit, then make it her business to haunt the hall all night . . .

Just entering her room, she was transfixed by a sound that made her head swivel violently toward her charge's door . . . nothing there, nothing at all. Then she realized: the sound had come from overhead. If she were not so deathly tired she would have known it at once . . . she remained motionless, still gripping the knob. After a long moment, since nothing else happened, she went in and closed the door behind her. A strong impulse to lock it, she resisted; it might be she would have to come out in a hurry, during the night . . .

In bed, all at once she had a long shivering fit. Reaction, that was all; now she would sleep. Her exhaustion being profound she did sleep, but a curious sleep full of sights and sounds. The wind outside was in it, the cold feel and sweep of wind, and the stones bruising her feet as she tore down the path, and the mist and spray off the water as she fought with something, formless, that struggled in her hands . . . a heaviness was there too, something she had promised not to tell but should tell, she should she should . . . and weaving in and out of all this the sound, the gentlest sound overhead, the door being closed softly, softly, so very . . . .

* * *

'Well,' said Mrs Dowling enjoyably, over the morning coffee, 'that must o' been a fine old to-do last night, what we saw of it.' She sighed with pleasure, adding, 'An' heard.'

'Not much o' one or the other,' complained Anna. 'When you wouldn' let us get close enough to listen, or anything.'

'I saw as much,' said Mrs Dowling serenely, 'as I needed to.'

'H'h! *I* didn't.'

'Who was it saw the old girl from their window, you or me?' enquired Mrs Dowling, calm with proprietorship. 'My, streakin' down the back garden wasn't she just, an' the girl tearin' after her. Not that you could ackshully tell who was who, in that light, but easy to guess. Then the old woman bein' marched back to the house—not all that much to see, not really.'

'We could of heard what they said, maybe,' Anna persisted, 'if you'd let us get a little nearer.'

'Any nearer than we got,' Mrs Dowling countered, 'we'd of got mixed up in it. You don't understand, girl, you don't understand how 'tis at all. Tangle yourself up in their mess, and what happens? Sympathy they'll want, that's what—askin' for your help all the time. S'posin' we'd went down when the old woman was brought back in, we'd of had to do what we could, wouldn' we? So work's what we get out of it, extra work and no extra pay. So just you take my word for it,' she concluded magisterially. 'We know nothin' about it, we don't know one bloody thing.'

'H'h,' sniffed Anna, unconvinced.

'We keep mum an' we go on keepin' mum,' commanded Mrs Dowling. 'Now if we're *ast* to do extra—well, that's different, that's more wages. So just you remember, you silly girl, we've no idea anything's wrong. We don't know one thing about it, we don't know nothin' at all.'

X

'Nice place,' commented Liz, looking about. 'Good whiskey.'

'And very good food,' said Jacintha. 'I've been here before. Don't see anyone I recognize though, thank God.' She looked about with satisfaction. 'The local has a nice-looking restaurant, actually, but I'd have been nervous about talking.' She sipped her drink. 'Do I need that!'

'You look half dead,' diagnosed Liz briefly. 'Come on, talk about what's bothering you—give.'

'Oh, not till we've had dinner—'

'Now,' interrupted the other. 'The way you sounded over the phone's the only thing that would've brought me here so soon.'

'Soon! ten days after I scream for help.'

'Well.' Liz shrugged. 'You know how *I'm* fixed. Now go ahead—begin at the beginning.'

'The beginning?' Her eyes quested desolate distance over the edge of her glass. 'Well, I suppose the beginning was a tramp or something, that she met outside.'

'By accident, you mean?'

'No, I'm fairly sure it wasn't.' Briefly she recounted the rest of the adventure. 'Then afterward, she was . . . she was *waiting*.' She paused. 'That's the only way I can describe it, always waiting for something or other. Then ten days ago—the night I rang you actually—I came home, from here it was—'

She paused again. 'And caught her trying to throw herself into what's a small river, practically, at the bottom of the garden.'

'Nice,' Liz nodded, attentive.

'You may say. And when I got her back to the house after a death-grapple more or less, she begged me not to tell anyone.'

'And—?' snapped the other, her voice sharpening.

'Well, she seemed in her right mind, terribly sorry and upset over it, she swore she'd never try it again if I wouldn't say anything about it—'

'And you *promised*—?'

'Well . . . yes.'

Liz looked at her silently, then sighed, 'Crackers, that's all.'

'But Liz, if you'd been there, if you'd heard her—'

'Crazy,' interrupted Liz. 'Whether the old woman's raving mad or not, you are.'

'I had to give her the chance.' Stubbornness came to her rescue and upheld her. 'In my place, I think you'd have done the same. She's not an ordinary . . . I mean, there's something about her . . . Oh, I don't know,' she supplicated. 'She promised she wouldn't do it again, and I . . . somehow . . . I *believe* her.'

'And since then, she's—?'

'She's been all right—she's been perfectly good.'

'How far,' asked Liz dispassionately, 'can you trust that goodness?'

'I don't know,' sighed Jacintha. 'With a thing like this, you wait—you go along with it. She practises, and I've played to her— Oh yes, I forgot to tell you. I said I'd hurt my arms over-practising, then I pretended she'd cured them with massage, and how I did pound away.' She sighed again. 'It was lovely.'

'And that's how the thing stands?'

The enquiry, sceptical, produced from the other a silence. 'She's tractable,' she answered finally. 'Only I feel sometimes as if she were still listening for something, waiting . . . Unless it's all my imagination.'

'About this suicide attempt.' Liz spoke after a meditative moment. 'If I may suggest it, you've picked the wrong thing to be quiet about.'

'Have I?' Yet she was strangely undisturbed, all at once; the mere relief of getting it off her chest it must be, of talking where there was no need of the caution that trapped her on one side or another. 'Anyway I feel much better, spilling it. Come on, you don't want another drink—I'm starving.'

* * *

'Lovely nosh here.'

'I told you.'

'Mm.' Liz chewed absently; her distant air, from the beginning of dinner, gave notice of attention still riveted on earlier topics. 'Look—I mean, unless you don't want to talk about it—?'

'I don't mind,' said Jacintha with prescience.

'You said the old girl had a son, didn't you?'

'Yes, she has.'

'What's *his* attitude in all this? How does he feel about having mamma at liberty?'

'He's—' To her own surprise she had to stop, in order to—to adjust, modify? control? '—he's the reason, actually, that she's not in some loony-bin or other.'

'Is that so?'

'Very much so.' She shrugged. 'When we had our first talk about her, he said he was sure she was all right, fundamentally —that loneliness was her trouble, she just needed someone with enough . . . imagination . . . to invent some interest for her, something to *do* . . .'

Her voice trailed off; Liz picked up the topic with peculiar caution.

'What's he like, the son?'

'Pleasant.' Beneath her careless accent her sense of dissimulation was more strenuous than ever, and more puzzling. 'Very nice, and never seems to expect too much.'

'And you say he doesn't think,' Liz explored tentatively, 'that she ought to be shut up?'

'He won't hear of it,' the other said indignantly. 'Certainly not.'

'And you're alone in the house with her?'

'Not alone, there's a cook and a maid.' Suddenly aware that she had forgotten the strange presence living above, simultaneously she resolved to continue forgetting it; if Liz became aware of this element in the background, the fat would be in the fire.

'What if,' Liz was asking, 'she comes at you with a knife?'

'Nonsense! you've got it entirely wrong.'

'Now look.' Liz's accent was of having made up her mind. 'Throw up this lunatic affair and look for something else. There're things much less dangerous, and everyone's frantic for help of some kind—'

'Not at this rate of pay,' Jacintha returned calmly. 'You won't be free for some time yet, will you? Say a year?'

The other was silent, her look suddenly empty.

'So this is a chance—' she had waited politely for an answer '—to get some money together. I told you I wouldn't let you take all the risk, nor will I. And beside,' she hesitated, 'I couldn't just walk out on the old thing. I'm too interested, at times I'm actually fond of her. Also I can't—' she hesitated again '—I can't seem to be *afraid* of her. She may startle me once in a while, alarm me a bit maybe, but it's miles removed from fear. Actually—' she stopped from sheer surprise '—I think she's fascinated me, ever since I've known her.'

Liz said nothing, her glance still withdrawn.

'And also—' Jacintha stopped herself just in time; she had nearly said *Hugh*. '—also this son, Hugh Kerwin, rings me every night or nearly as he can make it. If anything out of the way happened he'd come back straightaway, he told me so—' her voice broke off. 'Why! there he is!'

'Where?'

'All the way across, in that corner there.' Indicating the direction, she thought, *He must have got home just after I left.* 'With his girl, probably—that fat man's in the way, I can't tell.'

'*I* can.' It was a murmur, but emphatic. 'You didn't mention that the dutiful son was gay.'

'Of course he's not! Where'd you get *that* idea?'

'He's with a fairly slimy little queer, that's from where.'

'He's engaged, you juggins.' Jacintha, trying to manoeuvre cautiously for a view, and with a curious chill at her heart, was still obstructed by the restaurant's large patron. 'Engaged to be married, or all but.'

'Have you ever heard of marrying for a smoke-screen?' Liz was imperturbable. 'He wouldn't be the first.'

'Rot. If I ever saw a man who couldn't be a queer—'

'The funny thing is—' Liz interrupted, unhearing and still focussed on the table's second occupant '—I seem to know the lad he's with, in some connection.'

'What?'

'Can't put my hand on it. I'd say he was an actor, except that I should know him if he were. Still, there're so many of them in night clubs, sex clubs, blue films—that you never hear of in the theatre, at all.'

'Oh, go 'long.' The stubborn chill, weight, whatever it was, still lay on her heart. 'I'll bet you've never even seen him before.'

'I associate him with a woman, somehow.' Liz, ignoring her, was thoughtful. 'His partner in an act? Or a dance team, maybe?'

'Oh Lord! they're leaving.' Sudden panic struck Jacintha. 'They'll have to pass us, going out.' Falling into a trance of false absorption with the dessert trolley, now wheeled beside them, she yielded momentarily to a torturing urge to look up. The first presence was coming their way, a slight young man, not tall, with a fine-boned face and a sweep of blonde hair; a dark-blue satin shirt and skin-tight suede trousers moulded his elegant figure brilliantly. With his half-lounging, half-slithering gait he was compelling glances from everywhere, not all of them admiring by any means; he was insolently unaware—or insolently uncaring—of this attention.

Will he notice us? Aware only of the second man advancing, Jacintha sat with her glance stuck like a captive fly in the voluptuous display of sugar. *Do I hope he will, do I hope he won't . . .*

'Bee-yoootiful strawberries,' fluted Liz, her voice amused.

Do I hope he will, do I hope . . .

'Why, Jacintha—Miss Cory!' The footsteps passing their table slowed. 'Well, this is fine!'

'Why, Hugh!' With maidenly surprise, Jacintha raised her glance. 'When did you get home— Oh, excuse me. Miss Tennant, Mr Kerwin.'

'Miss Tennant.' He bowed, his smile of innocent pleasure enveloping them both. 'I'm just home for a few hours, this time.' On a quick significant look he added, 'And in a little while I'll have a few days off, maybe.' Seeing that the message was taken he beamed. ' 'Fraid I've got to be pushing along now. Good night, Miss Tennant.' He bowed awkwardly yet rather charmingly. ' 'Night, Cintha!' He was gone and their waiter was now upon them. . . .

'A baba, please,' she murmured. Still held in some sort of remoteness, with *Cintha* repeating itself like a charm, she failed to note Liz's sardonic face, then was startled to hear, 'Now what was *that* in aid of?'

'What—?' Her gaze relinquished vacancy and returned.

'Why the pause for conversation?' Liz was raucous. 'He'd every chance not to see us if he didn't want to. Why'd he stop at all?'

'Why not?' Jacintha queried, between blankness and antagonism. 'It's natural, stopping to talk to someone you know.'

'Balls. He didn't stop for a chat, he stopped for observation. Pretty sharp observation, too.'

'What rot.'

'He didn't like it, that you'd seen him,' Liz drove on. 'He didn't like it, but he was carrying it off.'

'Never,' Jacintha gathered herself for combat, 'never have I heard such rubbish.'

'Ripe,' sighed Liz. 'You're so ripe for being eaten up alive, that it's pitiful.'

'See who's talking,' Jacintha said nastily.

'Don't hit below the belt,' said Liz in a dead voice. 'By the way, this old girl of yours, I've been looking her up. She must be filthy rich, you know.'

'She married a lot of rich men.' Jacintha shrugged. 'Apparently.'

'Yes, but aside from that, the Mayan princess she found— buried in plates of gold plus emeralds—'

126

'Goodness!'

'Didn't you know? I mean, how she got on the track, how she found it?'

'I've never even thought about it.'

'Well, but listen, it's quite something. The Mayans were poor relations, sort of, of the Incas and Aztecs—no gold, no precious stones. The Spaniards tortured them to find out, and every word of it was put down officially and sent back to Spain. Plus details,' Liz paused, 'of the tortures—'

'Don't tell me!'

'No, no. But that's what your Mrs Tor dug her clues out of —testimony of Mayans being racked and soforth.'

Jacintha sat listening, her other preoccupations side-tracked.

'Most of the poor sods died under torture without speaking— but some of them did speak.' She regarded the other's riveted stare complacently. 'But the Spaniards didn't speak Mayan, and the Mayans' Spanish was so little that they couldn't make sense of it. So there lay the reports in the Spanish archives, mouldering away for over four hundred years.'

'And then—?'

'And then—Mrs Tor. She made sense of it, all right.' She gestured largely. 'It took her two years and over, sitting in the archives and putting bits and pieces together. But she got there in the end, so she did.'

'My old darling.' Jacintha was awed. 'I never knew that.'

'How would you? It was all in the early 1950s. You'd hardly been born.'

'So that's why she's swimming in money.'

'Yes—beside what she married. Books about the princess, and still being published—she must have made a fortune. Let's shout for coffee now, shall we?'

* * *

'A life like hers,' murmured Jacintha, still tranced.

'Mrs Tor?'

'Yes.' Coffee was now before them, plus a voluptuous display of *friandises*. 'Catch *me* letting anything get in the way of it. Including,' she shot a half-malicious glance at her friend, 'love.'

127

'You don't know what love will make you do or not do.' Liz was expressionless. 'Till it hits you.'

'Rot. Take people's thinking of love, as it was and is now. From earliest mythology it's been set up as something inaccessible almost—impossible to get. The barriers to love, my God— dragons, enchanted woods, wrong social standing, wrong religion or colour, loss of purity, no money.' She gave her companion a flaming glance. 'For how many centuries the world's swallowed that muck—just think!'

'I'm thinking,' murmured Liz pacifically.

'Sex is no longer inaccessible,' pronounced Jacintha. 'It's lost the priority that *men* have given it, the dirty dogs, not women. It never has come first, anyway—to lots of people.'

'I'm not arguing.'

'All right, I'm boring you speechless. But my point is, the thought of having an agency with you thrills me to the marrow, and love comes the hell of a long way second—' *Liar,* an inner voice startled her; she recovered almost at once and went on, 'Why, if sex were all I wanted—' She stopped again, suddenly.

'Pray,' said Liz politely. 'Continue.'

'Oh, nothing . . . there's a man, the old girl's solicitor actually, who's putting out discreet signals. If I gave him the come-on I believe he'd . . .'

'Quite,' said Liz. 'Is he nice?'

'Not too bad. The point is, I don't want him, I don't want *any*one—' She broke off suddenly. 'By the way, is Herbert still ringing you about me?'

'Regularly. And patiently.'

'My God, yes, I *know!*—I do apologize.'

'I always wondered,' murmured the other, 'what made you take up with him in the first place.'

'Oh, I was lonely I expect, I'd nothing else on. And he's terrifically intelligent. Not bad looking, either.'

'I can't imagine a waxwork like Herbert,' Liz soliloquized, 'in bed.'

'Now *that* was curious,' Jacintha admitted with unusual lack of restraint. 'It wasn't bad as it happened, rather good in fact, but all for himself. That I chanced to be in on it was just by the bye. And with it, he was so . . .'

'So . . ?' Liz prompted.

'—so kind. So amused and indulgent about my little female fancies, the damned fool. —More coffee?'

'No thanks.'

'A brandy, then?'

'Not when I'm driving back, you ass. And come to think—' she had glanced at her watch '—let's catch a waiter, I'll have to be shoving off.' She relapsed into silence, and when the waiter had come and gone said suddenly, 'By the way, your nasty hit about my being eaten up alive . . .'

She paused; her companion waited.

'—maybe it's nearly over—sooner than you think, maybe. The horror it's making of my life, never an easy peaceful moment . . .' Her voice failed briefly. 'You can't imagine.'

'I've seen how you look sometimes,' said Jacintha, 'and how you sound.'

'A first-chop producer,' the other brooded unhearingly. 'So filthy conceited and bad-tempered that his own actors can't discuss anything with him reasonably. And plenty of his lovely nature gets into his private life, I'm telling you.'

'How in God's name—' the other was suddenly waspish '—you've endured it this long, I don't know.'

'Of course you don't, you fool,' Liz returned dully. 'You've never loved anyone.'

'"I *have!*"

'You've had fancies, attractions, pastimes.' She was remote. 'You can't communicate this other thing any more than . . . sickness, say, or dying. And better shut up.' Her voice changed. 'The waiter's coming.'

They walked silently to the car park. As the car was being unlocked, Jacintha offered suddenly, 'Look. About this . . . involvement of yours ending soon . . .'

Liz turned on her a pale locked face, but said nothing.

'—whether it ends sooner or later,' Jacintha continued awkwardly, 'depend on me, there's no time-limit as far as I'm concerned. If it's more than a year, then all right. Count on me, Liz.'

'I do,' said Liz, expressionless. 'I do.'

She got in the car and slammed the door.

* * *

A little after ten; his mother's part of the house in darkness; a dull glow from his curtained windows . . . she hesitated, then whipped past Mrs Tor's as if pursued. Her knock at his door was of the most discreet, yet its opening, immediate, showed he had been waiting.

'Sorry I had to whip off, at the restaurant,' he explained eagerly. 'Some of these nightclub owners, they're queer fish all right. What will you drink?'

'Nothing, Hugh, nothing at all.' Even knowing Liz's estimate of this man as ridiculous, the relief was somehow profound, exquisite . . .

'You won't?' he was saying. 'Not anything—?'

'No thanks, I—' *I was half-drunk a few nights ago and that's enough,* went through her head; she substituted, '—I'd my limit at the restaurant. Hugh, if you're going away again tonight, I'd better tell you—'

'Yes.' He pulled up a chair, at the same time bending on her a curiously disturbing glance, so kind, so concerned. 'Go on.'

'Well, there's not much.' She set herself, at once, to navigate cautiously. The trouble was that if she left out the two main events—her dinner with Dennison, and above all the episode in the garden, there was little left. The suicide attempt though she *should* tell, she should . . . only not yet, not yet, she had given her word. And had already broken it by telling Liz, she reminded herself, but Liz was different . . .

'Not much, really,' she repeated. 'Your mother still practises with me.' *Without much interest,* she thought; added to his perfectly unreceptive look, it was enough to grind you to nothing. 'Quite faithfully.'

He sat obviously waiting for more; when she remained silent he asked, 'And that's all?'

130

'Well . . .' she racked her brains for any addition to the meagreness, and suddenly remembered something. 'Oh yes! she asked me if I could type.'

'You mean,' he asked blankly, 'letters maybe, something like that?'

'No-no.' Her answer surprised herself; never having thought about it she was struck, now, by her suddenly-distinct impression. 'Somehow I've the idea that—that she was talking about her writing. She has written?' she added a false question. 'She's written things—?'

'Oh Lord, yes.' His tone was weary, his glance far away. 'Tons of stuff in her day, didn't I tell you?' He shrugged. 'Well, all we can do is wait . . . for developments . . .' His bleak eyes returned to her; he achieved a smile. 'Thank you anyway, Cintha. At any rate, you can imagine what it means—having someone with her that's interested. And she still likes the piano, you say?'

'Oh yes,' she lied too positively.

'Well, that's something.'

'And see here.' She blurted it, driven on partly by his hopeless voice, partly by desire to make up for her dangerous, her inexcusable silences. 'If she loses interest in that, I'll see if I can't get her to work on this writing thing she's sort of . . . sort of hinted at. And if she's forgotten it—' she took a difficult breath '—I'll remind her.'

'Mh'm.' The shrug, this time, was in his voice. 'If it comes off, tell me.'

'Oh, I *will*.' Unconsciously her inflection combatted the listlessness of his. 'I will, Hugh.'

With a feeling that it was late, that he must be wanting to get away, she had risen to her feet. He followed slowly, yet remained motionless, looking at her. Then he smiled, and the smile made her heart lurch sickeningly, blissfully.

'Poor Cintha.' He smiled again, rueful. 'I've landed you with something, haven't I?' He reached out and touched her face lightly; the contact of his fingers, again, sent an electric shock splintering all through her. She had wanted to see him, for no other reason she had run the dark windows' gamut and knocked at his door. . . .

' 'Night now,' he was saying caressingly. ' 'Night, little Cintha, good night.'

XI

'Shall we practise?' she ventured—and at once knew the question to be ill-timed, ill-fated, or probably both. Since they had just emerged from the dining-room—*Too soon after breakfast?* occurred to her, yet on other days she had asked the same question as early, without rebuff . . . In the meantime she confronted the old woman's expression—secret, furtively hostile, with a sardonic twist not far from a sneer—and with failing heart remembered that breakfast had been unusually silent. Only silent though, not with this sudden restrained antagonism, amused contempt . . .

'Would you like to, a bit?' she continued bravely, and saw the contempt change to an undisguised jeering.

'And what,' Mrs Tor responded softly, 'if I wouldn't like?' An unnerving simper joined the other animosities in her face. 'If I wouldn't like to?'

'That's up to you,' said Jacintha with strenuous indifference. 'Entirely up to—' and paused as her charge moved with an insolent gait—of discarding a nuisance—into the living-room and slammed the door behind her.

Jacintha stood motionless, in the vacuum that follows rebuff; an emptiness of being thrown back on one's self, yet full of indistinct apprehensions. She listened for the sound of the piano; nothing came. The old woman's manner of closing the door indicated that she wished it to stay closed. Impossible, under the circumstances, to go barging in . . . *Oh Lord,* she thought, took a couple of steps with an indistinct notion of listening nearer to, then started violently. In almost the same instant, realizing what had made her start, she moved automatically to answer the door-bell.

On the step was the most unexpected figure possible; a gypsy woman whose aspect—after a moment—penetrated even her sense of trouble and woke her another degree. The woman was not only young and unusually handsome but possessed an elegance perfectly independent of her clothes, which were no more than the standard thing she had seen on women hawking bits of white heather in the London streets—immensely ample skirts in cheap colours with a big flounce at the bottom, just unclean enough to look faintly sluttish, with a doubtfully-clean shawl over it. This one also wore a shawl, not only around her shoulders but over her head, and closely held by invisible hands up to her throat; her skin was palest milk-coffee, her nose a strong aquiline, but the outline of her mouth was blotched with lipstick crudely applied. Beside this drawback she had one other; her eyes, in spite of being languorously long-drawn at the outer corners and shaded by long thick lashes, had badly reddened lids, so much so as to suggest some chronic infection or irritation. This perhaps accounted for another abnormality, the colour of the eyes themselves—not brown nor black as one might expect, but an unnatural hazel, muddy green; the whites noticeable likewise for being yellowish and distressingly bloodshot. Yet for all the drawbacks the first impression struck as fascinating, if not of actual beauty. Owing mostly to her silent eloquence of posture, appealing, ingratiating? but not servile, not in the least servile . . .

'Oh,' Jacintha blurted involuntarily; her survey was followed by the urgent necessity of getting rid of her. 'Thank you, I'm afraid not today, but wait, I'll get you something—'

'Please, my lady,' the gypsy put in respectfully, 'I shall see the mis'ess, please?'

'I'll get you something, just wait—'

'The mis'ess, please? I shall see the mis'ess?' The interrogating voice was low and gentle, with the usual sing-song quality. All gypsies she had ever encountered (to the best of her knowledge) had been English, yet English was not their native language. Their habit of speaking Romany among themselves, it must be, gave their English not a foreign accent precisely, but a foreign *intonation;* some of their constructions, too, were un-English . . .

'Yes, I'm the mistress,' she said brusquely; her analysis of the voice, taking a split second, had begun to be mixed with impatience. 'Now if you'll just wait—'

'No, you are the *y'ong* mis'ess,' the other contradicted with the most graceful and apologetic bow. 'I shall see the other, the other mis'ess, please.'

'Well, you can't.' Surprise had struck the embattled party dumb for an instant. 'Now please, if—'

'The other mis'ess, my lady?' continued the other imperturbably, half chanting. 'Please, the other mis'ess?'

'Now see here,' Jacintha began. In her anger was a growing dread that this curious altercation might penetrate to the living-room. 'You're being a nuisance. If you don't go this minute I'll call the—'

Her voice must have got away from her, for all her effort to hold it low; the next development was a harsh croak from behind her, 'Who is it?'

Startled, half-turning, she had let Mrs Tor see the visitant. Already consternated with defeat, she was further paralyzed by a cry of 'Come in! come in!' with the voice of someone hailing a deliverance. At the summons the gypsy glided past her—not with spiteful triumph, as might have been expected, but always with her former deference, soft and appeasing. Automatically Jacintha pivoted to stare after the old woman, now conducting the visitant toward the living-room door; just about to enter she waved the other ahead of her, and said, 'Miss Cory, you will please wait in your room.' Her accent was haughty and commanding, her smile small and spiteful. 'I'll call when I need you.'

Mechanically Jacintha moved to obey, her glance still locked with her employer's. Then with unbelief she was going up and up, knowing that her every step was followed by the stare of the figure below, motionless. Only as she got to her room did she hear the living-room door close; in a gust of anger she slammed her own door on an unhearing world, then stood considering what she had seen and what to do about it. This gypsy, undoubtedly another specimen picked up on the solitary walks whose solitariness Mrs Tor defended so fiercely; riff-raff like the bead-strung layabout. All this, incontrovertible, hardly helped. . . .

With infinite caution she opened her door again and listened hard. Nothing, absolutely nothing . . . or no, a low sound of voices reached her, so they must have come out of the living-room . . . and again, nothing but silence. Stealthily she moved to the stairhead, with heart in her mouth stole down to the balcony, and peered. The hall seemed empty; as she searched it with distracted eyes, it was the gypsy, alone, who came slowly out of the living-room, but why alone . . . ? Then the woman stood there, obviously waiting; just visible, foreshortened, was the black hair smoothed to satin with a big knot behind. While she stared, the gypsy with graceful gestures drew back over her uncovered head the shawl she had displaced. In her way of doing this was something strange, and yet—despite her catalepsy of attention—something that she missed, and could not call to mind afterward. Then Mrs Tor came into view again, no telling from where, and handed the woman something small, perhaps a folded envelope; it passed from hand to hand so rapidly that there was no chance of seeing it, and in any case she was too busy retreating from the balcony to get an adequate view. She sensed then, rather than heard, other sounds of movement before the front door closed, with nothing to tell whether the visitor had departed alone or not. If Mrs Tor had gone with her she must follow quickly, quickly, whatever the consequences . . . into her swimming wits came the sound of someone on the stairs; she dove back into her room, not a moment too soon.

The tap on the door produced a sort of stab all through her, though she was expecting it; when she opened, Mrs Tor stood there. Her look was not only odd but alien; sleepy yet sly, sated as it were, with the satisfaction of having put something over . . .

'Would you like to come now?' she enquired in a lulled, too-gentle voice. 'Come and play, now . . . ?'

'All right,' muttered Jacintha, stupefied. With no thought or feeling she followed the old woman down the steps, turned toward the living-room . . .

'In a moment!' came Mrs Tor's accents, decisive. 'First, I'll show you. Show you something, first.'

Dumb and acquiescent Jacintha followed her through the french door and into the garden. Ahead of her jounced her employer, and there flashed into her mind a new oddity; that whereas Mrs Tor was undeniably small and getting smaller, yet at times she appeared to gain in size, to be actually *inflated,* and now was an example of this mysterious increase . . . She had stopped suddenly in her descent; Jacintha stopped behind her.

'You see that?' With a wide triumphant movement she gestured toward the stream, dashing along between its banks. 'You see it? Well, I'm through with it.' A savage glee was in her voice. 'I've done with it, I've . . . I've *beaten* it!'

'I'm . . .' muttered Jacintha after a moment, again numb with incomprehension. 'Glad you . . . you've . . .'

'We'll play,' Mrs Tor cut her off decisively. 'Now we'll play.'

They accomplished the ascent to the house, the old woman still unnaturally strong and spry. The other came behind passive and blank of thought, except for an irrational . . . pride, of all things; she was illogically, unconquerably proud of this ancient warrior. In the same order they passed through the french door, into the small adjoining room, into the living-room. . . .

The moment she entered, her nostrils had twitched faintly; the nature of the smell seemed unmistakable, but she could not imagine the connection between it and this room. The instant she raised the lid of the piano it came at her more strongly, yet still her mind could fashion no bond between this humble utilitarian stink and a concert grand. Mrs Tor had just been in this room, how could she not have noticed it . . . ? Yet, apparently oblivious, she had drawn forward the rack and placed the album, open, upon it . . . Mechanically, still bemused by the inexplicable nastiness, Jacintha sat down beside her, delivered herself of the ritual counted bar, and the four hands, poised in readiness, struck. A curious sound resulted; instead of the full chords a few scattered notes answered hoarsely, with gaps between them like missing teeth.

'They won't go down,' the old woman complained, while the other stared at the keyboard, brilliant and shining clean as always, but most of it meeting her fingers with the resistance, almost, of a solid surface.

'Why won't it play?' Mrs Tor had not ceased to demand querulously. 'Why not? why won't it . . . ?'

Jacintha, after a moment, rose and peered into the piano. The music rack was in the way; she slid it toward her and out and propped it against the wall, then looked at the area it had concealed. Along the exposed length of hammers, the glue that had announced itself by its smell had been poured; not in a continuous stream, she could see, but here and there so that some notes were unaffected and others stuck together in clumps. Darkened felts, glistening stickily, blazed the ruinous trail to a conclusion.

'What's *wrong* with it?' the other was insisting, more and more temperish, and the companion had to wait before replying. The first bewilderment had been succeeded by a horror so profound—horror of unbelief, of senseless destruction, horror of evil nearby—that her head seemed to be coming off; she opened her mouth, found no words, tried again . . .

'What's wrong with *you?*' the old woman shot at her, changing course all at once, and into Jacintha's consternation came a remembrance that any sign of confusion in another person acted on Mrs Tor like a stimulant, rousing her not only to malicious pleasure but to unwonted alertness like an animal smelling fear, and that her own present state—of obvious nerves and shipwreck—was providing the spark for potential danger.

'You're white,' continued the accusation; the accuser was staring at her fixedly. 'White as a sheet,' and against the extortion of that stare Jacintha racked her wits and came up with a desperate invention.

'Mrs Tor,' she attempted huskily. 'Oh, what rotten, rotten luck. Old pianos . . . sometimes they . .' her heart was beating hard, her insides trembling '. . . sometimes the—the adhesive they use—it deteriorates from old age, liquefies, you know? I've seen it happen before in old pianos,' she lied with the boldness of despair. 'Dampness, we've had a lot—or rain brings it on, rain—'

Even before the end of her disjointed nonsense she had had the sense of an ear not only deaf, but purposely, contemptuously deaf. Like herself Mrs Tor had risen, peered along the line of hammers, and finally put out a hand to touch one of the felts. Then she turned on Jacintha a look that, for all its calm, frightened her badly.

'Dampness,' she echoed in a voice as inhumanly quiet as her aspect. 'It's glue. Why are you lying to me? Lying, like all of them?' A silence, deadly as her quietness, fell between them. 'Did I do this?'

Cintha produced a sound, meaningless; holding onto the piano for support she swam in some otherwhere, some clamouring, dizzy alienation.

'Did I?' pursued the voice, sinking even lower. 'Tell me.' Silence. 'Tell me.' Her look had turned inhuman, the whites of the eyes glaring, the eyes themselves distended and wandering. 'Did I? Did I do it . . . ?'

Cintha swallowed; her tongue touched her dry lips, her mouth opened to say God knew what, anything . . .

The nightmare exploded in a scream, then another and another, stuffing the companion's eardrums with unreality and beating against the walls and ceiling for escape. The large room seemed barely able to contain the pent-up violence, so great that broken window-panes, shattered ornaments, would be no surprise. Mrs Tor's ululation went on and on; she made random flailing motions with her hands, her mouth at times assuming the square outline of a Greek tragic mask. Yet strangely she was dry-eyed, no tear to be seen in this rending obscenity—of grief, grief and protest. . . .

Something, do something, beat on the companion; the limits of endurance had suddenly produced in her an icy composure

139

that did duty for thought. Afraid to come closer to dementia or the appearance of it, in one instantaneous and planless movement she had grasped a nearby vase of flowers, flung them on the floor, and dashed the water into the distorted face.

Silence fell at once. The old woman remained standing beside the piano with water dripping liberally off her head. Her mouth, caught in mid-scream, was still open with errant drops falling into it; she shut it. During another stillness, a change came over her; not so much the suggestion of awakening that was usual with her, as a sort of first return from chaos. She stirred a little, touched her face, then said, 'I've got wet.' Her voice was now merely fretful or querulous. 'Is it . . . is it raining?'

'It's just stopped,' Jacintha hazarded, with a glance outside. No rain as it happened, yet it had gone rather dark and threatening and supported her words; Mrs Tor had seemed not to penetrate the deceit. Yet not safe to assume this disability about her or any other, not safe . . . 'Don't you think,' she continued, with a good imitation of casualness, 'you should change your clothes?' She paused, holding her breath; the old woman took no offense, merely seeming to ponder the suggestion. Finally, nodding again like a mandarin, she said 'yes,' but the monosyllable, hesitant, seemed to contain a growing doubt. . . .

'Before you catch cold?' the other wheedled, then with consternation saw the doubt change, change into returning sense, recollection, sanity—and again stopped breathing.

'The piano,' came a voice, dry with absolute despair. 'The piano.' She fastened a look of torment on its ruined majesty. 'If I did that . . . *that* . . . I'm finished.' She gestured. "Better just . . . shut me up, shut me . . .'

'Rot,' said Jacintha boldly, then—all at once—with a stoutness born of sudden recollection: the spyer upstairs, the hidden enemy perhaps . . . 'Look, Mrs Tor. Sit down.' When the other made no movement she took her hand; the feel of it, cold and rigid, submerged her remnant of fear in a great wave of protectiveness. 'Come on, sit down.' With gentle force she pushed her into a chair, then sat down opposite and took both her hands.

'Look, I don't *believe* you did that, I don't believe it at all. You didn't do it,' she repeated with emphasis perhaps false, perhaps not. 'It wasn't you, it wasn't you at all. Let's forget it for a moment, we've other things to talk about.' She caught and nailed the other's distracted glance. 'Important things, much more important. Tell me now, tell me,' she urged with all her soul; this enquiry was her last hope. 'You've asked me if I could type, you've asked me more than once. Have you something you'd like us to work on? or—or put in order, or anything?' She breathed in raggedly. 'Something to work on, that I could help you with? anything like that?'

She stopped talking, and with bated breath attended on the answer. Had the poor old thing's attention been diverted from the piano, had she heard any of it . . . ?

'Something, yes,' she sighed at length. 'A . . . a book. Not . . . not finished, no. Only . . . only notes . . .'

'But you have it?' Jacintha followed up a long pause. 'You've got it here?'

'Don't know . . . don't know where,' Mrs Tor sighed vacantly. 'I . . . I must look.'

'Let's then, straightaway,' urged her companion, with a part-consciousness of victory. 'Come on, let's look for it—'

Again her words were cut short by the change visibly coming upon the old lady, the estranging spell.

'I want to go away from here,' announced Mrs Tor, her voice abrupt and strained by fear. 'Away, go away.'

'You mean . . .' She had had to take a moment to meet the deflected current. '. . . leave this house?'

'Yes,' the other agreed fiercely. 'You—you too.'

'Why though?' Jacintha pleaded. 'Why?'

'It's . . . it's *bad*.' She said it after a pause, as if struggling for words. 'Something . . . waiting in the dark. A . . . a bad thing . . .'

Staring at her with a feeling of helplessness, Jacintha saw again the phenomenon—always unsettling—of the return to sanity.

'My notes, yes.' She spoke weakly, but otherwise as if there

141

had been no interruption. 'I've got them somewhere. We'll look, yes, we'll . . .'

'Let's now,' the companion assented with a show of enthusiasm—cut off again by the glance her employer had turned on the piano, the look of remembrance and despair.

'But did I—*do* that?' With a tremulous voice and shaking hand she gestured toward it. *'Savage* it like that? Must think,' she muttered, beating her clenched fist on her knee, then rose. 'Must remember, remember . . . *No!*' she cried out, as Jacintha made to rise also. 'Must be alone, must . . . must *think,* alone. Alone, alone . . .'

* * *

Moments after the old woman had wavered from the room the companion stood with whirling wits, into which only one ray penetrated: she must have immediate help and thank God she had somewhere to turn . . . and even with help, hard enough to wait the long hours before Hugh could ring. And if he failed to ring, what to do now, what to do in this unbearable position . . .

In a sort of catalepsy she moved into the hall and listened, it seemed she was always listening. And as always, unbroken silence; its absolute quality reminded her that the two servants were off from after breakfast, that they were alone in the house, the two of them. No, the *three* of them . . . Something hardened coldly within her, a delayed but ironclad resolution. Ring first, and after that do a little investigating. Not too gently either, in fact the time had come to take off the gloves altogether . . . the steely glint in her eye vanished before the immediate grim necessity. Noiselessly she left the house, leaving the door on the latch, and sped to the phone-box.

'Just to be with her, and later on help her undress for bed, if it's necessary,' she explained, after a semi-incoherent account. 'She's never yet asked me to help her that way, but you've done it before, haven't you? I know it's terribly short notice,' she appealed, 'but—but c-could you, Mrs Williams?'

'Yes, I can do that. She's had a bad turn?' queried the steady experienced voice. 'By the sound of it?'

'Well, I don't know. Half off, and half on.' She laughed hysterically. 'Between being all right, and not all right. But I've got to be out of the house this evening for a bit, and leaving her alone's out of the question.'

'I'll be along, don't you worry, soon's I can. By the way,' Mrs Williams pursued, 'she'd part of a prescription left last time I saw her, tranquillizers or something. I might get her to take one at bed-time? If it's all right with you—?'

'Well.' Still scattered, empty of all but trouble, she fumbled. 'She's had them before—?'

'Oh yes.'

'Well then, if you think it'd help.'

'OK. And once she's in bed, you'll want me to stop for a bit?'

'Oh please, just for a while. So I'll—I'll see you . . . ?'

* * *

She stood a long moment before stepping from the phone-box, dizzy with combined relief, indecision and misgiving. If Hugh rang her reasonably soon, it might be all right. But if more catastrophe fell, if no Hugh appeared, if something occurred that was monstrously outside her experience and capacity both, she must go outside her instructions. She must, even to the point of confiding everything to the solicitor . . .

The unwelcome picture faded as the other thing took shape in her again, the former suspicion now heating to a glow, then firing up red hot. Who but one person in the house could have committed that unspeakable act upon the piano, that filthy vandalism . . . ?

With new resolves of action forming within her, more furious and more distinct, she made a stealthy entrance into the house and stopped. Still not a sound, not anywhere, if you listened to this particular silence long enough your ears cracked . . . She broke from the spell and entered the kitchen with a decisive step. Rapidly she put on coffee and a plump roasted half-chicken to heat, made a salad and cut an enormous wedge of Mrs Dowling's superb apple tart. While all this was in work, her disorderly swirl of thoughts settled about one object more and more single-mindedly. Who else in this house was capable of such spiteful mischief? Who else was so well acquainted with Mrs Tor's mental state, in which small worries became large torments and large ones had power to strike down, over-topple? And living just overhead, spying secretly and perpetually, who else had such opportunity to do harm, lethal harm . . . ?

The kitchen smelled deliciously of coffee; as she poured it into a thermos and added a jug of heavy cream she found her jaw set hard enough to ache. Get into Mary's room at all costs; have a good long look at Mary. Unlikely that the room would betray any evidence of her misdoing, but the woman herself might show uneasiness, furtiveness, she might make some illuminating slip as good as confession, almost . . .

She picked up the tray, and with her mouth in a hard line left the kitchen. As she ascended with the slowness imposed by its weight, she searched for some question that might startle the old bat into self-betrayal; her power of deception was clumsy probably, transparent. The only trouble was that no such question occurred to her, for all her attempts to frame something penetrating. Never mind, the important thing was getting into her room; she was counting more and more on the mere fact of encounter, of face-to-face confrontation . . .

Arriving at the door she struck against it with her foot, and called out, 'Miss Pargill! your tray.'

There was a dead silence, during which she thought she could hear a sort of flurry, and from well within the room came, 'Oh! Oh yes.' There followed an almost inaudible padding approach, and the voice spoke much nearer the door. 'Yes, put it down.'

'It's a bit hard, bending with it,' suggested the other speciously. 'Couldn't I just come in and put it on the table?'

'No, put it down, I'll take it in presently.'

'If you'd just open the door.' Jacintha, against her intention, had snapped. 'The thing weighs a ton.'

'I didn't ask you to bring it up,' the voice twittered with a sort of horrid gayety. 'Not I, not I!'

A moment passed before Jacintha managed, 'All right.' Her

defeat and rage impelled a useless, 'And *thank* you for your consideration.'

The peal of laughter that answered her, cackling eldritch laughter, gave her gooseflesh in the same moment that she longed to open her hands and let the tray fall. Conquering the temptation she bent and deposited her burden; going downstairs the continuing laughter was in her ears, spiteful and mocking. Or triumphant? and busily in her mind she attached this triumph to guilt, gleeful obscene guilt. The piano was done for, the duet-playing done for, trampled underfoot. . . .

She was in the hall again, vacantly, mechanically raising her head toward the stairs from time to time; submerged in the blankness of no further recourse, groping in a vacuum for what next, what next . . . Footsteps recalled her; footsteps at the same time hurried and shambling, terribly weak . . .

'I won't stay here,' was the greeting, dogged and a little hoarse. 'I want to go away.'

'All right.' Her dismay was overridden at once by a hopeful idea. 'But first—'

'I'm afraid,' the old woman broke in, unhearing. 'Afraid of . . . of . . .'

'Yes,' Jacintha agreed. 'But just sit down, won't you? just a moment?' Half compelling her, gently, she got her into a chair and dared to launch a question. 'Mrs Tor, is it because of Mary?'

The name produced, instantly, a silence; as instantly she drove into it. 'Mary Pargill? Is it Mary, Mrs Tor?'

'M-Mary?' stammered the other, after a pause. 'Mary . . . ?'

'Is it her you're afraid of?' Did she even recognize the name, it seemed not . . . all the same Jacintha pursued, 'You could send her away, you know. Just give her something to live on, and she'd go.' Killing two birds with one stone, she thought. 'She would, you know, she'd go away—'

'Mary,' said Mrs Tor suddenly. The vacant look was changing to something else. 'That old fool.' The name, as she had said it, had no association whatever with dread. 'Eats. Eats like a . . .' She laughed. 'I can afford it,' and even as she laughed it was coming back, the strained look, the fear . . . 'We'll go,' she half whispered. 'You—and I—we'll go . . . away.'

'What about your book?' Jacintha countered boldly. 'Oughtn't we to find your book first? Your manuscript that we're going to work on . . . ?'

'Oh.' A pause followed; the vacancy was infiltrated, little by little, with recollection. 'Yes, yes—we'll look. Look now . . . come.' She rose with surprising briskness, as if mention of the book had renewed her strength. 'Come.'

She hurried out of the room and began to mount the stairs; the other followed passively. This present aberration of wanting to flee the house, for all Dennison's reminder and prediction of it, had shaken her; with grappling powers in suspension she waited, merely waited. Mrs Tor achieved the landing, still with that unnatural vivacity, opened a door upon it that led to the back stairs, and started to descend. Down these in turn, on a half-landing, was another door. The next thing that dawned on her was a rattle of keys, hauled out from some hiding place in Mrs Tor's dress; did she carry them with her always . . . ? The door opened, the old woman passed inside; Jacintha followed.

The room, after its owner had pressed a switch with the ease of long familiarity, revealed itself as no mere glory-hole but a luggage room on a formidable scale, full of the paraphernalia of a wandering life. At the nature of some of it, it was impossible to guess; from its regimented look she could deduce the organizing mind that had arranged it. On the wall hung a board with more keys neatly labelled, and from this Mrs Tor took one, hardly pausing in making her selection. With similar promptness and decision she opened a small trunk, palpably knowing what she was doing and having, evidently, a firm grip on this bygone part of her life. Then she was fumbling and groping, muttering to herself meanwhile.

Jacintha, ignored, let herself relax a little. Instinct forbade her to intrude with offers of help, and about this search she knew nothing in any case. For what seemed a long time she stood there, presently beginning to feel somehow hypnotized, riveted, as if the hunt had gone on for hours; judging from its present progress and the constant inaudible soliloquy that accompanied it, it might go on all day. Still, it was all right; the old woman, so occupied, was far less alarming than when wanting to flee the house . . .

She withdrew her attention and let her gaze revolve idly over the trunks, mysterious canvas heaps roped up, cases arranged from large to small in orderly diminution. With nothing else to look at her eyes repeated the circuit idly, over and over . . . a bright gleam, bright brown, recurring each time at one spot, roused a languid interest. When her first step drew no least attention from the old woman, still rooting and talking to herself, she walked over quietly and peered into the source of the gleam, then inserted her hand into a narrow space, cautiously. Her way was blocked by some sort of thick strap; she hooked her fingers under it and pulled. Even before she saw it she had a sense of its texture—waxy yet velvety, somehow alive.

The thing came into a view; a briefcase, but a briefcase such as she had never seen. Entirely of crocodile skin it was the most beautiful colour, bright brown with subtle shadings, a regal object and a triumph of the leather-worker's art with its burnished seams and glossy strap that went all the way around and fastened underneath the handle. . . . About to unfasten this out of mere automatic curiosity, she stopped once more and glanced across. Mrs Tor was still fumbling, yet now there lay beside her a disordered mass of papers. As Jacintha looked she fished up another handful at which she stared in patent perplexity. *Oh Lord, she's tiring badly,* thought the spectator, *I should make her stop,* then at once the possible alternative—a renewed battle over her determination to leave—struck her down. *Wait then,* fleeted across her mind, *leave her to it for a bit,* and after a final uneasy glance she returned to her find. The strap fitted the brass buckle to a millimetre, stoutly resisted opening; beneath it was a tiny brass lock. No key, however . . . had the thing let her come as far as she could? She pushed at the lock, and was unreasonably pleased as it slid down with a click. She opened it and saw what must be, surely, an unusual

147

sight: on the inner side of the flap was a sizable brass plate covered with small running script.

To
Valeria Blakelie Tor,
from her publishers
Reynolds and Malahide
this case of a Bramla crocodile
estimated at fifty years old
Wishing her, her writings and her reputation
an even greater longevity
we offer this small token
with best wishes and profound admiration

Slightly dazed she reread it, then with a feeling of unreality glanced from it to the figure still crouched over the trunk, still muttering, its movements increasingly weak and vague; this poor dishevelled old thing, and the woman of the dedication, were the same . . . A pang, a greater pang of protectiveness and pity than ever before, smote Jacintha hard—along with another odd, unrelated knowledge. The buckle, the lock on the briefcase, the inscription plate within it: not brass as she had thought but gold, pale gold, as pure of blemish as the lustrous brown hide . . .

'Mrs Tor,' she essayed now, with the most cautious playfulness. 'You've found it, aren't you wonderful. Shall we take it down? Now?'

With utmost misgiving she waited; waited as the eyes, badly dulled, moved to the questioner. With no appearance of surprise or displeasure she viewed the object in Jacintha's hand, only saying after a pause, 'Yes, yes, you'll . . .' With a spent gesture she motioned toward the papers. '. . . put them in there . . . ?' Her voice gave out; she began to lift herself off her knees with a look of imminent collapse. In spite of this look the other, afraid to rouse the sleeping tigress, refrained from offering help. Mrs Tor, by now upright, stared at the briefcase. The sight, apparently, brought about one of those unpredictable and startling returns to herself; she fairly snapped, 'Where's the key to that thing?'

148

'It doesn't seem to be here.'

'Turn it,' rasped her employer. 'Upside down.'

The manoeuvre, carried out, failed to produce the key.

'Well,' muttered the old woman. 'Well . . .'

She's finished, thought the other with compunction, yet with relief. *For a bit, anyway.* She was quite correct; this was utter fatigue, a black cap quenching memory, intention, every-thing . . .

'Rest . . .' she was murmuring, 'mus' rest, rest . . .' Ob-viously no longer seeing or hearing anything she wavered across the room and out. Jacintha, stealthily hurrying to the door, followed her with her eyes as she laboured up the back stairs, then listened as she passed out of sight, standing rigid till she heard the sound of the bedroom door.

Still locked in strangeness she stood a moment before re-en-tering the luggage room. While stuffing manuscript into the briefcase (there was little room to spare when she had fin-ished) she thought again, with compunction, of the old wom-an's deathly exhaustion. Still, better that than her absolute, her immovable insistence on leaving the house behind her . . . *Hang on,* she thought, *hang on,* then realized something new: that only a short time ago she would have thought in terms of whether she could do this, and now thought in terms quite dif-ferent: that she must hang on, she must.

* * *

'Hugh—Hugh—oh Hugh!'

Her cry of relief, erupting at the sound of his voice, went on while he tried to interrupt, at last overcoming her incoherence with a strong, steadying, 'Jacintha! Cintha. Cintha.'

She fell quiet, trembling; a moment of silence followed.

'Now tell me,' the voice continued. 'Tell me.'

'I . . . oh God, where to begin, I don't—' she broke off, try-ing to impose order on the disorderly tumble of event, and gulped at random, 'The piano's ruined.'

'What?' he was evidently nonplussed. 'What's that you say?'

'Someone poured in glue—all over the felts.'

'Good God,' he said, after a moment. 'When was this?'

149

'This morning.'

'But *who*—' he broke off; with all her desire of accusation, she suddenly felt that he had the same thing in mind . . . all at once the ugly glee of the upstairs recluse, the spiteful laughter, were ringing again in her ears . . . 'Go on,' he was saying. 'Go on.'

'Your—your mother took it badly, very badly, and said that . . . that if she had done it, just to put her away. Just shut her up.'

'And then?' he prompted, as she tapered off.

'Well, I talked to her as well as I could, brought her around a little bit, then I reminded her she'd asked me about typing—'

'*Did* she?'

'—and it turns out she's got a book or something, notes for a book I mean—and I got her to hunt them up.'

'Yes, go ahead.'

'Well, she did. She'd been saying she wanted to leave the house, but then she went to that sort of luggage room—'

'Luggage room?'

'Oh Hugh.' She was a little impatient. 'It's halfway down the back stairs, simply crammed with trunks, you must know it—?'

' 'Fraid I don't remember it all that well, Cintha.' His tone was of perfect simplicity and patience. 'I haven't been in that house all that much, and I wasn't encouraged to explore. I've next to no idea of her—well—arrangements—'

'Well, at any rate.' She was apologetic. 'She got a whole mass of papers from there, simply masses, and I've got it all in a briefcase in the study. We'll tackle it tomorrow, I suppose, unless she . . .' her voice dwindled '. . . has another spell of wanting to go away, or something.'

Her mind was suddenly engrossed with something else, unforeseen. Crisis; the time of crisis had evidently come. Reservations and part-truths, doubtfully permissible before, were now no longer to be considered. Nothing for it but to clear her conscience at least partway. Suppressing the suicide attempt had perhaps been excusable then, in view of Mrs Tor's painful entreaty; now it was impossible, it must be told . . . She had

got as far as opening her mouth for a tremulous 'Hugh . . .'
when he came in ahead of her.

'Cintha.' He said it in a tone that all at once made her weak;
it was not only the entreaty in it, but something else. 'Hang on
for God's sake. I can't get back tonight, I can't possibly, but
hang on till I can. Will you? will you stay——?'

'Yes,' she promised. 'I'll stay.'

'I'll try to be home not later than six tomorrow night—at
least I'll make every effort. Not later than six, I swear——'

'Don't worry.' Unbelievably, into her disjointedness of moments ago, flowed a wonderful steadiness and courage. 'Don't
worry at all.'

'Promise? You won't let yourself be frightened away——?'

'Nothing like that—I'll be here.'

'Bless you,' he groaned. 'Bless you.'

'But Hugh, suppose—suppose she——'

'What?' His apprehension echoed hers. 'What?'

'—suppose she still wants to leave the house, tomorrow
morning? Suppose she rings John, asks him to help her? If he
agrees——' she was nearly clamouring '—can anyone stop her
from going? or stop him from helping her to go——?'

His stillness was the stillness of a lethal blow: then, after a
moment—

'Cintha.' His voice was thick, almost gasping. 'Prevent it. At
all costs, prevent it. Think of something, anything. If she's actually gone by the time I get there—with her own consent,
when she doesn't know any better . . .' His voice failed for a
moment. 'Get her interested in this new book or whatever—
jolly her along till I get there.'

'I'll try—I'll do my best.'

'I don't put it past Dennison to—to butt in somehow, take
her away and shut her up with her own consent——'

'He won't,' she broke in. Suddenly she felt again that surge
of strength and assurance; she was equal to Dennison, equal
to all the world. 'I'll see to that.'

'But if she——' He was troubled, doubtful. '—if she *asks* him
to come——'

'There're things I can do,' she broke into his uncertainty.

151

'He can't just whisk her out in five minutes, I'll find some way of . . . of delaying, impeding—'

'Thank you, thank you. Oh darling—!'

The endearment was followed by a new silence, an utter suspension. She listened to it, and to his breathing, and to her own.

'Darling?' he repeated, almost too softly to be heard; she still listened, rapt and unbelieving. 'Cintha, are you . . . angry with me . . . ?'

'Angry! Oh Hugh.' Her voice was fragmented with the moment. 'Hugh, Hugh.'

'My sweet, my sweet. And to think—' a broken laugh escaped him '—that I've always been afraid of you, a bit.'

'*Afraid?*'

'Well, there's something about you—I don't know, high and mighty—that says keep off.'

'Nonsense, you should have known better.'

'Why?' He was reasonable, equable. 'I've never expected that my love for anyone would be returned. You don't, you know—if you've been on short commons from the beginning.' He was impersonal, without self-pity. 'All your life, in fact.'

'Yes,' she muttered. 'Yes, I . . .'

'See you tomorrow then, early as I can? Good night for now, my sweet. Good night, my lovely sweet.'

'Good—' Sudden recollection cut her short; her earlier intention resurged in a wave. 'Hugh, there's something else, something I ought to tell you—'

'What?' He was alarmed again. 'What's that?'

'Your mother tried to commit suicide.'

Having hit him with it full force, she was stopped by the mere impact—the full realization—of the folly of her original promise to the old woman; the foolhardiness of it, the screaming danger . . . He at his end maintained a silence that she felt as stricken; after this pause he made a sound that she interpreted as *Go on.*

'She tried to throw herself in the stream, it's terribly high now, fast. If she'd been another two feet ahead of me, I couldn't have got her.' She was ready to humble herself, grovel,

152

take the blame for what she had done. 'She fought, it was pretty bad, but I managed to get her back to the house. And once she was there she . . . she practically swore she'd never do it again. She *promised*—and made me swear, practically, not to tell anyone. And I know I shouldn't have done it, Hugh, I know, but . . . as things were, and she seemed, I don't know, actually desperate . . .'

Her voice trailed off; she braced herself anew for whatever form his reproaches might take, his justifiable displeasure.

'When?' His tone was rasping, yet barely audible. 'When was this?'

'A few weeks ago.'

Once more there followed a wordless gap; this she felt as a black pit of condemnation for her concealment, unjustifiable, unforgivable . . .

'Well,' he muttered finally. 'Well . . .'

Suddenly hollow with fear, she listened to the beating of her heart.

'See you tomorrow, then,' he achieved finally, his voice cold and dull. 'Soon's I can make it.'

* * *

Closing her mind against the sound of the voice, against everything, she walked back to the house. Gently as she had let herself in, Mrs Williams appeared on the balcony almost at once.

'She's asleep,' she announced, coming down. 'Fast asleep.'

'Well, that's good.'

'Had her pill, they knock her right out, always.'

'I see.' A dim shape took clearer and clearer form within her; anything to put off thought, the gnawing fear . . . 'Mrs Williams,' she propounded suddenly. 'If she's actually *sound* asleep—'

'Oh, she's that.'

'—then I wonder if we could both—I mean together—do something that's been worrying me—'

'What would that be, miss?'

They had been all but whispering, in spite of this being obviously unnecessary; yet Jacintha's voice fell another degree as she explained, 'I think, that is I rather suspect, that Mrs Tor may have drugs or . . . or stuff like that, actually dangerous. If you could help me go through her things, if she's as far under as you say . . .'

Mrs Williams could be seen to reflect on this proposition, then finally nodded. 'We'd better do it now, straightaway,' she suggested. 'The pill shouldn't wear off for a good while yet, but you never know.'

'You mean, she's drug-resistant—?'

The other, already moving toward the staircase, nodded.

* * *

'Nothing so far,' said Mrs Williams, stepping soundlessly into the bathroom. 'Anything here?'

'Not a thing. Nothing that shouldn't be, at any rate.'

A baffled silence succeeded to their exchange.

'Better not talk here,' mouthed Mrs Williams, hardly moving her lips, and Jacintha got up and followed her into the bedroom. There, with a new consciousness of the place which she had not seen before, she stared about her at the furnishings, ornate, of past fashion, and somehow, though not actually, shabby; stared also at the occupant of the big double bed, unmoving from the moment they had entered, lying on her back and breathing regularly, deeply and noisily. Preparing to follow Mrs Williams who had gone ahead and was now at the door, all at once she stiffened, her heart dealing a violent blow on the side of her chest. The figure on the bed gulped, snorted irregularly once, twice, showed every sign of being about to waken . . . Mrs Williams's violent gestures hardly penetrated; in some corner of her mind she was frantically making excuses for her presence here . . .

The sleeper stirred again, uttered an inarticulate moan, again lay still and began breathing heavily.

* * *

'That was a near thing,' she said on a shaky laugh, as they reached the bottom of the stairs.

154

'Well, I don't think actually,' returned Mrs Williams. 'It's just I was afraid she might open her eyes an' half-see you, and that *might* wake her up full. But we were all right,' she reassured. 'This time.'

'Her breathing,' said Jacintha. 'Is it always so terribly heavy?'

'After a pill, yes— 'most any sleeping thing'll do it. But I've heard her breathe very heavy in her sleep, pill or no pill.'

'And so,' the other reverted moodily. 'You didn't find anything there, at all?'

'Nothing that oughtn't to be there. But there's such loads of stuff, and I couldn't turn up the lights for a *good* look, you know. But so far as I could see . . .' Her voice trailed off. 'Nothing you could find either, in the bathroom?'

'Aspirin.' Jacintha's laugh was at once hollow and grim. 'A couple of bottles. I turned them both out in my hand, and far as I could see they were just what they said they were.'

'Miss Cory.' Mrs Williams spoke after a moment of silence. 'If I might ask you, for why d'you think she might have anything that's . . . well . . . harmful?'

'I don't know.' She spoke after a pause. 'It's just a . . . a feeling . . .' The self-irritation that had sharpened her voice fell to another note. 'I'm scared to death, to tell you the truth.'

'Of her doing away with herself?' The sceptical voice was hearty. '*Her?* Not much.'

'How do you know?'

'Well.' Mrs Williams, by no means nonplussed, all the same hesitated. 'Well, it's the feeling she gives me, that's all. She's too alive in . . . in *herself*. I mean, she's too full of herself, too stuck-up.' She had turned half-apologetic. 'That kind doesn't commit suicide, not much. I shouldn't go upsetting myself over that, miss.'

'I suppose you're right.' She should be comforted, but somehow was not. 'You know better than I do.'

'Mind you,' the good woman pursued, 'I don't say there *isn't* trouble ahead, you know. She's going downhill, sometimes fast and sometimes slow, like with all old folks. But that's nature, my dear, there's nothing we can do about that.'

'Gypsies.' Jacintha had spoken suddenly, after a pause. 'She's met a couple of them—she even had one of them, a woman, here in the house. No later than day before yesterday—!'

'What of it?' Mrs Williams was tranquil. 'She loves 'em, she'll always buy their trashy bits of heather and stand talking to 'em, anytime.'

'Mrs Williams!' Jacintha cut in, spurred by a new idea. 'Do you think the woman, the gypsy woman—would she have spoiled the piano?'

'Spoiled?'

'I didn't tell you. Someone poured glue in it.'

A curious expression—an uncharacteristic hardness—settled on Mrs Williams's features, after the first shock; she stood a moment totally unmoving, then cast her eyes aloft for a single, significant instant.

'Do you mean Mrs Tor did it?' the other demanded; it was time for plain speaking. 'Or Mary Pargill?'

'Well.' Mrs Williams, however forthright, would not commit herself. 'I don't mean Mrs Tor, that's certain.'

Jacintha opened her mouth to cite her employer's own self-suspicion, then for sheer weariness—of this house, in which everything was uncertain—closed it.

'I'll be pushing along then,' Mrs Williams was saying. 'And you better get some sleep yourself, Miss Cory, by the look of you.'

XII

*Well, chum, the day of freedom has dawned or words
to that effect. I'm through with him, I've walked out.
What I've taken from him no one knows, but enough
is enough. Will you believe that* three *of his clients
are bringing a joint action against him. Thank God
they have the nerve, everyone's so terrified of his
success, but two of them are Viola Carberry and Rex
Trenholme and you can't write* them *off, not with
their reputation. I told him he'd lose the case and
better settle out of court, and he fetched me one
across the mouth, a fourpenny one, it's a wonder I've
any front teeth left. All right, let him go ahead, he'll
pay them a packet and pay another packet in costs
—damn him to hell, I hope they twist the balls off
him. But* listen, *sweetie, here's the big lollipop, Rex
and Viola are giving him the push of course and coming with US. Do you* realize *it, a baby agency with
two first-string people like that, always in work and
offered more than they can do, and that's only the
beginning. We'll make a big thing of this, big big BIG.*

So listen, drop everything and come, *I'm way over
my head already. Shove off that ridiculous job, you*

can give them a couple of weeks notice but not more.
Hurry hurry, what fun we'll have, I can't wait.

L

*PS Just realized something. I hate him so, now, that
I can't even bear to write his name. Yet when you
think for how long I was his worshipping door-mat,
funny hahaha?*

* * *

Having read it once, always with her ear out for Mrs Tor's
morning descent—having left the door open for that purpose—
she sat enclosed in a sort of hollowness, a vacuum of consternation threaded with intermittent despairs. What if, after all, he
were through with her; what if he regarded her silence on the
suicide attempt as an utter breach of trust, for he had every
right to so regard it . . . Yes, if it had happened like that—
and it had sounded like it—then this summons was a lifeline,
something for which she could be grateful, abjectly grateful
. . . So wait, she counseled herself over her leaden heart;
wait till her first sight of him told her the best, or the worst . . .

Descending footsteps sounded from the hall; she shoved the
letter into a pocket and emerged, her face hastily composed
along lines of cheer, and caroled, 'Good morning!', meanwhile
with every faculty of attention fixed—riveted—on her charge.
From this surveillance, however, no absolute conclusion could
be drawn. The old woman, always rather careless as to dress
and hair, now appeared a little more careless than usual. On
the favourable side her manner was tolerably amiable but—
at the same time—wandering, as if she waited to . . . remind
herself of something? or be reminded . . . ?

'Good morning,' she responded in a voice rather blurred, always looking about for that thing, that unknown invisible
thing. The dining-room door now stood open and Mrs Tor
turned toward it absently; Jacintha followed, with an unpleasant fluctuating chill all through her. The other ate little
and fast, as if anxious to get at some more important task. At
least she had not yet referred to her project of leaving the
house; could this failure be the result of the sleeping pill last

night? Whatever or however, fervently the paid companion thanked God for every moment of delay . . .

'The papers, now,' she said in a bright eager voice, as the old woman's scant consumption was patently approaching its end. 'We'll be getting at the papers this morning, won't we?'

'Papers . . . ?'

'That you had out of the trunk-room yesterday,' she prompted cautiously. 'Your notes, you know. Your *book*.'

'I—I'll pack,' responded Mrs Tor in a voice ineffably wandering. 'Pack . . . first.'

'But the papers,' she insisted charily, her heart falling lower. 'You must go over them, mustn't you? The papers for your book, you know? for your *book*—?'

The repetition of *book* had an effect, but one too capricious, too variable, to define. Hesitation was in it, a half-hesitation accompanied by a half-blankness; while being distracted from her idea of packing, she still kept or was trying to keep some sort of grip in it . . . a flash of something new passed over her face. Irritation perhaps? with the person who interposed this obstacle . . . ?

'We could begin,' Jacintha pressed on nevertheless, carefully. 'Now—?' and held her breath, trying to follow the confused play of emotion on the old face. It had changed again, indefinably; she was reminded of a clouded sun half-appearing, submerging, then appearing again with gleams of sulkiness, of threat . . . 'Shall I get them?' she asked, and was struck dumb by the other's look of intense amusement, sly and baleful. While she sat wordless, Mrs Tor announced, 'First get . . . get my cases. Get them—first.'

She rose and made for the door, moving fast; with equal speed Jacintha rose to follow. At once the old woman turned on her with a distorted face of fury. 'Don't follow me!' she screamed. 'I *won't* be followed! No! No!'

*   *   *

She stood motionless, reduced to listening. The footsteps went up, crossed the balcony and then—she could hear it

159

distinctly—opened the back-stairs door and went through; dimly she heard the first steps of descent, then nothing.

In another moment she was going through the serving pantry, her first check and blankness succeeded by a strange cool resolution and unbreakable purpose. In the kitchen she began at once, 'Sorry.' Both women had risen from their breakfast. 'Very sorry, but I wanted to tell you both. If Mrs Tor tries to leave the house by the kitchen door will you manage to prevent her somehow, Mrs Dowling, and send Anna to tell me at once? I'll be in the phone-box outside.'

'I'll do that, miss,' said Mrs Dowling agreeably. 'I better lock the door now, shall I, an' take the key?'

'But it's a Yale lock—?'

'Yes, but the old keyhole's beneath, *with* the key.' Following the words with the action, she turned and slipped it into her pocket. 'If Madam tries anything, I'll stop her an' send Anna along.'

'Thank you,' said Jacintha fervently, 'thank you,' and withdrew, racing to the garden door, locking it also, and pocketing the key. In the hall once more she listened hard, decided against the risk of ringing from here, and finished by letting herself softly out of the front door; if Mrs Tor tried escaping that way, she could see her from the phone-box.

'Mrs Williams?' she said after a moment, her voice breathless and very low, though now there was no necessity for it. 'Could you possibly, as early as you can . . . Oh, not early? . . . Well then, from about two o'clock? . . . Oh thank you, *thank* you.'

Re-entering the house noiselessly she stood for another long moment, listening. Except for that sense of something stirring, out of sight—imaginary perhaps—again there was nothing. She took the untouched morning paper from the table and retreated into the small room from where she could see the stairs.

Here she passed, incredibly, almost two hours. With eyes that swivelled from the paper to the hall, with ears straining to catch the least sound, with nerves ready to bring her to her feet at the least need, she waited. Four or five times she could hear, unmistakably, the sound of Mrs Tor gaining the balcony;

she followed by ear the sounds of objects labouriously humped up the remaining stairs and into the bedroom. The old woman must be amassing a ton of luggage; piteous, yet this extended effort had the great and overriding advantage of taking time, *time,* the essence of the whole thing. Let her spend hours selecting and more hours packing, in what confused and tumultuous manner one could guess; every moment that passed, till Hugh's arrival, was that much gained. Reviewing her charge's scattered and ominous behaviour of the morning, only then did she realize—realize fully—what a blow the damaged piano had dealt her shaky understanding; what a cruel, hard blow. . . .

After this she found she was bankrupt, thrown back without recourse on thoughts of herself. His voice last night, the sound of it; first in endearments (a shiver passed over her, involuntary) then his silence all at once when she admitted the suicide attempt. The *quality* of that silence . . . of anger? or at best consternation, a withdrawal, deathly, a . . . a finish to her hopes? Yet his voice only a moment earlier, *my sweet, my lovely sweet:* Could all that be quenched by her single stupidity, turned to nothing?

Rowelling herself with alternate hope and destroying fear, she sank at last into a comfortless certitude. In love, especially in the early stages of love, there was no telling what trifle, what small accident, might stop the whole thing in its tracks. The mystery of desire, the greater mystery that severed and killed it in a moment, she was not likely to guess at. Not when the greatest poets that ever lived, the greatest writers, had circled the puzzle round and round without solving it. . . .

The sound of footsteps brought her up standing. Mrs Tor, carrying a small case, came in sight and started to descend unhandily. The instant she was down she brandished the case at Jacintha and demanded, 'Are you ready?'

'Well,' demurred the other. 'I haven't packed.'

'No? Well, hurry—I'll wait here.'

'All right.' The mere answer of the old woman had been informative; time and passage of time were misty to her, otherwise she would have reproached her companion for not being ready. 'Yes, I'll go at once. Only—'

The vague fragrance that was in her nostrils, impelling a stealthy glance at her watch, was the next life-saver. Hard to believe that it was one or all but . . .

'—I mean,' she continued plaintively, 'couldn't we have luncheon first? I'm starved.'

Mrs Tor, visibly given pause, turned visibly displeased. 'No,' she said decisively, and flourished the case. 'Must be . . . be going, going . . .'

'But just some coffee?' Jacintha wheedled. 'It won't take long.'

'I—I should like—' the wafts of odour, stronger now, must have reached her. '—yes, I should like some coffee.'

'I'd love some,' fervently Jacintha helped the cause, then ventured, 'Leave the case in the hall, wouldn't you rather?' and in return got a black look of distrust, accompanied by a double-handed grip on the case; evidently they were not to be parted.

What followed was, on the surface, the routine of a meal, with below it an ordeal of lively and variegated torment. Mrs Tor, between abrasive remarks on the local train service, kept muttering under her breath *No time, no time* . . . She had finished her coffee at once and spurned everything else while Jacintha, on purpose, lingered and lingered over her food, always aware of the old woman's feverish impatience . . . and aware, simultaneously, of something else, ludicrous and infinitely touching: that although Valeria Tor had lived by no rule and no convention, yet some strand of her earliest training forbade her to hurry anyone at table, least of all at her own table . . .

She sprang up as Jacintha finished her dessert, with the look of an arrow ready to fly. 'Now, now,' she said on a gasping note. 'Go—we'll go.'

'Where?' enquired the other easily, with most entire good humour. 'Where are we going?'

The question stopped Mrs Tor dead; it also administered to the companion a thrust of hope. Stop her often enough on one pretext or another and it might work. Lunch had reduced the waiting time to a little over four hours; still an eternity, but if it could be bridged . . . she had now settled on a chain of trip-lines she could use, and furthermore knew in what order she would use them. The old woman's appearance of purpose and hurry, she realized increasingly, was the merest shell; beneath it was a trembling infirmity, some breakdown not far off. *So don't oppose her, not for anything,* she thought. *Keep asking questions, spin it out . . .*

'Where?' echoed Mrs Tor, vacuously. 'Don't . . . don't know . . . decide later!' she blurted. 'Decide on the way, yes . . . on the way.'

'And how did you say we were going?' Jacintha pursued tranquilly. 'By train?'

'Train! No good, no good. A car—we'll have a car.'

'Will it come here? Have you got one?'

'Got a . . . a . . . ?'

'A car,' Jacintha prompted. 'Did you order one?'

'You!' cried Mrs Tor. 'You order—now.'

'All right.'

'And I'll . . . I'll pack.' Evidently she had forgotten all about her morning activities. 'I'll go pack.' With a sort of tottering haste she moved to the stairs and up, saying under her breath, 'Pack now, pack, pack . . .'

In a couple of minutes she was floundering down again, with an effect of being ready to fall at each step. 'All done,' she said breathlessly. 'All done. Have you got a car?'

'Yes, but first you'll want me to go to the bank, won't you?' she queried. 'Have you enough money?'

'Money, money—I've cheques.'

'But you can't give cheques everywhere—'

This was the beginning of a long, incredibly involved argument, all of it accompanied by her own inner refrain, *Another five minutes gone, now another thank God, now another . . .*

'I'll go to the bank,' announced Mrs Tor at the end of the debate. 'Go . . . go now.'

'Yes. Only—'

Quite clear in her mind was one fact: that her employer

163

was not to be allowed on the street alone or accompanied. To prevent it she had one single card more to play, and if it failed . . . . averting her mind from the picture of actual physical compulsion, she played the card. 'And the book, Mrs Tor, what about it? We'll take it along, won't we—your book?'

The first bewilderment on the old lady's face had given way, indistinctly, to partial recollection and understanding. 'The book,' she repeated, her pronunciation increasingly affected. 'Oh yes! I'll go . . . go get it . . . where? Where is it?'

'I'll show you, shall I?' Jacintha began, and was cut off by a strident outcry of *'No!'* As she stood taken aback the other shouted again, 'No! no! Keep your . . . your hands off . . . you've *hidden* it! you've hidden . . . hidden . . .'

'It's on your desk,' said the other carefully, and watched in silence as the figure with its hat on askew, its increasing look of dishevelment and desperation turned about and—at first with some little uncertainty—made for the study.

There followed other blank moments. What to do next would depend on the old lady's reappearance and her frame of mind; wait, that was all, simply wait . . . A very slight sound of the bell, hardly pressed, drew her to the door and the blessed relief of the presence waiting for admittance.

* * *

'What's wrong?' she asked the moment she entered. 'You look like a ghost, you do.'

'She wants to go away,' returned Jacintha in a rapid undertone. 'I've been trying to prevent it. She's wanted to go since yesterday.'

'She's bad then?'

'Worse than I've ever seen her. Mr Kerwin'll be here about six, so if you could stay till he comes—?'

'Oh yes.' Mrs Williams, with her peculiar gift of composure unaffected by her rapidity, had stowed her coat in the closet and come back. 'Where's she now?'

'In the study, getting some notes—' her involuntary jump revealed to herself her degree of tension. 'What was that?'

164

Mrs Williams listened. 'Like as if she's talking,' she diagnosed after a moment. 'Sounds that way, at any—'

'Shhhh!'

Scared rigid with formless misgiving she waited as the sounds came nearer, nearer, as the door was pushed open, as the sounds became loud, hideously loud . . .

The apparition itself smote her with a reeling terror, a momentary blackness in her head. It looked fragmentary, about to disintegrate, with the appearance of being blown about by a strong wind; its eyes brilliant within two circles of chalk, its expression and motions having passed some invisible line that bound it to sanity. 'Where . . . where . . .' it was crying indistinctly, on a note of wild outrage indistinguishable from weeping. 'My book . . . wha' you . . . *do* with it, my book—!'

'Your desk!' shouted Jacintha without intention of shouting; anything, anything, to check this monstrous grief. 'It's on your desk!'

'No! No! *No*—!'

'Go see,' Mrs Williams mouthed quickly. I'll take care of . . .'

As she advanced calmly upon their employer Jacintha slipped from the hall with her legs giving way beneath her, hearing in those furious *No's* the first sound of what could only be called a howl. With a feeling of craven thankfulness mixed with collapse she shut the door between it and herself, yet paused again to realize the new disaster. Full lunacy and its meaning she was totally unarmed to confront, seeing that never in her life had she any experience of it . . . Still weak, yet convinced that the old woman had not known what she was saying, she walked forward quickly and stopped dead as quickly. On the desk were the usual oddments, and except for these was as bare as the back of her hand. She began pulling out drawers, knowing that no drawer would admit anything so bulky as the briefcase, yet if the papers had been taken out of it and stowed away . . . ? Nothing in the drawers; a rapid search of the solitary bookcase was fruitless. Most likely the old girl had taken it up to her room and forgotten; try to search there, also in her luggage if she would allow it . . .

Still casting about she was struck by something new, a changed quality of the silence felt but not yet seen . . . she looked up and with a creeping chill saw Mrs Tor standing in the doorway, regarding her fixedly. At once the chill deepened, spreading through her body in a wave of realization and terror; terror different from the shock of lunacy, for this was the shock of something else. Even while she tried to realign her shaken perceptions, Mrs Tor spoke first.

'It's true,' she said in an unmoved voice, almost conversational. 'They were right. It's true, true, true.'

'Mrs Tor,' she croaked, vacant of what to say further. Not that it mattered; the old woman bore relentlessly on.

'When it happened before . . . and they . . . hinted about it . . . I didn't believe. But now, now . . .' The faintest shiver traversed her. '. . . yes, now I believe. Yes. Now.'

The other, devastated beyond speech, accepted the crowning disaster. By some cruel and wicked paradox the old woman's frenzy, instead of casting her into worse dementia, had knocked her back into cold sanity. *The lightening before death,* the people of two hundred years ago had called this process? Faintly there invaded her the memory of Melbourne's son, retarded all his life and waking to full, sound sense a few hours before his end, and the pen falling from his father's hand to hear him . . . Even as she grappled futilely with these shreds, Mrs Tor took a single step forward. This partly revealed to her Mrs Williams in the background, making urgent gestures. Of this she was hardly aware; all of her was riveted, concentrated, on one sole object.

'They knew,' said Mrs Tor, after taking the step. 'All the while, they *knew.*'

Wouldn't you . . . like to . . . rose in Jacintha's throat, and stopped.

'But I . . . didn't know. They wouldn't tell me, in so many words.' A discordant sound came from her, belatedly recognizable as a laugh. 'Too polite. Much too polite.'

'Mrs Tor,' actually got past Jacintha's lips, for all the good it did her.

'I can even remember—now—the times when I was mad.

166

What I said . . . what I did. It's not clear—but clear enough, enough. So . . . so that's all.' Her inflection on the last word was curious; not of one meaning but of infinite meaning, not of one finality but of total finality. 'It's true and . . . that's that.'

'Please, please,' burst from Jacintha. 'If you'd—if you'd rest—'

'It's all right, you know,' said the old woman, on an accent of surprise. She seemed to waken another degree, and with the wakening to pass into a new degree of clarity. 'It's all right.'

'Don't let anyone,' pursued Mrs Tor, unhearing and implacable, 'tell you differently. You won't, will you?' She fixed Jacintha with an eye suddenly hawklike. 'Will you?'

'No,' faltered the other, with no least idea of what she was agreeing to.

'You promise? . . . *promise* me?'

'Yes.'

'Good girl, then. Good girl. You . . . you were . . .' Her mysterious objective accomplished, the urgency that had kept her vocal and upright had disappeared; once more she was old, failing and terribly shrunken. She put out a faltering hand and administered to Jacintha's wrist—vaguely, clumsily—a quick pat, quickly and clumsily withdrawn. 'Remember!' she warned. 'Remember!' Then with utmost composure, for all her feebleness, she walked toward the door as if it were unobstructed, forcing Mrs Williams to step hastily aside. In silence they watched the small figure, its hat still perched crookedly on its head, mount the stairs slowly, pass the balcony, disappear . . .

'She'll lay down without taking off that hat,' said Mrs Williams. Humour was in the words, but no trace of it in her voice. 'I'll be bound.'

'Her door!' A dire thought started the other, belatedly, toward the stairs. 'What if she locks her door—'

'She won't,' said the peaceful voice. 'Last night I took the key from her door—from every door that had a key in it. She didn't complain about it to you—?'

167

'No.' An immense relief took all the stiffening from her arms and legs. 'Oh thank you.'

The blank that fell between them, Mrs Williams was the first to break.

'I shouldn't wonder if this was a . . .' her cheerful face had gone sober, her voice subdued '. . . a turning point, sort of.'

'How? how d'you mean?' Jacintha murmured, knowing perfectly well what was meant.

'It's like one time when our dad seemed to—to realize all at once—how it was with him, what the end of it must be. And after that he went downhill all in a rush, you might say. As if the—the realizin'—did something to him.' She meditated. 'Yes, this reminds me of him, exactly. Better for him—' she gave a short unamused laugh '—if he'd stayed out of his mind. Kinder.'

'Yes,' muttered Jacintha. 'Oh yes.'

Mrs Williams regarded her in silence for a moment. 'Now see here,' she said persuasively. 'Whyn't you lay down a bit? You've been having a rare old time of it. Go on, lay down awhile before you're dead beat.'

She stood swaying, suddenly dizzy, then asked in a loud voice, 'What time is it?'

'Four, all but.'

'Oh! yes.' The watch on her wrist presented itself suddenly. 'Yes . . .'

'Do,' urged Mrs Williams. 'Have a lay-down.'

'All . . . all right.' A dozen vague fears swam up suddenly. 'And you'll . . . you'll be . . . ?'

'Sitting outside her bedroom door, nor I won't move from there,' the other assured her. 'And I'll look in on her every now and again.'

'But Mrs Williams.' Desperation flared in her weakly for a moment. 'Those papers, where can they be, *where*? I put them on that desk, on that very desk, yesterday afternoon. Didn't you see them there last night, didn't you notice them—?'

'Well no, I didn't, I'd no call to.' Her tone was unmoved, judicial. 'As to who's taken 'em . . .' She paused. 'There's

not all that many people in this house, that you could suspect.'

'No,' she muttered blankly. 'No.'

'The two of 'em used to fight, that's long before you came
here,' pursued Mrs Williams. 'My, how they did go on.' She
paused. 'On the other hand, *she*—' again there was no mis-
taking the inflection '—she's put things away more'n once and
couldn't find 'em again, ever.'

'You never told me that.'

'No, miss, it just didn't come up. If I was wrong, I'm sorry.'
She was imperturbable. 'She'd pretty near tear the house up
looking, she would. Now.' Discarding these old rags of event,
she returned to the present. 'You go stretch out miss, do.
There won't be any trouble for a bit, I'd say.'

'Yes, but if there is—'

'I'll call you, no fear. Now you go an' have a lay-down, take
the weight off your feet, that's right.'

* * *

'What they might do with the old lady,' speculated Mrs
Dowling thoughtfully, 'is cart her off to the loony-bin.'

'Onless she dies,' Anna contributed.

'Die? her? she's tough as old boots. But they're a'most sure
to take her away this time,' the other pursued, 'judging by the
rumpus.'

'There's been other rumpuses, 'fore now.'

'Not so bad as this one,' Mrs Dowling returned. 'The son, he
might take over this side of the house. On'y,' she added with a
sinister inflection, 'he better be damned sure she's not comin'
back.'

'I think it's a shame she's took against him, crazy old bat,'
sniffed Anna. 'Her own son, an' him such a nice fella.'

'Well, we'll see, we'll see. Now about dinner, Cory only
picked at her lunch, an' why waste the lobster casserole? So
you an' me can have that. An' with the lobster . . .' Her voice
had turned self-communing; Anna's heathen darkness, on questions of wine, was better not invoked. '. . . a bottle of Sancerre
I think, with lobster you want somethin' with guts to stand up to

it. An' Cory, she can have whatever I can dig up, if she wants it—cold chicken, or anything.'

* * *

Of sleep there was no question; lying down obediently, with eyes closed or staring at space, there was nothing but trouble and still more trouble. Liz; her letter; her expectation of a speedy return to London; the damaged piano, the old lady's sudden deterioration, the disappearance of the papers; her own rampant suspicions divided between the spiteful laugher on the second floor and the gypsy girl, woman, whatever she was. Then circling back again, Liz, the thought of Liz . . . *Oh God,* she groaned in silent despair, and with a violent motion turned over in bed. If not for Hugh, the thought of Hugh, she would sink, sink without a trace . . . *My love,* she said experimentally, moving her lips without sound, *my sweet, sweet love,* till she remembered the possibility of his anger against her—and remembered too, with a violent start, the old woman's voice cawing *Remember!* that harsh demanding *Remember! . . . What shall I remember?* she asked dazedly of Mrs Tor, of herself, of the silence about her, *Remember what?* as she slid below the level of waking to a lower one, then to one still lower, lower. . . .

She woke with a start and a violent motion of scrambling off the bed, then recollected the state of affairs and lay still for a moment. No sound anywhere, the house so deathly quiet; the daylight was different too, departing with calm, majestic and relentless indifference. . . . She got up and tidied herself. Only after this did it occur to her to look at her watch, and her heart lurched furiously. That late was it, he would be here soon, soon, any moment . . . Cautiously she opened her door, stepped into the hall, and at once was fortified by the sight of Mrs Williams planted four-square in her chair; she had turned on the hall light and was leafing a magazine.

'How is she?' Jacintha mouthed, and for reply the other rose and laid hold of the door-knob with infinite caution. Noiselessly the door opened; Jacintha had one glimpse of the old lady lying there beneath a light coverlet before it closed again. Now

170

Mrs Williams was making signs; together they retreated to the end of the hall.

'I let her get to sleep first,' she murmured low and rapidly. 'Then I went in and took off her hat an' shoes an' covered her up. She'd laid down in her hat, I told you she would do.'

'And she hasn't woken up at all——?'

'Not her. Dead to the world, and a good thing too.' Mrs Williams compressed her lips firmly. 'Let her sleep, miss, that's my advice. When she wakes up she might've forgot everything what's happened. It's likely, going downhill quick the way she is.'

'Yes, I . . . suppose so.'

'And after all, she's only been asleep a couple of hours, that ain't much after what she's been through. So just let her be, even in her clothes,' she concluded robustly. 'It won't do her any harm. Our dad, after he'd had a real bad turn, he'd go off for nine, ten hours. Sleep's the best thing, after those kind of upsets.'

'But have you had anything to eat?'

'I sneaked downstairs just the once and Mrs Dowling gave me a tray to bring back, Anna came for it later on. You wouldn't want tea now, I s'pose?' she pursued interrogatively. 'It's pretty near dinner time.'

'That's all right, I don't think I could eat.'

* * *

She jolted slowly downstairs to wait; only twenty minutes now, more or less . . . settling herself in the hall so as not to lose a moment of his coming, she retreated into blankness and sat in its comfort a few moments. Then, angrily, she forced herself out of it to face what had to be faced, to walk the inexorable treadmill . . . She took the letter from her pocket and again read and reread it, the phrases urgent but full of expectation above all, absolutely assured expectation . . .

There escaped her an unconscious laugh, slightly hysterical. She was penned; penned in shameful, ignoble calculation. The first glimpse of Hugh would be enough; whether his feeling for her had survived the tale of her omissions, her deathly, fatal

171

suppressions . . . yes, one look at his face would tell her. And if its message were of rejection, she would need Liz. Liz and the job, how bitterly she would need them; at all costs she must keep this resource in view if the other failed her . . .

She started, her head suddenly raised toward the stairs; anything, was there . . . ? After a moment it seemed not, but her current of thought had been jolted back to Mrs Tor asleep, Mrs Tor in her stunned, exhausted sleep. *Don't let anyone tell you differently. Remember, remember* . . . valedictory somehow, a desolate goodbye without goodbye being said . . . Sighing, giving it up, her eye fell on her watch. Twenty past six. Six at the latest, he had said. What if the old lady woke up now, again started her clamour to leave the house . . .

'He's not come yet?' queried Mrs Williams softly and urgently from the balcony. As the other shook her head she pursued, 'I'll have to be getting back, you know.'

'Is she . . . still asleep?'

'Oh yes.'

'Well, but could you wait,' she implored. 'Just a few minutes more? If Mr Kerwin hasn't come by then, I'll have to think of something.'

As Mrs Williams nodded and withdrew—*think of something, think,* began beating in her head. Think of what, of whom . . . ? If Hugh failed to turn up, and soon, there was only left the person whom she rejected as soon as she thought of him. . . .

The sound had escaped her; only on its repetition did she start up and go toward the door, toward the repeated knocking on it, soft and discreet. Before she found a word, in her disorganized state, he had somehow come in, asking, 'Is she about?' His voice was hushed, hurried, half appeasing. 'Nearby?'

'No,' she said automatically, her resistances just beginning to form; once more he cut her off on the same hurried, apologetic note. 'Quickly, we've no time to waste,' gently eased the door from her hand and shut it, then asked again—still with a gentleness that made no secret of its urgency—'Where is she?'

'Asleep,' she answered, for all her resolve to answer nothing.

172

'Quickly then,' he urged. 'What's been happening?'

Her pause was a welter of urgency and conflict. Hugh, suppose Hugh failed to come after all; suppose there were a sudden waking upstairs, sudden uncontrollable violence . . . Mrs Williams was anxious to go, this visitor would then be the only prospect of help she had, she must not antagonize nor send him packing too promptly . . .

'How'd you happen to come here?' she asked, to gain time. 'Just now?'

'Well.' The question had deflected him for a moment. 'It's been my habit to drop in now and again, for a long time now.' *Long before you came here,* she heard, yet felt nothing abrasive in his inflection, nothing at all.

'Especially when I haven't seen her for any extended period,' he was continuing. 'Only repetition of an old habit.'

'Oh,' she said half ashamed, trying to recall whether, in her own question, there had been any abrasiveness.

'Something's been happening.' He did not ask but stated it, watching her keenly. 'You've had trouble.'

'Yes.' All at once resistance, the will to dissimulate, ran out of her completely. 'We . . . we've had . . . a little.'

He did not say *Tell me:* it was unnecessary.

'It began with—with the piano.' His gaze alone drew it from her with the compulsion of a magnet. 'Someone . . . destroyed it.'

'Destroyed—?'

'Poured glue in it.'

His start, his half-smothered ejaculation, delayed his question for a half-second only. 'And you know who's responsible, don't you?'

'Well, I thought . . . Mary?'

'Mary? Mary Pargill?' The first *Mary* had been incredulous, the second pitying. 'Now Jacintha, let's not—' He stopped. 'Was there anything else?'

'She's been upset.' His compulsion was still upon her. 'Some papers were lost. I mean, they were here yesterday and today they aren't.'

'Mh'm.' His tone, reflective, woke up rapidly and cast off

reflection. 'Jacintha, look: all this means, to anyone who knows her, that her condition has deteriorated and is redeteriorating —badly, it seems, and rather rapidly.'

She was silent, with her first opposition reviving again, yet faintly.

'Has she ever, recently,' he was asking, 'expressed a fear of this house? said she wanted to leave it?'

Impossible to dodge this; reluctantly she answered, 'Yes.'

'Another old story.' He pondered while she watched him with something growing and growing in her, something indefinable, guarded . . .

'Now my dear girl,' he was saying.

In her spoke a sudden, silent voice, *I'm not your dear girl.*

'I advise you to leave this to me,' he had continued. 'I'll wait for a bit, now, till she wakes up, then I'll have a little talk with her. Don't worry about it—everything will be taken care of.'

Still silent before his positive and conclusive manner she felt, joined to her opposition—now fully formed—a grim amusement. What was he proposing, suggesting to her . . . ?

'When you say "everything'll be taken care of,"' she murmured, 'just what do you mean by that?'

'Mean by that—?' He was pulled up short; now his way of speaking, markedly more careful, denoted an abrupt cognizance of possible resistance. 'Well, I mean that whatever procedure is followed, it would be in accordance with Mrs Tor's own wishes.' He stopped a moment, then added, 'At this stage.'

'Oh?' she queried cryptically, blandly.

'*At this stage.*' His voice, though lowered, had no less emphasis. 'Consulting her own preferences is still possible, I imagine.' He stopped again. 'Later on—to judge by your account —it may not be possible.' Another pause. 'I should like to spare you, or anyone else concerned, the sight of a forcible removal. Because it'll come to that.' He gave it the force of imponderable truth. 'Sooner or later.'

Not in Hugh's absence, she told him without speaking, *and you can depend on it, chum,* then said aloud, 'How would Hugh feel—about his mother's being removed while he's away?'

174

'Hugh?' His slighting repetition of the name even had an amusement in it. 'If Mrs Tor leaves by her own desire and with her own consent, Hugh's feelings are neither here nor there.'

'I see,' she murmured, deliberately luring him on. 'It wouldn't take much to persuade her—she'd agree to go quite easily, I think.'

'*There's* a sensible girl!' The approval in his voice did not conceal a shade of jubilation. 'Now why not just see if she's awake, Jacintha? If I could see her now—'

'No,' she interrupted, her voice very low and shaking. 'You won't see her now, you'll see her in Hugh's presence. It's the only way you'll see her—that is, if it depends on me.' Too roused to enjoy his look of having something flung in his face, she bore on with pleasurable anger. 'And I take exception, the very greatest exception, to your asking me to help you in such a plan behind Hugh's back. The meanness—!' It broke from her on a higher note, instantly caught back. 'To suggest any— any such doings—when Hugh's too far away to say anything, much less do—'

'Far?' he tried to interpose; she trampled him down.

'—and to suggest that I'd be a p-party—' she was breathless '—to any such goings-on, b-behind Hugh's back—!'

The rush of her denunciation had completely obscured the new development, the sound of the key in the lock. Yet almost without a pause—in a high sweet voice, now hardly stammering at all—she said to the new presence among them, 'Hugh! Mr Dennison came to discuss taking your mother away.'

XIII

The newcomer's face, after his first perplexity and surprise, at once became expressionless; from expressionless, it became grim. At the same moment, the urgency in the other man's look was wiped out and replaced by a blankness, but a *minatory* blankness; though he did not glance at her, even, she felt how she had become his enemy. For a longish moment there was silence, till Hugh said finally, 'You've plans then, John?' His voice was as polite as ominous. 'For taking mother away?'

'Miss Cory has . . . ah . . . perhaps misunderstood me,' the solicitor replied impassively, with no perceptible hesitation. 'I was discussing probabilities, rather than making suggestions.'

A lie, she thought, yet not exactly . . . ahead of her fiery yet unformed wish to challenge it, Hugh had said, 'I'd only like to know one thing. Was any of this—what you were discussing—supposed to take place in my absence?'

'Not necessarily,' said the other, a form of answer that brought *Liar!* to her lips, only she dared not say it.

'But from previous experience of your mother's condition, more than one experience let me tell you,' the solicitor was continuing, 'I was trying to look forward a little, suggest how to provide for emergency. That's reasonable, isn't it?' he asked so smoothly that the mockery in it was problematical. 'Fairly unexceptionable, shouldn't you say?'

'You talked about an immediate removal,' she broke in, unable to keep still another moment. 'A *forcible* removal—!'

'Only in extremest emergency—'

'I've been *fighting* to keep her here!' she cried, rounding on Hugh. 'Hanging on by my fingernails, it's been desperate! And then he came without being asked, he's been talking and talking about her leaving here—'

'Ah.' Hugh cut her off with the syllable, his eyes nailing the other man; in his slight dangerous smile was complete, if belated, understanding. 'You came on your own, did you? Harassed Miss Cory, talked her down—?'

'I discussed possibilities,' returned the solicitor, again imperturbable. 'In view of the situation—'

'Also, since it seems you're not here by invitation,' Hugh cut him off, 'may I ask why you're here at all?'

The question imposed a check, a complete silence. At the end of it Dennison shrugged, smiled slightly, and straightened in a movement of obvious departure. Yet his attention, previously nailed to his more immediate antagonist, again returned to her, then all at once included both of them; his eyes continued to bracket them together, while his very faint smile deepened balefully.

'Ah yes, a charming picture,' he murmured, and raised his eyebrows. 'But not likely to find favour with—' He cut himself off with a look of withdrawal, at once resuming his air of composure, even of ascendancy. 'Good night,' he said politely, and walked out.

* * *

A silence followed, empty with the emptiness left after acrid collision; in its taint, still on the air, neither of them seemed to breathe. Then simultaneously they had turned, with an imminence slight yet violent, were about to move toward each-other . . .

'Miss Cory,' called a voice, soft yet pressing; during the immobility with which it had again transfixed them, its owner had crossed the landing and begun to descend. 'Sorry, I'm very sorry,' she was apologizing. 'But I—'

'Mrs Williams.' Hugh had gone at once to meet her with his hand out. 'You've both been having a bad time of it, haven't you? How can I thank you for standing by Miss Cory?'

'Why, that's all right, Mr Kerwin, glad to oblige,' she answered with her usual composure, and turned at once to Jacintha. 'Miss Cory, I'd better be going now—'

'Of course, of course,' she interrupted fervently. 'And thank you so much for standing by, your husband must be worried.'

'Well, not all that worried, he knows about this job. But if you think you can manage now, without me—'

'I'm here now, Mrs Williams,' Hugh put in. 'I'll be taking over—let Miss Cory rest a bit.'

'She's had the worst of it,' said Mrs Williams unexpectedly. 'The very worst.'

'I know, I know. You're a couple of heroines, that's what.'

His voice, the mere sound of it; reassurance, salvation, a dispeller of terrors . . .

'I looked at her last a few minutes ago, sir,' Mrs Williams was saying. 'Shall I . . .'

All at once the words were coming to her as if from a vast distance, alternately fading away, coming back, fading again . . . dazedly she strove to follow them.

'. . . take a last peep at her, if you like—?'

'No, no, you cut along . . . I'll rush up now . . . have a look, and if there's anything . . .'

How strange, the voices dying out and returning, strange . . .

'Miss Cory.' That was Mrs Williams; she was alone with Mrs Williams, how odd, where could Hugh have got to . . . 'You'd better sit down,' someone's voice was continuing, 'don't you think . . . ?'

Deaf, stupid, she swayed a little but kept her feet.

'It's all right.' Another voice, Oh yes, Hugh's; she had somehow missed his return. 'She's asleep. 'But Mrs Williams . . . possibly come back tonight? Miss Cory's in no condition . . . and I'm . . . pretty ignorant, so if . . .'

The rest of it was receding again; dimly she caught, 'Well, yes sir . . . do that . . .' then a door opening somewhere, closing. . . .

178

'Cintha?' The voice had come close to her, gentle, hesitant. 'Cintha?' In the fog that was closing about her she somehow knew he had put out his hands uncertainly, beseechingly; after an instant she fell against him, literally, feeling his arms tighten as he held her up. He began kissing her almost fearfully, gentlest feathery kisses that drew her out of the daze of fatigue, out of the fear of his displeasure, out of the threatened nightmare of his estrangement. She began returning his kisses and in that moment the miracle happened, the fusion of lips and arms became electric and incandescent, unbearable; she had entered—and knew herself to have entered—into a land foreign to her, foreign and terrifyingly unknown. What had this to do with what she had called affairs, passing attractions, yieldings to flattery, ways of killing time? In this single consuming flash, in submission at once despairing and exultant she yielded up will and identity, happy to be nothing and have nothing except in this one person, this one, single being . . .

'Cintha,' came a harsh whisper. 'Come to me. Come to bed with me, sweet. Now, now . . .'

With no will but his, she tightened her clasp on him. Or at least thought she did, it was very strange but the cloud had returned, it was carrying her away, away . . . She returned, aware of lying on the couch; through the pleasant semi-fog Hugh was there, indefinably busy somewhere out of sight; she felt a wetness on her temples, drops running down into her neck . . . 'What?' she murmured half-wittedly. 'What is it . . . ?'

'You keeled over.' He was still applying a wet cloth to her forehead. 'Lie still now.'

Wrapped in the agreeable haze she closed her eyes again, ministered to by him; lovely, lovely . . .

'I thought you were through with me,' she said in a loud unfocussed voice.

'In God's name, why?'

'I didn't tell you . . . about that . . . that suicide thing . . .'

'Hush. I let you in for too much, too brutally much. I ought to be kicked.'

179

He was not angry with her, not angry; she began closing her eyes.

'Look, sweet.' He was bending toward her. 'You'd better go to bed—'

'The book,' she interrupted, again in that loud uncontrolled voice. 'Your mother's book, her—'

'What?' he asked, obviously nonplussed, then remembered. 'Oh yes, what about it?'

'Gone. It . . . someone took . . . took it . . .'

'Took it! But who—' suddenly his look was of grimmest understanding. 'Ah, yes.'

The conviction in his voice had the unforeseen effect of rousing her from her lethargy. 'You mean . . . Mary?' she asked on a wavering accent. 'D'you think so, really . . . ?'

'Who else?' Angry, his concern for her seemed to vanish momentarily. 'Who else in this house? First the piano, now these notes for the book or whatever they are?' On his good-natured face was a look she had never seen before. 'Well, as things are now . . .'

She waited; when the silence became too ominous . . .

'What?' she asked fearfully. 'What do you mean?'

'I mean, maybe I'll have a free hand at last. And if I do—' an unfamiliar cruelty hardened and tightened his features '—she'll be out of this house before she'll know what's happened.'

'But what'll she do?' It broke from her independent of will and thought. 'What'll become of her?'

'Who cares? She'll do all right on what she's saved.'

'But she won't, Hugh, she's got nothing—'

'Who told you that?'

'She did.'

'Pah! My love, don't be the complete mug, mother paid her well for years—'

'No!' What perversity was driving her to argue with him over a repulsive and mischievous old woman, she could not imagine. 'She hasn't a penny, she—'

'Cintha.' He was gentle again, suddenly. 'We'll save it for later, shall we?' In his mastered annoyance he looked so hand-

180

some, so dominating, that her heart bowed before him again, with the accomplished submissiveness of a slave. 'H'm?' he was asking. He took both her hands and kissed them, then bent and put his lips to hers for a long moment; not with passion, only with utmost gentleness. Beneath this healing touch her resistance faded away, she closed her eyes once more and lay drifting in peace, heavenly peace, happiness . . .

'Shall I carry you to bed?' he whispered.

'I'll carry myself, thanks.' Having crawled before him in her mind, and not used to crawling, she repossessed herself a little, even with a show of asperity. 'I'll just lie here a little . . . while . . .'

'All right. I'd better put the car away, my traps are still in it.'

'Yes,' she murmured. Again she was drifting, drifting. 'Yes . . .'

* * *

An interval, timeless. He had gone, why . . . ? Oh yes, his car, put it away . . . Her success in remembering this seemed —strangely—to jolt her a little from her lethargy, to waken her a trifle to . . . to remembrance? No, not remembrance, it was *failure* of remembrance; something she had heard or seen that she could not bring back, more than one thing? Recent or long ago? She stirred impatiently, and as if the small movement had had some power to unlock, all at once she saw, with piercing and painful distinctness, Hugh advancing through the crowded bar of the Wheatsheaf, Hugh with his hand on the girl's arm, the tall handsome girl . . . at the same moment she saw and heard Dennison's farewell of only moments ago, the mocking look that joined her with Hugh, the parting innuendo, *A charming picture . . . not likely to find favour. . . .*

A weight fell so heavily across her heart that it wiped out everything else, the other forgotten thing if there were one. *I must ask him,* revolved in her like a deathly sickness, *Must ask him, must . . .* The sickness took her under again like lead, she floated like a corpse beneath brackish water, then woke vaguely to sounds, to a presence . . . he was standing there, looking down at her.

'Hugh,' she said at once. Her voice came back to her loud and unclear. 'Hugh, that girl I saw you with—'

'Who? what girl?'

'At the—the inn. Tall and . . . and beautiful, blonde . . .'

'Oh.' Recollection was in his face. 'What about her?'

'I only mean—if you've someone else—tell me now, at once, I—I—'

'Fool.' He had gone on his knees and pulled her against him. 'My God, you fool.'

'—no, no, but I mean—if you're just amusing yourself with me, I couldn't—I couldn't bear—'

He silenced her, again putting his lips to hers in one of those long gentle caresses. 'Are you telling me,' he asked finally, 'that *you've* never kissed anyone? slept with anyone?'

'No. But I—but I—'

'I'm over thirty.' A hard gleam of mockery, uncharacteristic, showed for a moment. 'And so what?'

'Sorry . . .'

'I should damned well hope so.'

'—I'm so *sorry*—'

'Shut up,' he said ruthlessly. 'Or I'll beat you. And by the way, this blonde siren of yours, she's been married recently, or so I hear.'

'Oh.'

'And now you *are* going to bed, whether you like it or—' he stopped suddenly at the sound, released her and went to the door. 'Ah, Mrs Williams, this is very good of you.'

'That's all right, sir.'

Curious how the atmosphere changed with the entrance of that invincibly tranquil and sensible figure. Mrs Williams now vanished into the cloak-room, returned, and asked, 'How has everything been, sir? all right?'

'Absolutely all right.'

'You've been up? looked at her?'

'Twice. I didn't go in, I was afraid of waking her up,' he explained. 'Just peeped in, for just a moment.'

'Oh.' Mrs Williams had turned thoughtful. 'Well, I'd better get her undressed and properly put to bed. She won't like it, but laying all night in your day clothes, not much comfort in it.'

'Just as you say, Mrs Williams,' he returned submissively.

'Oh.' Mrs Williams had taken a step toward the stairs, then stopped. 'If it turns out there'll be trouble, d'you feel well enough, Miss Cory—'

'Of course.' Jacintha, as if galvanized, sat up. 'Of course I'll help you. No, no—' peremptorily she drowned Hugh's objection '—I'm perfectly all right now. Tell you what, Mrs Williams, I'll go up with you now and—'

'No, you stay quiet.' The two women, banded together in the nursing instinct, had excluded the male from their conference. 'I'll leave her door open and call if there's need— you'll hear me all right.'

* * *

She was alone again, still lying on the sofa. *Just finish up next door,* Hugh's voice floated vaguely in her mind, *be back in two two's.* Sighing deeply, she lay divided between listening for Mrs Williams's possible summons and a longing to sink again into darkness, down, down . . . an obstacle prevented her, some indefinable interference. *That thing I was trying to remember,* came back to her suddenly, *that other thing, what was it?* The growing conviction that it was important rowelled her. *What was it, what was it . . .* her inability to bring it back, maddening, plowed and woke her up another degree. *Something else, there was something else . . .*

'Miss Cory!' The voice from overhead brought her twisting about and up, before she had time to define its quality.

'Miss Cory, ring the doctor,' Mrs Williams continued rapidly. 'Quick, there's something wrong up here.'

'Yes, yes . . .' making for the phone, she threw over her shoulder, 'W-which doctor, whom shall I—'

'Oh Lord, she's had a string of 'em. Dr Wallace, try him.'

Cintha, with shaking hands, was already leafing the address book.

'No, bring me some brandy first, quick—'

She had no memory of tearing upstairs with a bottle, tearing downstairs to the phone, no memory of hearing the key in the lock. In a gabble of words she had thrust the responsibility of the call upon him, before scudding wildly into the kitchen to make strong black coffee, the second command of Mrs. Williams.

XIV

Morning, it must be morning; she could feel light past her closed eyes. She opened them, and simultaneously remembrance, striking her like a club, immobilized her. With vacant look and half-open mouth she stared past the present day into the past night, grotesque and hideous and not quite distinct. Hugh and Mrs Williams striving with the inert body, lifting, turning; liquid being poured into its sagging mouth and spilling out again, the limbs highly relaxed, the eyes in a constant half-closure scarcely to be maintained by living eyes; above all Mrs Tor's incredible lack of objection to the liberties they were taking and the indignities they were forcing upon her. Still the two of them laboured, still they strove and rubbed and pummelled, and still Mrs Tor responded to their efforts with that indifference not distinguishable from mockery, *contemptuous* mockery . . . Thank God she had been employed in humbler tasks, getting this, fetching that, she had been spared touching the . . . the body . . .

The doctor too, the presence suddenly among them, not that she would know him again . . . then after awhile the figure on the bed with covers drawn up over its face, then all of them herded from the room; again by some progression that escaped her, they were all in the downstairs hall. Someone was making phone calls, more than one, then they were waiting . . . During this waiting the doctor, still the doctor, had asked them abrupt questions, unimportant; the real questioning was yet to come, she remembered thinking. Also she had had the impression, or had it now, that he was one of those medical men dismissed with contumely by Mrs Tor, and was not grateful for being pulled in on this final stage of her journey . . .

The shock of two police officers suddenly among them lanced her reminiscently; if her life depended on it she would not know them again, either. What she did remember was her awareness, her new knowledge—like a hard blow—that your house was yours under certain circumstances only; let those circumstances be broken and strangers could come in, tramp upstairs and down, conduct inquisitions into your utmost privacies . . . The doctor seemed missing from this part of it, apparently he had gone. Then all of them summoned in turn to be questioned, then Hugh—his face drawn and shocked—sending her peremptorily to bed. And long after she was there her awareness, hazy, that movement still went on in the house, broken movement somewhere, somewhere . . .

She pulled herself out of bed, in dull surprise that her joints were not creaking; mechanically dressed, mechanically descended in the silent house. At the foot of the stairs Mrs Dowling, obviously on the lookout, came to meet her.

'Oh, Miss Cory,' she mourned, her voice unnaturally low, 'Oh, ain't it terrible.'

Jacintha nodded.

'Them pills,' the other pursued. 'Nasty things.'

'Yes.'

'And people taking too many by accident, tch—!'

'I shouldn't wonder.' Let it rest at this version. 'Mrs Dowling—'

'Yes?' The other was all respectful solicitude. 'Yes, miss?'

'—I wonder, could you plan to stay on here? I mean, till Mr Kerwin's decided what he'll do?'

'Oh yes ma'am, and anyway—' fruity expectation was in her voice '—we couldn't none of us just walk out, could we now? I mean, with the coroner and all—?'

186

'Oh.' She gaped at Mrs Dowling. 'Do you know, I'd forgotten that.'

'Naturally, ma'am, you're too shook up, but we'll all be called as witnesses, won't we?'

'You're right, of course you're right.' A stray fragment from her shaken universe touched her. 'And could you—just for a while—see that Miss Pargill gets her trays?'

'Don't you worry, madam, we'll see to that. Now you come and have breakfast, you'll feel better with something inside you.' She bustled off.

* * *

Still there was something else, the thing hidden from her by last night's exhaustion, the thing in her half-dream defining itself now, only now. The footsteps, irrhythmic shuffling of stretcher-bearers negotiating stairs, balcony corners, stairs again; Mrs Tor departing from her house . . . A strange recollection struck her, not thought of for years; the memoirs of an ambassadress, over a century ago, viewing the Hapsburg tombs in the Capuchin Church in Vienna and curious to examine the tops of their catafalques; demanding a chair, swarming up, and seeing—to her astonishment—the sculptured cadavers of the dead royalties below, the naked bodies stripped of earthly pomp with the scars of embalmment undisguised, and upon those scars—minutely, exquisitely executed in marble—the fine stitches that held them together. Mrs Tor leaving her house for the last time with the privacies and reserves of her body about to be cut apart, scrutinized . . . with the cruelest pang she recalled her reassuring, even affectionate gesture, clumsy . . . And now Mrs Dowling had appeared in the dining-room door in summons sober, respectful and lugubrious, suited to the occasion.

* * *

'Does she know anythin'?' Anna demanded hungrily.

'No more'n what I already heard,' responded Mrs Dowling. 'Old girl took a big dose of something or other.'

'By accident, did she say?'

'She didn't, I don't reckon any of 'em knows, yet.'

'Listen, Mag.' Anna's voice was abrupt with initiative, a rare thing with her. 'All this coroner's thing you been talking about —let's get out o' here.'

'Get out! What for?'

'I don' know, I don't like it—'

'We can't go if we want,' the other informed her loftily. 'The police won't let us, we'll have to be goin' to the coroner's court an' testify—'

'Ooh *no!* I couldn'—'

'Shut up, such a juggins I never did see. Of course we'll go, it's nothin to do with us reely. Golly, what larks, I wouldn' miss it for anything.'

'Well.' Anna was unconvinced. 'Then let's go right after, shall we?'

'My God, talk about stupid. Look, the son'll get married, won't he? What'll you bet?' She gave her a look, intensely significant. 'He'll ask us to stop with them, you see if he don't.'

'Who'll he marry?' asked Anna with bated breath. 'The Lor' Lieutenant's daughter?' Both women always had, in shortest order, an unfailing grip of any titles in the immediate neighbourhood. 'Her?'

'If not her, then another.' Mrs Dowling spoke abstractedly. ' 'T'wouldn't surprise me neither if he'd been sleeping with Cory.'

'Ooh! how'd you know?'

'Never mind, and just you keep your mouth shut,' said Mrs Dowling cruelly. 'But leave *now?* Wild horses wouldn't drag me.'

* * *

Feeling a little better for coffee and toast, now she was passive; merely passive, waiting . . . The key in the outer door woke her a little, the sight of him moving toward her woke her still more; the feeling of being held very gently, kissed very gently, began reviving and healing her . . .

'How are you?' he began, then—having released her a little too abruptly—had to take her arm, saying, 'Steady there!' He smiled at her, yet the smile (she realized later) was abstracted. 'Just looked in for a moment,' he explained. 'A hundred things to see to, be back later—' already turning toward the door he paused abruptly, hesitated, then demanded, 'Tell me, did mother ever say anything to you about a—'

'What?' she hazarded; he had stopped as suddenly as he had begun.

'Oh nothing, nothing, it'll probably turn up . . . see you, sweet.' He had gone hastily toward the door and out.

On a sudden impulse, after a moment, she followed him outside. Already he was in his car, and having started it made a furious full circle—reckless, considering the narrow road and the amount of traffic on it—then straightened skilfully and swept away without noticing that she stood there at the front gate.

A moment of let-down followed. It would have been nice if he had not been so absorbed in making the turn, if he had waved at her . . . And by the way, was he always such a reckless driver? She had never been in a car with him. Never been in bed with him either . . . a half-smile touched her lips. It would come, everything would come . . . She lingered at the gate, waking enough from her dream to note for the first time the quality of the morning, the most exquisite May morning. After the unfriendly spring this sudden warmth, this pouring sunlight that would be actually hot if not for the ceaseless moving air that leavened it . . . enveloped, restored, she stood half drowsing, turning her head this way and that, letting the warmth and the coolness stroke her in delicious alternation . . .

The far-away sound, ominous at all times and not less ominous with distance, startled her awake and staring toward the village centre. The violent screech of brakes, even if diminished; the *crump,* the instant of stillness . . . Already she could sense rather than hear an uproar, could see one or two running figures and nothing else, thank God, it was all out of sight except for the outer edges of the tumult. A life or lives, perhaps shattered by catastrophe; frightful, too frightful . . . Well, these things happened and what was one to do. Again with closed eyes she turned her face to the sun, basking and immune with a security that hardly let in the sound of rapid footsteps approaching, tranced with a happiness that was pierced only by the sound of Mrs Williams's voice lamenting, 'Oh, Miss Cory! Oh Miss Cory, isn't it terrible, isn't it *terrible?*'

* * *

She stared like an idiot; the other continued pouring out broken phrases, '—a big lorry—and not his fault, Mr Kerwin's I'm afraid—the light against him, he'd just started going through it—a fast driver and known for it, I heard that much—'

Her insides cold and dissolving, her legs turning to water, she continued to hold on to the gatepost; hearing what was said but as if from a next room, with the door closed between them.

'—the shock when I realized who 'twas, my, what a shock—' The ruinous recital halted suddenly; Mrs Williams appeared not only to regain self-control but to realize, belatedly, the devastation before her.

'Come, let's go in,' she said briskly. 'Come now.' She had to pry stiffened hands from the gatepost, needing considerable effort to do it. 'Come along now, I'll help you.' She supported the sagging burden up the path, again needing all her strength. 'Too bad, the shock last night and now this. Don't trip now, that's it, that's fine.' She half lifted the puppet over the threshold and managed to get it to a chair before it fell on the floor. 'There we are, fine, that's fine . . .' a blank fell, a glass of water was at her lips, the kindly monologue was going on and on. 'My, you're cold.' Her hands were being chafed. 'And your teeth chattering, my goodness, let's get you a hot-water bottle.'

Through a mist, and with that resilience forever mysterious, the remnant in the chair was fighting its way out of collapse and becoming, if not an entity, the ghost of one.

'I'm . . . all righ',' it croaked. 'Don' . . . want lie down. Thank you, no more . . . water, I'm . . . all right, I'm fine. Thank you ver' . . . very much.'

Mrs Williams, palpably unconvinced by the declarations of

190

well-being, continued to stand with a tumbler of water at the ready.

'Is he . . .' appealed the remnant. 'Is he . . . badly hurt? I mean, did you *see* . . . ?'

'No more'n I could help,' said Mrs Williams with strong distaste. 'I just fought my way through the crowd, I didn't want to look. Bless me, how people do gather for something ugly like that, I never!'

'So you don't know . . . at all? Where . . . where he is . . . ?'

'Oh, he'll be at Cottage Memorial,' said the other, with the assurance of indigenous knowledge. 'Just a mile down the road. Lucky for him it's so near, other places he might of had to be driven ten, twelve miles with that awful siren going.'

'Please,' Cintha implored huskily. 'Please ring them . . . find out . . .'

'Oh Miss Cory, not yet.'

At once, on the protest, the atmosphere changed. The elder, solicitous for a stricken fellow being, now expressed in silence an intensified compassion, albeit a little awkwardly; Cintha, seeing her remember that earlier interrupted gesture, the kiss imminent if not accomplished, had no time to care one way or another. 'But couldn't we,' she entreated, 'just ask—'

'They won't have finished examining him yet, not near,' her companion objected gently. 'Anyways, you know *them*—hate giving out information, 'cept it's family. Now Miss Cory, why don't you lay down just a—'

'No, no,' she gasped. 'I couldn't. I'm all right really, I'm quite all right.'

'But shan't I get you some tea, a nice—'

'No, nothing. You have some though, you're pretty pale.'

You should see yourself, thought Mrs Williams, while admitting, 'Well, I am a bit shook up.'

'Of course. Have tea, take your time over it.'

'Well, thank you. Then afterwards, there's nothing I could busy myself with, and—I mean, you'll be paying me for doing nothing, and I don't like—'

'Don't go!' The mere thought of it jolted her not only awake, but into near-panic. *'Please* don't, you don't know what a comfort—and anyway—there may be things to do, all sorts of things,' she babbled incoherently. 'We don't know yet.'

'I s'pose not,' said Mrs Williams, with more indulgence than agreement. 'That may be. Then I'll ask Mrs Dowling for a cuppa, shall I, and meanwhile you take it easy.'

* * *

Ability to get to her feet was a great thing, ability to stand without falling on her face a greater; she wavered a moment then took a feeble step, another, and by their combined feebleness was gaining on the front door . . . something puzzled her, a livid flash somewhere to her side; she took a step backward and saw it again, her own chalky face in a mirror, her expression vacant.

In the street, unsteady on her pins, righting herself occasionally without knowing it, she was—again without knowing it—engrossed with annihilation. The end, by various names; the finish, all over. One moment you had everything, the next moment nothing. She was absorbed, taken up and swallowed, by the strangeness of bankruptcy, unaware that this was preparation: preparation to have nothing, to accept nothing, to endure and survive having nothing, nothing, nothing. When she passed the junction of roads where she knew the accident must have happened she averted her head, unaware that the traces had been cleared away and cars were flashing up and down merrily in the sun. The world could come to an end, yet people were walking up and down enjoying the delicious air, warm yet cool . . . A mile to the hospital, Mrs Williams had said? A terrifying distance to crawl with spinning head and watery limbs, terrifying . . . At least no one would stop her with questions, she knew hardly anyone . . .

The hospital became, as she had known vaguely it would become, a battleground. The coolness of the entrance must have revived her; she held out against the reception-nurse, strenuously uninformative behind her desk, she was prepared to hold out till Doomsday. The nurse, having expended her utmost powers of waspishness and repulse, was driven at last to leave her desk and seek reinforcements. These arrived in the person of a tall formidable woman, her starched garments rattling like a dinosaur's armour. No one seeing the type, in fullest flower of offensiveness frequent among the English nursing hierarchy, would take it for the same person when it was cringing before an eminent specialist. This one initiated proceedings by demanding metallically, 'Who are you?' and continued, on having been answered, 'But surely you know that no information of this sort's given out, except to the patient's immediate family? *Are* you of Mr Kerwin's family?'

'No, but—'

'*Any* relation, then?'

'N-no—'

'No relation at all?' Swiftly the woman had cut off her wavering attempts, and now gathered herself for denunciation. 'Then by what right do you come bursting into a hospital and creating a disturbance? How *dare* you? Waste the receptionist's time and force her to call me and waste *my* time, d'you suppose I've nothing better to do? Are you the only person in the world that's got someone sick? Now be off with you immediately, or else I'll—'

'Please, please,' Cintha besought against the fusillade; its insolence, its arrogance, passed over her unheard. 'We're marrying, we—'

A pause fell among them like a flung stone; a silence heavy with unknown ingredients, except for the stupefaction in it.

'—we were going to marry,' she continued pleading. 'So if you could just tell me, Sister—'

'Matron,' snapped the other. Still bound fast by whatever it was, she reacted equally fast about rank.

'—Matron. So if you'd—if you'd . . .'

The woman's manner had changed very much, yet enigmatically; a sort of concession, restrained by a sort of wariness, was the best one could call it.

'I see,' she observed finally. An uninvolved spectator might have divined how strenuously she and the other nurse avoided glancing at eachother. 'Well, you understand I'm taking your word for this?'

Cintha, not breathing, nodded.

'Mr Kerwin was lucky,' the other continued in measured tones, obviously against her professional inclinations. 'The empty seat alongside saved him from the worst of it. His left shoulder and left arm are broken and his left temple and cheekbone are badly bruised. That amounts to very little, he's a strong youngish man.' She paused. 'There is, however, a degree of concussion. We'll know more about it when he regains consciousness.' She paused again, with a pleasure—genuinely not suspected by herself—in airing her knowledge and keeping people on the rack. 'Which he should do, within twenty-four hours.'

After the mendicant had thanked her and wavered through the revolving door, the matron turned her head slowly. She made big eyes at the nurse, who made big eyes back. The matron then spread her hands slightly; the nurse replied with lifted eyebrows, also the ghost of a shrug.

* * *

The world that had become fragments, meaningless and obscene, reassembled itself to some degree. Once more it was possible to walk without danger of falling, to breathe without fighting for breath, possible even to admit thoughts of the future unclouded by total despair. The sun's warmth flowed into her and strengthened her for the hardships ahead; she began, in concrete terms, to face them. A broken shoulder and broken arm, to begin with; he would be incapacitated for weeks. Then the concussion . . . how much of the truth had she been told about this? Concussion was unpredictable, or so she had heard somewhere. And with concussion came ravages of shock, also unpredictable; able to kill without leaving a sign of injury on its victim, opening dread lesions far below the surface. Or from a victim who had lived, who knew what dire resurrections might surge, years later . . . ?

One thing was plain. He would be dependent on help when

he came out, as never before in his life; tireless help reinforced by love, the sort that no money could buy. At the thought a high resolution and courage lifted her heart. When she got to the house she would ring Liz at once, she would stand firm against the outcry of disappointment, anger, abuse. He would need her; to that need everything else must give way . . . her strengthless walk had changed unrecognizably; she was now moving at almost her normal pace. Call Liz at once, get the few bad moments over with while this imperious strength upheld her. She let herself into the house quickly, a different person from the one who had left it; strong with the thought of his need, strong with the thought of herself ministering to that need.

* * *

She faltered at sight of the man in a hall chair, who rose as she entered.

'Good morning, Jacintha,' he said, his impeccable manner shaming her awkwardness. 'I've been rather anxious to see you.'

'But why are you sitting in the hall?' she asked. 'Why didn't Anna show you into the living-room?'

'She offered, but I preferred to wait here.' Inwardly he smiled a wry smile at her unconscious assumption of a hostess's role; her self-betrayals were all so perfectly innocent. Divining where she must have been, he pressed on, 'How's Hugh?'

'Not—not too bad.' A furious resentment scalded her suddenly. *Why did it have to happen to him,* she thought, *why to him,* and continued, 'His left shoulder and arm—' she stopped abruptly, finding that she grudged him even this much '—they're broken.'

'And that's all?'

Isn't it enough? she raged inwardly, while replying, 'Some . . . some concussion. He's got to be kept quiet.'

'It was a nasty smash, from what I hear. He's lucky.'

'Very,' she murmured ironically. *'Very* lucky.'

'You're quite right,' he agreed disconcertingly. 'Idiotic expression, and I beg your pardon. I only mean, considering the circumstances we're in . . .' His face, impersonally pleasant till now, became worried. 'We can't find the Will.'

* * *

'Oh,' she said witlessly. Not yet detached from her single passionate focus, the words had made no impression. 'Well, I suppose it'll turn up sooner or later.'

'Sooner or—!' he echoed staring, then smiled. 'My dear girl, it's got to be found *now,* not later.'

'I don't know anything about it,' she disclaimed with finality.

'I didn't expect you to.' He was changelessly, undisturbedly, pleasant. 'But if you'd begin searching the likeliest places in the house—'

'*I?* goodness no,' she broke in without apology. 'I wouldn't have the least—' her partial recovery from shock, in truth, had been followed by a usual sequence—desperate hunger for solitude, utter solitude. '—not the vaguest idea where to look, I'm afraid you'll have to get someone else.'

'There *is* no one else.' Gently he ignored her dismissiveness. 'Sorry, but you're stuck with the job.'

'But I'm no relation, I'm no—'

'You were Mrs Tor's companion, her friend as I see it, you've more status in this house than anyone else. Anyway, what do you suggest I do—send over one of my typists, who doesn't know the house at all? Taking charge of the search is something Hugh should do, if he were able. Seeing he's not able . . .'

Her stubborn inclination to refuse gave way all at once before the sound of a name. Here was a chance, a first chance to be useful to her love, to serve him. And instead of seizing on it she was shrinking, evading . . .

'He rang me early and said he was coming down,' the solicitor was saying. 'I'd assumed he'd have the Will with him. He didn't though—I've already asked at the hospital.'

'All right.' In the same moment she felt the surge of false energy drain out of her as quickly as it had risen; weakness reduced her again. 'I will tomorrow, I—'

'Tomorrow!' he exclaimed. 'At once, if you please, we've not a moment to lose.'

'What difference,' she contested fretfully, 'can one day make—'

'All the difference in the world.' His interruptions were not impatient, only firm. 'The deceased may have left instructions as to the disposal of her body, whether she wants burial or cremation, whether a religious ceremony or not and so on. We can't possibly proceed without the Will.'

'Oh,' she murmured defeated.

'It shouldn't be too hard to dig up, a sizable affair like that— seven or eight folio pages in a blue legal cover.'

'All right,' she said again. 'I'll look.'

'Thank you, Jacintha, thank you very much.' His voice changed to soliloquy, together with his worried, indrawn look. 'I'd no chance to tell Hugh we hadn't a copy. It must be in the house somewhere.'

'All right,' she repeated.

'By the way, I've put two hundred pounds to Mrs Tor's credit at the Merchant Weavers, and arranged for you to draw cheques. Her funds are all stopped, as you know.'

'Thank you,' she said tonelessly.

'Also, any of her cheque-books that you find, gather them up and let me have them, would you?'

'I will.'

'And when you're hunting,' he said in a changed voice, 'be thorough. Don't let scruples or delicacy keep you from going through everything with a fine-comb. Death is like murder in one respect—most ordinary privacies go by the board.'

'I won't do it alone.' She spoke suddenly, without previous knowledge or intention—for what reason she never knew then or later. 'All this rooting and digging you've wished on me—I'd like Mrs Williams along.'

'The nurse? by all means, she's an old retainer, practically.' He was turning toward the door. 'So you'll get down to it, at once—?'

'Yes,' she said. 'I will, straightaway.'

* * *

She gave him time to be out of sight, then shot from the house and into the call-box, wanting no possible hearer of what

197

was going to be a comfortless affair. Ranging silver on the shelf, she dialled with cold shaking hands and breath coming short. Too soon the ringing sounded, then the voice, the crisp business voice so different from the voice of friendship, 'Liz Tennant here.'

'Liz—'

'*Cintha!*' The voice changed electrically to joy and welcome. 'Oh sweetie, it's so *good* to hear from you! I didn't like to ring where you are—'

'Liz—'

'—but listen, a dozen things are popping here, I'll wait till you're back to put you completely in the picture—'

'Liz—'

'—but hurry now, get away from that damned hole, don't let them hang on to you with hard-luck tales and all that. You're in a call-box, aren't you? Ring off and I'll ring back, I want to tell you just a few—'

'Liz! Liz!' By dint of a near-shout oddly leavened with a near-sob, she stemmed the torrent. 'I'm not coming, Liz, I . . . can't come.'

The silence was instant and deep, as if all her force, and not only hers, had been used up. After a moment—

'Cintha?' Liz essayed. Her voice was barely audible with fright. 'What's wrong? you're ill? or—or—'

'No, no, nothing like—'

'But what then? You're scaring me to death. Tell me, surely I can—'

'I'm—'

'—do something, something—'

'I'm—oh God.' A hail of beeps had intervened. 'Wait, I'll put money in.'

'Ring off, you fool, I'll—'

'No, there, it's all right.'

'Now what's all this, what's this nonsense—'

'I'm going to marry!' she bayed desperately, with all the force of her lungs. 'I'm getting married!'

Again the silence was instant, again profound, only of a different quality. At the end of it Liz said, 'To whom?'

198

'Hugh.' As the lack of response this time was of obvious in-comprehension, she was forced to add, 'Hugh Kerwin.'

'The one at the restaurant?' She had remembered. 'With the queer? the old lady's son?'

'Yes.'

'Well, of all . . .'

'Liz, please, please,' she supplicated. 'You yourself—when you said being in love makes everything else nothing . . . it's true, it's true, don't be angry—'

'You mean this?' Liz cut across her. 'You mean it?'

'Yes. I know it's happened at a bad time for you, I know, I know, but I couldn't help—'

'Shut up.' The voice, grating and unrecognizable, made her jump. 'For Christ's sake don't give me the soul's awakening and that shit, you—you sicken me. Do you *know* what you've done to me, maybe cooked the whole thing at the outset—'

'Liz—'

'—Diana Howarth wanted to come in with me, put up two thousand quid—and she an experienced agent's secretary and damned useful, more so than you, and I told her no—'

'I'll send you every penny I've saved,' she broke in franti-cally. 'You'll have the cheque tomorrow—'

'Why, damn you.' It was a high incredulous note, stretched tight. 'Damn you. It's not just the money, you know that per-fectly well. We can *work* together, what's the use of having Diana when I know we wouldn't get along!' Harshly she drew breath and re-launched herself. 'You knew I was counting on you, you knew I couldn't handle it alone, then you do this rotten thing to me, leave me high and dry for what, a big, flashy—'

'Liz!'

'—ambisextrous wonder. Your intended.' The voice had turned hateful and malicious. 'Accomplished fella, what? Here's hoping you get your fair fifty per cent, but don't count on it. Why, my God, I *still* can't believe—'

'Liz,' she implored against the lash that struck on and on. 'Liz—'

'Don't talk.' From railing the voice had dropped to endless

weariness, endless contempt. 'Be quiet, just be quiet, it's all I ask of you.' The phone crashed in her ear.

* * *

There was no pain, she noted wonderingly, pain would come later. Everything would come later: awareness of loss, of scorn, of her own shame in betrayal. It would all come later and when it came she would have to endure, that was all, endure till it passed. And if it failed to pass, if it left scars . . . *the price of love,* she thought, a passing smile of self-mockery barely touching her face. She left the call-box and let herself into the house again; another cry for help she could make from here. She dialled, waited, finally saying, 'Mrs Williams?' Her voice was the curious hushed voice imposed on her by this house emptied of its owner. 'Mrs Williams, could you—'

XV

'Yes, Miss Cory speaking.'

'Miss Cory, Miss Faversham here.'

'Miss . . . ?'

'Matron at Cottage Memorial.' Faint annoyance and incredulity. 'We spoke yesterday.'

'Oh yes.' Shivering suddenly, she clutched the phone harder. 'Is he—is Mr Kerwin—'

'I told you yesterday, if you remember, that he should recover consciousness within twenty-four hours, which he—'

'Yes? yes . . . ?'

'—has in fact done,' loftily the other overrode her. 'Also I told you that the extent of the concussion would reveal itself, which it has also done. The centres of speech are affected. Temporarily,' she added rather fast. 'But at the moment he cannot speak intelligibly—nor, of course, write.'

Hanging dizzily in space, she waited. *Temporarily* echoed and re-echoed in her ears, she clung to it as to a last hope . . .

'However, something is on his mind which is disturbing him seriously,' the measured voice went on. 'This prevents him from getting the full benefit of treatment, and may even delay his recovery. To interrogate him on the nature of his trouble is of course out of the question, so we can only—' another pause, betraying her unwillingness to ask layman's help, this layman's above all '—try to find someone who knows what's worrying him, someone who could reassure him—'

'I know what it is, his worry,' she broke in curtly. 'Shall I come now?'

Seconds later she was running down the street, barely stopping for breath then running again. Nothing had importance, nothing had meaning but this urgency, overwhelming, tremendous . . . a female Mercury with wings on her feet, she sped to bring healing. It was another lovely morning of sunshine, of cool balmy air, if she had had time to notice it.

* * *

'He's not in extreme pain,' said Miss Faversham.

'N-no?' Quavering and terrorstruck she stood nailed to the spot by the sounds coming from behind the door. 'He . . . ?'

'Some discomfort in the arm and shoulder,' the matron assured her briskly. 'It's not that, it's the state of mind he's in— I've told you.' She put her hand on the door-knob. 'But remember, *he must not talk.*'

'No,' she assented, fighting her panic. He was in need, in supreme need, her wretched body must not betray her, she would die of shame if she fainted . . . Yet, never having seen the victim of a car smash . . .

'Just so you understand.' Miss Faversham, a little restored by the assertion of her authority, opened the door.

* * *

A linen screen concealed the bed. Still with an imminent swooning all through her, all at once she nerved herself and stepped quickly around it. He lay on his back with massive dressings on his left shoulder and arm; slighter bandagings on his head failed to conceal the outermost edges of a cruel bruise, or the fact that his abundant cap of hair had been shaved off. Worse than this however was the restlessness that pervaded him—the vague movements of something nailed down and struggling uselessly in torment. A faint sound, continuous and awful, accompanied this movement of something impaled; not crying, not moaning nor groaning, but a mixture of all three.

202

And at the sight and sound, her own contemptible weakness dissolved and was forgotten. He lay here in bitterest distress, distress that she alone could lift from him. Her heart broke with love and dedication, she was his, utterly his; apart from serving him existence was emptiness, a living grave . . . Her head had cleared as by magic; she was strong, steady and intent, upheld by her knowledge of what rowelled him and her ability to lift it from him, to heal him . . . Taking a deep breath she leaned toward him; it would have to be quick.

'Darling,' she said in a low distinct voice. 'Darling. Darling.'

The lamentation had stopped all at once, he seemed to be listening; the unbandaged eye, not looking at her, was suddenly distended as if alarmed.

'We'll find the Will,' she pressed on in the same muted voice, with exaggerated distinctness. 'We'll look everywhere, we'll find it. Don't worry about—'

She stopped aghast; the eye was glaring wildly, the cry broke out still louder, the heaving and threshing renewed themselves with a weak violence, incalculably distressing.

'—we'll find it,' she repeated, distraught. 'We'll look, we'll take care of everything, *everything*—'

She broke off again; someone had touched her shoulder.

'Miss Cory.' The matron's voice was heavily fraught for all its softness; she must have been listening outside, and on the new outcry had come in at once. With a gesture she indicated the door, mouthed, 'Wait outside,' and snatched up the phone.

Obediently she went out; a flurry of nurses appeared, passing in and out. After another waiting, Miss Faversham reappeared.

'He's worse,' she accused balefully. 'What did you tell him?'

'Not to—to worry.' Thunderstruck, she stammered a little. 'I said everything was being taken care of.'

'No more than that? you're sure? Then why's he so upset?'

'Because he didn't understand.' Anger, to her own astonishment, swept away her timidity. 'You let me speak to him too soon.'

'We—' She swallowed a plainly furious denial, and continued more calmly, 'He appeared to come back to himself this morning—before this new upset, whatever it is.'

'It still seems to me that you called me too soon.' Cintha allowed herself a moment of pleasurable iciness. 'Much too soon.'

The matron's face rigidified anew as she sought for combat
on this point; failing to find it her manner altered, palpably by
an effort of will.

'Would you say,' she asked disparagingly, 'that Mr Kerwin's
condition is connected with Mrs Tor's death?'

'I know it is,' said Jacintha, uninformative with intent.

Miss Faversham's face assumed, undisguisedly, its original
dislike. She would love to explore the nature of her patient's
unrest, she knew she would get nothing out of this girl, and cast
about for something, anything, to restore her status in her own
eyes.

'Well, let's hope he hasn't taken harm,' she said with under-
keyed spitefulness. 'Since what you told him wasn't very successful, was it?'

* * *

'Jacintha? You sound a bit windblown.'

'Do I? Sorry.' She saw no necessity to mention where she had
been. Nor did he ask, probably he knew anyway . . .

'I've been trying to get you earlier.' His voice sharpened.
'Have you found anything?'

'No.' Her voice, also, changed. 'We've torn the place to
pieces—there's nothing.'

'You're sure though? you've looked carefully—?'

'Everywhere. Her closets, wardrobes, her old hatboxes—every drawer in the house, everything that's got a drawer in it—'

'I believe there's a safe,' he interrupted. 'A wall safe—'

'We found it—took down all the pictures in the house on the
chance. It was open anyway, almost nothing in it.' She took a
deep breath. 'We've opened every trunk in the luggage room,
untied every bundle, turned out her study—and I couldn't
have done it without Mrs Williams,' she added. 'She was wonderful.'

'Mmm.' His voice was abstracted. 'Yes.' A pause. 'Jacintha,
you're not going to like this very much, but I've got to ask

you—' he paused again '—to go through Hugh's part of the house.'

'Oh, *no!*'

'I'm sorry,' he repeated. 'But whom else can I ask?'

She said nothing; against her wordlessness he continued battering.

'There's no relation that I know of, there's no immediate family but Hugh. And Hugh . . .' he left the rest of it, deliberately, to her imagination.

'All right, I'll . . .' she said after a pause. 'All right.'

'Thank you.' As deliberately, he refrained from overgratitude. 'I'll ring the hospital at once about his keys, and bring them to you as soon as possible.'

'Mrs Williams, though,' she croaked. 'I must . . . have her with me again.'

'Certainly, if you like. That's all right.'

* * *

She rang off with unsteady hands, also with a renewed tremor all through her. In the house she was being asked to ransack, there must be evidence of former love affairs; in what form—letters, photographs, other things—made no difference. Feebly she put it to her craven heart that such relics could have no resemblance to what she was seeking, she had only to avert her eyes and it would be all right . . . In the meantime, with sickness growing in her, she must ring Mrs Williams, see if she were available today. She would not enter that house without Mrs Williams; stubbornly, mindlessly, she was resolved on it . . .

An unmeasured interval after making the call she heard the car draw up outside, and like an automaton went to anticipate his ring.

'Here we are.' He handed her a handsome leather folder, open; it had a fair number of keys in it. 'Make a thorough job of it, will you?' As she nodded he pressed on ruthlessly, 'Have you ever heard Mrs Tor express a preference, or a dislike, for any particular method of disposal after death?'

'No.'

'She had a horror of ground burial.' He said it half to himself, already turning to go. 'That much I do—'

The door-bell interrupted him; she went to answer, had a sudden feeling of hope and reassurance as she admitted her stay and support, and all at once heard herself saying, 'Mr Dennison, would you please repeat, in Mrs Williams's presence, that I'm to go through Mr Kerwin's side of the house?' What impelled her to this precaution, foreign to her nature and her experience both, again she had no idea. 'Just tell her what I'm supposed to do there, so she'll know it's . . . it's all right?'

XVI

Almost all talk had died between them by now. Methodically and rigorously they continued to hunt, turning on all lights as they went along. By a sort of common consent, unspoken, she and Mrs Williams were never out of eachother's sight, both of them entering and leaving a room at the same time. The small house was turning out to be an infinitely more complicated job than could have been expected, what with its elaborate luxuriousness, not to say comfort; the growing awareness of this had struck her with a curious unease, quickly opposed with a silent *Well, why not, why not.* Meanwhile, downstairs, she had searched the handsome desk, averting her eyes from the numerous envelopes in feminine writing; the two of them had investigated every drawer in every piece of furniture that possessed one, rifled every pocket in the lavish assortment of coats in the hall closet. They had explored the small dining-room then rummaged extensively in the kitchen, this latter prefaced by Mrs Williams's doubtful, 'I don't reckon this will be any good,' but they had searched microscopically, all the same. Everything was open and unlocked, there had been no need for the keys that Dennison had pressed upon her. Once, after a glance at her wrist had startled her, she had volunteered, 'It must be past your dinner time, Mrs Williams, would you like to stop?'

'Well,' was the reply, unruffled, 'I'd rather get this over and done with. My, it *is* a bit of a big job, isn't it?'

* * *

It was evening, even though early evening, when they mounted the steps to the first floor. Her ascent was companioned by the swooning cowardice of her earlier shrinking. A man's private life: where might it be expected to leave its traces, if not in his bedroom? And by what cruel perverseness had she, of all people, been chosen to conduct this miserable prying and rifling? . . . She turned on the lights at the top, and saw at once that this level was a sort of half-floor, consisting of no more than the tiny hall and bedroom with its bath. No chance of dodging this main part of the search, no chance of putting it off on any pretext whatever . . . and what was she shrinking from, she asked herself furiously, what entitled her to this . . . jealousy, deathly gripping jealousy as if she herself had been an untouched virgin, which she certainly was not?

* * *

'Well,' said Mrs Dowling. 'No use lettin' all this go to waste.' Venison pâté, *escalope cordon bleu* and peaches with sabayon deployed themselves luxuriously on her imagination. 'We might as well polish it off.'

'You think it'll be all right?' breathed Anna, always the timorous one.

'Lord yes, I can always dig up somethin' if it's called for.' Mrs Dowling's voice had gone meditative, as always when deciding on the wine. 'And if you ask me, she don't even know what she's eating, not the last day or two anyways. Now with this, I think . . . a Muscadet, that's what, a nice Muscadet.'

* * *

Vigorously they had embarked on the last of their ferreting. The bedroom was in fact much larger than it had first appeared, owing to the amount of furniture in it, expensively designed for the accommodation of expensive clothing. Again, at sight of its elaboration and refinements, she had felt that return of distaste, even a . . . a revulsion? . . . which she had pushed out of sight even more quickly than before. Through quantities of fine underlinen, through sports shirts, business shirts, formal shirts plain or ruffled they rooted; through mountains of scarves and socks where the questing hand brushed against textures of silk and cashmere. By now their silence was utter, broken by nothing more than the sound of drawers opening and shutting, the rustling of fabrics intruded upon.

This was the point at which she confronted the two enormous wardrobes centrally joined by a dressing-table with a huge mirror, the whole a commanding example of built-in fitments. Doggedly she slid back the doors of one, doggedly went through the array of suits on padded hangers, and yet with a reviving hope: they had found nothing elsewhere, they would find nothing here and it would be over . . . She finished with the coats and the trousers in their presses, again compelled to note how very fine were their materials. She knelt and ran her hand between and beneath ranks of polished shoes on stainless-steel racks; she mounted a chair and had down every hatbox on the shelf. Hats for every occasion, not only a high silk one— somewhat rare nowadays—but a handsome grey topper. *Just like Prince Philip,* she thought with an involuntary mocking smile—which faded at once to a faint, desolate smile of understanding. The child deprived of childhood, the boy starved of love, the man who had been (almost literally) without father or mother; if he compensated himself with *things,* later on, how could she find it amusing? Shameful, shameful . . . Now she had progressed to the dressing-table drawers, crammed with aids to grooming; again they inspired her with no more than her newly learned, indulgent tenderness as she moved on to the second wardrobe and pushed at the door . . .

Which refused to slide back; the unexpected check was followed by a return of fainting, sickening jealousy; she thought she had reasoned with and conquered it. Then, since there was nothing else for it, for the first time she took out the keys, made a couple of trial casts, found one that fitted . . .

The first thing was the odour that came out, a blast of heavy perfume with undefined undertones of some kind. This, administering another violent check instantly countered with *All right, all right, he's had no time to clear out this junk,* was quickly accompanied by her recognition of the lesser smells, the smell of leather wedded to a faint, the very faintest, decay . . .

She took a moment to let her head clear, glanced surreptitiously at Mrs Williams who was unmaking the bed and probing beneath the mattress, and bent again to the closet. At its far right-hand end, whose door she had not touched, were shadowy pastel colours, filmy textures; rigidly fixing her attention on the opposite end she went through the array of sports coats and jackets that took up most of the space. Beneath them more shoes stretched away and away. Easier if she slid back the right-hand door but she would not, she had rather die than give Mrs Williams a sight of what hung there. Having to reach beneath the silks and satins, she experienced a crawling of the nerves as the long delicate fabrics brushed her hand. Shoes, still more shoes . . . she came to the end of them and encountered something different and large, sitting flat against the far end; something, for all its being invisible, familiar at first touch to her questing fingers. Or no, there could be two of them, Mrs Tor's was not the only one ever made . . . Yet her fingers moved with old knowledge over its proportions, found and grasped its handle, then—after another glance at Mrs Williams, unconsciously full of fear—half-pulled, half-lifted toward her a considerable weight.

* * *

The premonition that was advance knowledge, wildly denied till the last moment, exploded like a bomb whose light, as it destroys, gives one instant of ghastly revelation. There was a splitting inside her head, a violence of focus wrenched upside-down, the shock that pitilessly strips, exposes, lays open . . . She must have made some slight sound, crouched there gripping the thing's handle; Mrs Williams had looked her way.

'Have you found it?' she asked, her eyes on the object. 'Would that be where he's got it?' and by her tranquil gaze it was plain she had never seen the briefcase before; thank God for that much, anyway . . .

'I'll have to take it downstairs,' she managed out of a face stiff as wood and a chest cruelly squeezed. 'Look at it carefully.'

'Handsome thing that is,' Mrs Williams said without interest, turning again to the bed. And in spite of what she had said, forced by some hunger for self-destruction, again she had taken the keys from her pocket, singled out the tiny gold one (by instinct knowing it would be there) and unlocked the thing. It was packed tight with notes for the book as she had left it, but crammed farther down were other objects . . . With caution she fished some just short of the surface; the medals of course but also some rings and brooches, on whose loss—before her own advent—Mrs Tor had undoubtedly raised hell. And meanwhile—to her own wonderment and incredulity —her shipwrecked mind had steadied and begun calculating, shaping determinations and procedures. . . . .

'Is it there?'

'Not so far.' Mrs Williams's voice had startled her. 'I think we're through here, though. But first—' again strange, how her moment of near-insanity had been replaced by total composure '—would you just sign a little memorandum about when and where I found this case, and in your presence?' She tried to get up, almost fell, and ruthlessly pulled herself erect. 'That pad beside the phone—' she wrote. 'Read it before you sign, would you?'

'Well, let's hope you've turned up something—' Mrs Williams, having signed cheerfully, broke off with belated consternation. 'Miss Cory, you look—' *like death* was on her lips; adroitly she changed it. '—you look done in. Hadn't you better—'

'No, no, I'm all right,' she began to interrupt, then stopped as another thing, all at once, overwhelmed her. 'Mrs Williams,' she said in a stifled voice. 'When you found Mrs Tor, the other evening—' she stopped again, afraid to go on.

'Yes?' asked Mrs Williams mildly. 'Yes, miss?'

'—I mean, was she dead . . . already . . . or still alive, or . . .'

211

'Bless you, she'd already cooled off a bit. Couldn't you feel it?'

'I didn't—' she had to stop her teeth from chattering '—I didn't actually touch her.'

'Is that so? I don't remember. But from the way she felt, she must of died before Mr Kerwin got home.'

He left plenty of time to make sure, she thought.

'I hadn't touched her all afternoon, myself,' said Mrs Williams, her voice faintly desolate. 'For fear I'd waken her, you know.'

'I see.'

'Miss Cory,' resumed the other, after a silence. 'Hadn't we better quit now, and go on tomorrow—'

'Thank you very much, but I'm all right.' And strangely, she was all right, relieved at least of the hideous suspicion that would have taken the whole thing out of her hands; she stood tall and composed, shorn of tomorrow, shorn of everything.

'Actually, I think this is all,' she went on. 'There's nothing we haven't been into. Thank you for everything, Mrs Williams, for your wonderful help. I've put you out a lot, I'm afraid, but that's all over now. Come on, let's go down—come along now.'

* * *

In Mrs Tor's house, she wrote a cheque and handed it over.

'Dear me!' exclaimed Mrs Williams at sight of it. 'But I haven't been here all that much nor worked all that hard—'

'Hush,' she interrupted. 'You saved my life, that's all.' Carefully she was avoiding the accent of valediction. 'I'll be seeing you. And thank you again, Mrs Williams, I can't thank you enough, I've never—' it had come to her lips irrepressibly '—never met anyone so good and kind as you are.'

'Well.' Still nonplussed by an atmosphere she could not define, the stout comely woman remained undecided. 'But you'll ring if you want me—?'

'Goodness yes.'

'Bye-bye then. —Oh, would you know when the funeral's to be?'

'No—no one's told me yet.'

212

The instant Mrs Williams had gone she sat down again, wrote briefly, then marched into the kitchen.

'Mrs Dowling, Anna,' she began without preamble. 'Here are your cheques, and thank you very much.' Suddenly aware that she was lapsing again into what she wanted to avoid—the accent of departure—she altered course. 'I mean, thank you for standing by, it's so terribly good of you.'

'Well thank *you,* madam, and I'm sure we were glad to, weren't we, Anna?' In Mrs Dowling's mind, as she stowed the cheque away, was a vague awareness both of some unfamiliar accent and of the ghost of *escalope cordon bleu,* still floating on the air. 'Shall I do you some dinner now, a bit of—'

'Oh nothing, thank you.' She had spoken too quickly and with too much repugnance, but no help for it. 'I hope you haven't put a lot of work into it?'

'Well, that's quite all right, madam, that makes no difference.' Conscious virtue had returned to her voice and demeanour. 'We've just been making out as best we could, haven't we, Anna? Seeing as no one's given any orders.'

'I know, you've done wonderfully. Now if you'd be willing to carry on, till someone tells y—us—differently—?'

'Oh yes, madam,' they replied in dramatic unison, the senior adding, 'And the funeral, madam, would you know when it was?'

'No, not yet.'

'Ah well.' Mrs Dowling was enjoyably, mournfully ready. 'Whenever 'tis, we've got our blacks laid out all proper, it's a mercy we both wear black a lot. It's sad, ain't it?' she added with gusto. 'Sad for all of us.'

* * *

With her departure and her consequent absence at breakfast next morning elided, she stood motionless for a long moment. The silence, the special and terrible silence that had oppressed her before, she did not even notice; what she felt and what she thought were different, because she herself had become different. A chaos of things to do beat upon her, and which of them to do first, first . . .

On a wild movement toward the stairs to go up and pack, she stopped dead. By the same savage light that had stripped her of her idiot delusions she looked backward and saw other things, disregarded when they had happened; inexplicable bits and pieces crowding upon her with voiceless, insistent demand. . . .

One of these, indistinct as it was, drove her to the phone. If he were out she would ring again, she would keep ringing till she got him . . .

A voice answered; a sudden awareness of the hour made her ask, 'Were you just having dinner?'

'No,' he answered without pause. 'Long over.' His voice quickened. 'Have you found anything?'

'Nothing, absolutely nothing, but—'

'Lord,' he muttered.

'—but there was something I wanted to ask you,' she drove ruthlessly past his interjection, then stopped short. 'That is, if you don't mind.'

'Ask me,' he said dryly, 'and we'll see.'

'It's such a small thing that you probably won't—won't remember—'

'What was that?'

'Well, do you recollect saying—not so long ago—' the memory, uncomfortable, stopped her for a moment '—saying something about . . . about . . .'

'Yes?' he prompted patiently.

'—about Hugh's . . .' the name brought an uncontrollable spasm to her lips '. . . his territory, would you call it, his representative's . . . ?'

'Yes?'

'—and you said it wasn't far from here or something like that, don't you remember—?'

'As a matter of fact, I don't,' he responded, after waiting politely. 'But it's true that he's never very far from home, not more than a couple of hours driving, at most. Actually I believe he's refused to change this job for a better one, I've heard him say it myself—because this way, in emergency, he could get home fast.'

214

'I see,' she said collectedly. 'Yes.'

'Was that all?' he asked, after a silence.

'Yes.' She girded herself. 'Thank you.'

'Well.' He was obviously perplexed, but too courteous to pry further. 'I'll see you tomorrow, then.'

Not in this house you won't, she told him silently, and said, 'Good night, and thank you very much.'

* * *

In her room she fell at once on pen and paper and began writing, bowing over it hungrily and driving along without reflection, almost without thought.

> *You had keys to her house and she had none to yours. That was all of it, the whole thing.*

She stopped for the fierce pressure of things to say, too many things crowding and jostling . . .

> *You were never more than two or three hours away from home. You could drive here at night, you knew where everyone slept and that it wasn't likely they would hear you. It was easy for you, you never had to go above the ground floor for what you wanted, or for what you'd come to do.*

She hardly paused now under the clarity of sequence in her mind, like whitened bones signposting a desert.

> *It was all there from the beginning. You wanted someone with imagination enough to create little interests for her, so you could destroy them. And found me, didn't you? I got her interested in the piano, and you ruined it. I got her to find those notes, and you stole them. You knew what she'd think—that she'd hidden them herself, during her bad spells. And you knew she couldn't bear the thought, YOU KNEW IT. And put the blame on that poor creature, on Mary—*

She flung down the pen and with both hands pushed violently back from the table and got to her feet. With this rage

215

flagellating her she could not sit still, not another moment
. . . Feeling his ring of keys still in her pocket, all at once she
thudded downstairs and flung out of the house; in delirium of
hatred longing for fiercer self-punishment, for more vitriol to
pour on the memory of her smiling complacence, her unbearable stupidity. The thought of her physical longing for him, of
how she would have been in bed with him yesterday if not
for her collapse, were eating her with a sort of madness as
she let herself into his house and turned on lights. Not the desk
in the living-room, no . . . she sped wildly upstairs like an
animal smelling fresh blood.

The elegant desk in the bedroom, from which she had
averted her eyes, offered a generous selection. All the envelopes—she saw now—were addressed in the same hand,
and she had not disturbed their order. Snatching up the top
one in the first drawer she opened, she reft out the heavy
paper.

> All right, if you can't think of anything, it's your
> neck. I'd better marry L and get it over with. It won't
> stop the fun for long, darling, the poor sweet's so
> thick. But I've said no to so many eligibles that the
> Ps are sitting up on their haunches and yelling, the
> old man won't throw me out but he can cut my allow-
> ance to damn all and he will too. So there you are,
> my red-hot poker, that's the position. I'm not taking
> any job either, definitely not my caper. By the way,
> that female you got for your old blight, have you slept
> with her yet? If so, will it do any good? What use
> you thought she'd be, I never could understand. Well,
> next Tuesday then, usual place, but after that no
> more for a bit. Can't help, sweet, I'm under pressure.
> 'Bye.

Restoring it to its envelope, she happened to glance at the
postmark. *Next Tuesday,* yes, the night he had rung her: *I
can't get back tonight, I can't possibly.* . . . Stock-still, she
listened to his voice: *Hang on till I come, will you? will you?*

216

and to hers: *Yes, I'll be here.* Delivered ardently, with what fervour. . . .

* * *

Now she felt nothing at all; strange how the raging current exhausted itself. Instead, another urgency was coming to life in her, urgency matched by an equal dread . . . She left the alien house, turning all lights out carefully, and made with driven steps for the call-box. Do it, do it, get it over with . . .

The ringing had commenced; it went on, on . . . A swooning relief came first, then a swooning despair. If not done now it must be done some other time, postponement only meant twisting her courage once more to this point, a point of life or death . . . In her abstraction she actually missed the *Yes?* till its second repetition; in mindless terror she blurted, 'Liz.'

* * *

Silence: empty or full? favourable? ominous . . . ?

'Liz,' she tried again. 'W-will you . . . s-speak to me?'

Another silence, before there came a curious sound, a sort of snuffling too weak to define; against it she went on petitioning, 'Will you? will you, Liz?'

'You mean—will you—speak to *me*.' It came after delay, in muffled jerks; she took a moment to realize it as crying.

'Ah don't,' she begged witlessly. 'Ah Liz, don't—'

'I can't *bear* it,' the muffled voice cut across her. 'Oh God when I think how I spoke to you, the rotten filthy things I said—'

'It's all right.'

'Don't tell me it's all right!' yelled Liz. 'Oh Christ, how could I be so cruel about it, all you'd done was fall in love like I did. And you so patient about it all, so patient—'

'It's all right—'

'—please forgive me, please please forgive—' Liz was weeping undisguisedly; her emotion, curiously, killed the other's emotion stone dead.

'Listen a moment,' she put in forcibly yet carefully. 'She's

217

dead, Mrs Tor's dead.' She took a long breath. 'Do you still want me?'

'Don't be a fool. —But did you say—' the voice had changed from fierce to avid '—the old girl's dead?'

'Later, I'll tell you later. I just wanted you to know, now, that I'm moving out of here. I'll find something else and let you know where.'

The briefest pause followed before Liz spoke, her voice hesitant. 'Cintha—don't mind too much, you aren't the first.'

'Mind . . . ?' Momentarily she was displaced by the change of subject.

'His . . .' Liz struggled on '. . . his being that way.'

Catching up, she waited.

'I was sure of it the moment we saw him with that queer— you know, in the restaurant—?'

'Yes,' she murmured passively.

'He's not the first who wanted to marry, for a smoke-screen.'

'I suppose not.' Let the wrong turning be pursued, it was not worth contradiction or discussion.

'And on top of that, I've remembered. About his boy-friend, you know—?'

'What?' she asked, now mystified. A memory shaped itself vaguely, a presence blonde, graceful and insolent, but without a face.

'I thought I'd seen him before, but it took me a few days to catch up with him. He does a turn in nightclubs, smokers and whatnot—men's clothes but also in drag and very good apparently. His stage name's Dudalli, with an *i*, how's that for coyness—' A strange sound burbled up in her all at once, a gust of laughter broken by hiccoughs. 'W-what a thing to remember just now, what a thing—' a louder giggling took possession of her, rising and boiling over. '*Mad,* isn't it? c-crazy, hahaha—?' She went off into peals of laughter, hysterical and broken. 'S-sorry, sorry. I'll see you then? soon? s-soon . . . ?'

* * *

Your friend Dudalli. The layabout, the gypsy woman, he was both of them. And sold your mother the stuff that killed her, whatever it was. Were you paying him off, that time at the restaurant? We both saw you and Liz Tennant recognized him. I rather think he'd give you away to protect himself, if the police caught up with him.

Breathing as if she had been running she flung down the pen once more, started to her feet and in a sort of delirium attacked her cases, pushing things into them, slamming down lids, plucking them up again for stray bits . . . all the while with furnace heats rising in her again, the sense of fathomless outrage. His love-making: if not for her collapse, she would have been in bed with him. *Something to remember,* she thought gritting her teeth, then was struck motionless under an ultimate knowledge: that as his dupe she had penned an old woman in the house she was struggling to escape, had led her gently, inexorably to her death . . . Her first interview with him flashed on her. A year, he had insisted, she must take the job for a year; giving himself a wide margin of time for his work. But he had not needed a year, she had supplied him at once with a double attack, the piano and the papers . . . His phone call, she thought suddenly, his silence when she had told him of the suicide attempt, a consternated silence she had thought, which was actually murderous; how he must have damned her . . . another hysterical laugh escaped her, muffled at once by another reflection. Her betrayed and derided love, it was nothing beside this other thing: that in his plan to destroy his mother he had made her not a passive, but an active, partner.

*　*　*

She began thinking of what she planned to do. At once, for all her new coldness and detachment, she found herself in serious indecision, even fear. Hand him over to justice, it was her plain duty. A pleasant thought but it left out other things, essentials. He might slide out of a legal trial, he might evade significant penalties . . . her face cleared at the same time that it hardened. Keep justice in her own hands. Wrong, it was wrong, and she gave not a damn. What she planned for him was *real* punishment, long punishment too unless she had guessed badly at a life-span, and this particular life seemed to her to have every sign of deadly longevity . . .

Flinging herself again on her letter, she was struck motionless for an instant by a thought strange, and at the same time strangely remote. Dennison, he had liked her, she had begun to like him, what might have happened between them if . . . she shrugged, already free of him, in the same moment absolving him of harmful intention. He was too used to having the upper hand in any situation, used to controlling things, no more than that. Time to make plain her intention to the other one, who—only now—she diagnosed in one word. Odd that it had not occurred to her before, but now it was blindingly clear and simple. He was a coward, and in his cowardice lay her safety.

> *The briefcase. You've been wondering when I was coming to that? Mrs Williams saw me find it, I had her sign a statement about it. Photostats of this and my own statement about everything will go—sealed —to John Dennison, to the bank here, and to my own bank. I'm keeping the briefcase. Try to get it from me or have anything happen to me, they'll all have had instructions to open the statements on my death.*

She stopped suddenly at a vision: herself bending over the hospital bed pouring out her soul in reassurance, *Darling, we'll find the Will, we'll look everywhere.* And he had understood, he was able to understand her . . . A sound broke from her, a laugh.

> *What were you going to do with the briefcase? Have it discovered among my things? Ah, your shocked surprise, your sadness when you broke off with me, can't I just see them.*

The savagery of her expression faded before another savagery—of retribution intent, collected, and ice-cold.

220

Mary Pargill will lose her home and she's got no-
where to go and nothing to live on. You are going to
make her an allowance of one thousand pounds a
year for the rest of her life. I'll be in touch with her
always, I promise you. The first word I hear of your
not paying, I'll put the briefcase and statements into
Dennison's hands and let him take it from there.
Judging by the relationship between you, I wouldn't
risk anything if I were you. He won't lose the chance
of making you sweat, not if I know him. Remember
it all depends on your paying Mary. REMEMBER!

And now, at this unlikely hour, she sat down to violate the
two silences—silence of the house and silence of night—with
the clacking of her typewriter as she made copies and signed
them all. Putting them carefully into a side-pocket of her
largest case she thought that tomorrow she would go to London
if necessary, and have them photograph Mrs Williams's state-
ment.

XVII

And that was all, all of it; what she had to do was done. A shivering took her for no reason, then a sort of relapse, a fall into blankness of exhaustion, an extremity—combined, still, with frantic wakefulness. She glanced at her wrist, and at the same moment the hall clock struck half-past two. Go to bed, turn and twist trying to keep off the thoughts that prowled underneath, the lesions waiting to reveal how deep they went, deep . . .

Violently and unconsciously shaking her head, she fell back into her waking stupor. Her features, only just now carven by hatred into an unrecognizable mask, had gone slack and pale; her eyes roamed without purpose, seeing nothing, seeking nothing . . .

Into this vacuum crept, by degrees, what made her frown intermittently with puzzlement till she recognized it: loneliness, undeniable loneliness. But for whom? Liz? . . . Unconsciously again she shook her head, casting about, and then—muzzy, half-unbelieving—admitted the source of this loneliness. Still, why not? In all the commotion attending on the death she had thought only of this commotion, she had lost sight of the crux of it, the solitary, central figure. Yet again, now that she identified the cause, why this sudden feeling of guilt, this sense of terrible shortcoming? She of all people had served this difficult

old woman well, beyond obligations of pay or sense of duty
. . . or no: she had done it not for Mrs Tor but for someone
else . . . she flinched; no escape that way. Or could it be that
Mrs Tor was reproaching her for her refusal to attend the
funeral, whenever it might be. . . ? In the night silence, she
laughed briefly. Considering Mrs Tor's attitude to such for-
malities, funny . . . Yet still the feeling gnawed her, like un-
developed toothache. She had failed to do something, *something,* if only to take proper leave; to offer Mrs Tor something
however little, the courtesy of a goodbye that should be hers,
hers alone . . .

She was on her feet, passing with a sleepwalker's gait into
the hall, then into Mrs Tor's bedroom. Here without hesitation
she opened the door on darkness and felt for the switch. The
room sprang out under the lights, larger even than she remembered it; a room really huge, containing with ease the rank
of three wardrobes, the desk, bureaux, dressing-table, chairs,
the bed; the bed empty and still, with an embroidered coverlet
drawn up over its pillows. All of it waiting till a new mistress,
with a new scheme of decoration, should consign it to second-
or third-hand dealers . . .

Having just passed the threshold, she stopped dead. Into
every corner and cranny of this room her yesterday's ferreting
had led her. What new impression waited for her therefore,
what new feeling or emotion, nothing. This pilgrimage of
goodbye had turned out to be nothing, a lost cause. All the
same, for no reason she slid open the door of the nearest
wardrobe. Having done this, she looked at it blankly. What
had she expected to see but what was familiarized to her yesterday, a coal-mine vista crammed with soberest colours, and
the same true of the second wardrobe. Into every pocket of
these her searching hand had gone, into every inch of the
shelves above or the floor below she had peered or felt her
way . . .

On an unconscious sigh she moved—with the aimlessness of
no objective, of failing purpose—to the third and last wardrobe. On this, and for good reason, she had spent less time than
on the other two; here hung evening dresses only, patently

hopeless as containers or concealers of large-size legal documents. All these she had pushed to the left-hand end in the course of her search, and there they all remained crowded together. Now with different eyes—since now she had time—she regarded the limp and fragile finery that testified to countless formal functions. All those silks, organdies and chiffons full of beading or sequins or diamanté, whose dingy flashing caught the light; all those frills and furbelows and pastel colours, cut very low and ludicrously at odds with those strong shoulders, sinewy weatherbeaten arms and astringent personality . . .

'Oh God,' she murmured aloud, thinking that Mrs Tor's achievements must have lain between her forties and fifties, so she would not even have had youth in her favour to carry off these testimonies of pathetic bad taste. Then as if in apology she began pushing the dresses apart and spacing them more evenly; a vague and useless propitiation, done gently and fondly. *She must have looked like hell in them,* she thought, and again visualized—with a melancholy half-smile—the figure of a woman in khaki shirts and shorts, striding through the jungle. . . .

Her hand had encountered opposition as she drew the dresses apart; an obstruction suggesting a considerable weight, unyielding, but what on earth . . . ? She slid back the door at the left-hand end and saw what she had not seen before: that the very last dress on the rod, a dress specially offensive for its fluffiness, had something hung inside it, something dark and well concealed by floating gimcracks; heavy as lead, too heavy in fact to lift down easily. Taking the bottom of the dress, pushing and crumpling it upward ruthlessly, she saw a dark linen jacket, well worn, with bulges at its sides. Galvanized with cold, with premonition, she reached into a pocket—and withdrew her hand as if she had touched a snake. Still pinioning the dress high on its hanger, motionless as if transfixed by an arrow, she stared. Not at the dress nor what it hid, not at anything in the room, but at dark tumbling water; night-haunted water racing past at the garden's end, its current swollen with spring and deep, deep . . . Mrs Tor, taught by her frustrated

224

suicide attempt apparently, was leaving nothing to chance. If the furtive purveyors of sleep should fail her, she now had a promise of sleep that would not fail her. In fact, a double promise: that once she had consigned herself to the rushing stream, wearing this jacket weighted with stones, she was sure not only of sleep but sure likewise that no last-minute change of heart, no struggle, would do her any good at all. The matter would have been taken out of her hands.

* * *

Standing before the wardrobe, still holding the crumpled finery above the jacket, she was crying. Without sobs or other emphases, with an endless welling of tears from an innermost pain, she saw a succession of pictures. Mrs Tor labouring earnestly over a child's piano piece and counting aloud; Mrs Tor massaging her arms; Mrs Tor seizing on the thought of her notes for a book, in her need battling always, with indistinct hope, for her shaken mind. And all this gallantry doomed, defeated in advance, by what bored underground, silent and faceless in the dark. *I can't bear it,* she thought, *I can't bear it but I have to bear it.* Before the rack of expensive trash, before the forlorn glitter of yesterday she wept and wept with the same soundless and strengthless weeping, and in this manner said goodbye to Mrs Tor.

XVIII

For the twentieth time her eyes swept the confines of her room, searching with savage intensity for anything overlooked. The thought that any trace of herself might remain in this house, any least trifle, drove her to frenzy. She wanted it bare of herself, bone-bare as if she had never set foot in it. Actually it seemed that she had been as thorough as she could wish; wardrobe, drawers and shelves gutted and empty, surfaces bare of so much as a hairpin or trace of powder; even the wastepaper basket tipped into a bag and crammed into a holdall.

After this survey she stood still again, then again looked at her watch. Its message struck her into near panic: a quarter to four. Hours yet before she could tear free, hours like iron bars pinning her in . . . and no chance of sleep, she was in torment for sleep yet jerked awake by the drumming and throbbing in her deepest nerve-centres . . . *I'll go mad,* she thought, then snatched at an idea: perhaps something of hers remained downstairs, a book, anything. Going to see, at least, would wear away some of these interminable seconds, unmoving . . .

She thudded down at a gait perilously unbalanced, first having pressed every switch that served the staircase and hall. Not out of fear, fear was remoter from her than ever; to have lights crazily blazing at this time of night chimed with her semi-craziness. Nothing of hers in the hall or morning-room; she flung back a door with unnecessary force, again turned on all lights, and entered the living-room. Nothing of hers on any table or chair; with a revulsion half occluded by her half-sleeping state she hesitated a moment, then raised the lid of the savaged piano and saw—what luck, she had forgotten it altogether—the edge of the duet-album protruding from under the lowered music rack. She seized it, pulling it free with such violence that it flew from her hand, spreading its wings like a bird and landing on the floor, open. Bending to retrieve it, she saw the music on its exposed pages and above it the title: 'The Jolly Miller.'

* * *

The thing that turned her to stone, bending over the book, was no more nor less strange than what can happen in the mind or spirit under stress. Every emotion in her, grief, anger, fatigue, had been raised to the pitch of madness; when she straightened after taking up the album, she was sane again—sane, cool, and—strangest of all—reflective. Now faintly surprised by the lights glaring from every side she turned them out one after another on her way upstairs, still possessed by the sense of something approaching; something so complex, so compounded of a thousand things realized or unrealized, remembered or hardly remembered, that the shape of it had not appeared when she regained her room. The best she could make of it was a . . . a prism? a prism not light but dark, dark and shifting; revolving slowly and turning toward her now one dark facet of itself and now another. The 'Miller,' the 'Jolly Miller' reviving a long-gone episode, reviving also the outrage it had evoked from her, the desire to hurt, punish . . .

The prism turned subtly so that another of its dark facets confronted her—with something so unfamiliar, so detached from memory of the neat and prim little pervert of the library that she stood before it vacantly, groping for any handhold. Even when the nature of it began to emerge, or seemed to, it came as something incomprehensible, ludicrous even, and yet —as she stared at it—more and more immutable. Words, that was all, the meaning of words, and the words were *dirty* and *unclean, dirty* and *unclean* . . .

Dimly she heard the clock striking downstairs; four o'clock. What a time of night to wrestle with shades of nuance, enough to make a cat laugh . . . yet with mysterious weight they pressed on her, the weight of words demanding to be explored to their last, their very last point of significance inward or outward. . . .

In fact she was undergoing, without knowing it, the process by which accepted fact is turned upside down or inside out, made into something different and unrecognizable. By this light of bewildering revelation she set the library exhibitionist against the frank and open-mannered schemer and wondered by what stretch—what possible stretch—the past corruption could be compared with the present corruption. The earlier offense, by this revelatory glare, had shrunk all at once to pitiful insignificance, a nothing, silly childish dirt . . .

Again one single word caught and compelled her to another grapple with definition unknown and unthought of. *Dirt,* in itself, had a host of meanings harmless and unobjectionable. A playing child got dirty, gardeners and labourers got dirty, a woman cleaning an attic got dirty; mild adjective with little reproach in it, something easily washed away. But *unclean?* Did any similar exoneration exist, for any shade of . . . ?

With eyes remote and mouth sagging a little she set herself against the secret, since every word (she began to realize cloudily) has secrets. *Unclean,* suggestive of buried taint, of filth in secret darkness, of evil buried deep, deep—yes, that was it. Divided from the lesser word of harmless meanings, *unclean* had no such exoneration, no single facet that could bear the light of day; deep within it lay its distinguishing mark, its infamy.

And yet the library thing, not nice . . . she was somehow trying to revive her earlier vengeful disgust, then realized—with another shock—that not only had she failed, but knew the nature of her failure. The pervert's offense had been physical, a misuse of the flesh. Flesh with its thousand elements and components that give it life, flesh whose every cell pos-

228

sesses its giant secret of self-healing and self-renewal, flesh with its silent alarm-signals that send help flying where help is needed; flesh whose mysterious knowledges lift the burden from an afflicted part and divert it, by instant and intricate re-routings, into channels able to sustain it . . . And by these unflagging powers that create and re-create the body every moment of every day, flesh appeared to her innocent, innocent, triumphantly and indestructibly *clean;* untainted in every animal, except the one animal with power of base imagination . . .

Something in her head seemed to give way; in a swimming blackness, annihilated, she managed to reach her bed, fell on it fully clothed, and at once was a thousand miles under.

* * *

After a while she began to dream. An old dream, very old and yet with shadowy differences, and because of these differences more grotesque than ever. In this dream as in the earlier one, she was running. Not through endless library corridors this time, but through a solitude noisome and frightening. She was flying from something behind her, something toward which she dared not turn her head for an instant lest she see its face and its shape. She heard herself moaning with fear—of what, exactly, was indistinct. She only knew that in the earlier dream she had been running after the gentlemanly pervert in his black coat and snowy scarf, and in this dream she was running away. Yet even in her deathly panic, the shred of reality that persists in the worst fantasies of sleep told her it would fade like the earlier one, she would not have to run away like this forever . . .

Only again, and still in the dream, she wondered how long she would have to keep running.